NO ONE IN THE WORLD

In

The Beginning

By

Colandra A. Blackwell

Play List

**No One In The World- Anita Baker

- What Have You Done For Me Lately- Janet Jackson
- The Men All Pause- Klymaxx
- Pop, Pop, Pop, Pop Goes My Mind- Levert
- Peter Piper- Run DMC
- Word Up- Cameo
- Sussudio- Phil Collins
- Brass Monkey- Beastie Boys
- The Show- Doug E. Fresh
- Computer Love- Zapp
- Sweet Love- Anita Baker
- Billie Jean- Micheal Jackson
- Tender Love- Force M.Ds
- Candy- Cameo
- Girlfriend- Bobby Brown

- Fly Girl- Boogie Boys

- I'm Bad- LL Cool J

- Fresh Is The Word- Mantronix

- I Ain't No Joke- Eric B. & Rakim

- Looking For The Perfect Beat- Afrika Bambaataa & Soulsonic Force

- Bad - Micheal Jackson

- On Broadway - George Benson

- Something Just Ain't Right - Keith Sweat

- Nite and Day - Al B. Sure

- Saving All My Love For You - Whitney Houston

- My Fantasy - Guy

- Poison - B.B.D.

- End Of The Road - Boyz II Men

DISCLAIMER

THIS IS A WORK OF FICTION. UNLESS OTHERWISE INDICATED, ALL THE NAMES, CHARACTERS, BUSINESSES, PLACES, EVENTS AND INCIDENTS IN THIS BOOK ARE EITHER THE PRODUCT OF THE AUTHOR'S IMAGINATION OR USED IN A FICTITIOUS MANNER. ANY RESEMBLANCE TO ACTUAL PERSONS, LIVING OR DEAD, OR ACTUAL EVENTS IS PURELY COINCIDENTAL.

DEDICATION

TO MY DEAR SWEET LOVING PARENTS, LEWIS AND ALBERTA BLACKWELL, WHO ARE BOTH CHEERING ME ON FROM HEAVEN. I WANT TO LET YOU KNOW THAT I APPRECIATED THE LOVE AND THE ENCOURAGEMENT YOU GAVE ME WHILE HERE ON EARTH. YOUR LOVE IS STILL SO POWERFUL, THAT IT IS PRESENT IN MY LIFE TODAY.

IT IS MY HOPE THAT PURSUING MY DREAM OF WRITING AND BECOMING AN AUTHOR WILL MAKE YOU PROUD. NEVER STOP BELIEVING IN ME FOR THIS JOURNEY WILL BE A REWARDING ONE WITH YOUR BLESSING. I LOVE YOU MOMMY AND DADDY FOREVER!

Acknowledgement

First and foremost I want to give all praises and honor to God. I am so thankful that HE has blessed me with an imagination and the ability to be creative. I am fortunate to have such a wonderful support team and I want to acknowledge each and everyone of you. To my family, thank you for being my strength all the way through this process. You all have been my rock.To my children Timmy,Tyuntra, and my grandson Noah, thank you. You all are my inspiration. To Mama Mary, thank you for your motherly love.

To my book review crew: Janet Allen, Camilia Anderson, Kimberley Blackwell, Shonda Bonner, Rachel Brown, Denise Frederick,Tyuntra Fuller, Deloris Johnson, Rhonda Miller, Kimberlyn Moore, Cynthia Robinson, Lauren Robinson,Shontae Young, thanks so much for taking the time from your busy schedules to preview my book and giving me quality feedback.

To Lillie Nesbitt and Isaac Tate III, I am so grateful to have friends like you. The two of you are always so supportive and encouraging and I thank you for that.

Last but not least I want to give a very special thanks to my real life Tyler, thank you so much for being the man that you are. Life is so much sweeter with you.

NOITW!

Chapter 1
Tan
1986

It just hit me, it's October! The prom is only six months away, and I will be there! With whom? I don't know, but what I do know is I'm going to look like I have just stepped out of the most fashionable magazine. Oh yes, ma'am! I'm going to put this 5 '5, 96 lbs., brown sugar slim fine body in the flyest dress on this side of creation! And what in the world will I do with this hair? It's crazy thick without a perm, naturally curly and wavy, jet black, and down my back! People always say, "girl, you got good hair. I wish I had it!" Yeah, I can wash and wear, but that look is old and tired. I want my hair to be straight, bouncing, and behaving!

Who knows, I just might lose my mind and get rid of this black by coloring it honey-blonde! Who am I kidding? John Sr. and Cathy (my lovely parents) would never go for that! Maybe I will just shock the Hell out of them and just show up one day as a blonde! Or maybe I need to find a new place to live because that is not going to work well, and I will still be able to reside at 1238 Danson St. OK, I won't risk it. I'll play it safe and just get my hair straightened and perhaps cut me some bangs, or maybe not.

Now that the excitement has erupted in me, I have to get some concrete plans together. Let me get on the phone and call my best friend, who lives next door. The phone is ringing. "Hello," Deon, whatcha doing? I'm on my way over! I didn't give her a chance to say anything because sometimes she had a way of making things about her when this time it should be clearly about me.

Dad's deep voice filled the air, "Tan!"

"Sir!"

"Whose turn is it to wash dishes?"

Now, why does he feel the need to bother me about some rag-gedy dishes right now? I DON'T HAVE TIME FOR THIS RIGHT NOW!

"Daddy, I don't know whose turn it is. All I know it isn't mine."

While I'm opening the closet, grabbing a jacket and putting on my shoes, and getting ready to touch the door knob to go out, I hear my sister Kerry's quiet voice whisper, "Daddy, I washed dishes last night. It's Tan's turn."

In slow motion, I turned around with my left brow pointed up, giving her the meanest look I could dig up.

Daddy said, "Getcha butt back in here and do these dishes!"

"Daddy, can I do them later? I'm about to go over Deon's."

Daddy stands up, with about ten frown lines accompanying his forehead, and he looks over at me like, "Try me if you want to!" So that is my cue; I immediately snatch my jacket off, kick off my shoes, and make my way into the kitchen before World War III happens!

The frustrated me is now in the kitchen, slanging pots, pans, and suds everywhere. "Alright now, break a dish if you want to!" When I heard those words come out of my mother's mouth, I knew she meant business! So, I managed to come to my senses quickly, finished the dishes, and wiped off the table, stove, and bar. After the kitchen passed a thorough inspection, I was able to make my getaway next door.

As soon as I get to Deon's porch to ring the doorbell, I hear Janet Jackson blasting, "What Have you Done for Me Lately." Well, there's no need for me to ring the doorbell. I will just twist the door knob and walk on in. Deon's room is located at the front of the house. I'm knocking on her door and she yells, "Come in!"

I'm dancing my way through the doorway.

Deon jumps up from her chair, and now she's beside me, snaking to the left, then the right! We both are dancing, laughing, and yelling, "Hey!" while jamming all over her bedroom floor. After that Soul Train tribute, we both fell down on the bed, laughing hysterically and trying to catch our breath.

"Whew. Girl, I'm here on business. Dee, you have to help me! You have to help me figure out how I can go to the prom this year!"

"Hold up! How do you think that you are going to the prom? It's only for seniors!"

"That's what you and I are going to figure out!"

"Who are you planning on going with?"

"Again, that's what you and I gon figure out!"

Deon throws her head back and bursts out laughing, "Tan, you are always up to something, and you always make me be your partner in crime."

"I just gotta go to the prom!"

Dee has this puzzled look on her face. It's almost like she is afraid to tell me something.

"Dee, why do you have that look on your face?"

I don't know why, but I am brave enough to inquire. "What's on your mind, Dee?"

"Well, since you asked, what's up with you and Tyler?"

"Oh, my goodness! Why are you asking me about him? We are just friends!"

"Really? Not the way y'all be looking at each other, and another thing. Doesn't he walk you home every day? Now, that's someone who secretly has a crush on you. Look how far you live from him after he walks you home. He has a long journey to his house. So, you really want me to believe that there's nothing going on between y'all?"

A big smile just covers my face, and I'm trying not to look goofy while I try to convince her that he's just my friend.

"Besides, I have been looking at Tyler since the 6th grade. I remember he was so short and cute in middle school. He agreed to be my little boyfriend while I also had a big boyfriend, and now that was some agreement we had. Also, I've fixed him up with one of my friends. How could I do that if I wanted him for myself?"

Now that I'm saying these things out loud, I'm realizing at this very moment that I have a lot in common with Tyler. We are always on the phone, talking for hours, and he's always over here. WAIT! Am I trying to convince her or me?

"He is cute, Tan!"

"Yes, he is, but we are good friends, and I never really thought of him as anything more." *Hmmmm, I'm consumed with all kinds of thoughts about Tyler right now.*

My mind is racing. It's hard to focus. I hear Dee saying something, but I'm not able to respond. What has she started? The doorbell rings. I'm thinking, who could that be? We both are running to the door, "who is it," we both say in Unisom.

"JJ," said a small voice from the other side of the door. I am thinking, what could my little worrisome brother want? He gets pleasure out of delivering messages from our parents.

Dee opens the door.

"Daddy said come home!"

"Did he say why?"

"No, he didn't! You better hurry up before I tell him you said you are not coming!"

"You make me sick with your big head! Dee, I'll be back, or I'll call you."

"Ok, girl!"

I'm taking my time as I walk across The Franklin's well-manicured yard. I took a deep breath and walked through the front door, and the pleasant aroma of fried fish filled the air. One thing about the Breakfield household: before the end of the day, no matter what Mama cooked earlier that day, you were going to get some fried fish before you went to bed. My dad truly believes that fish is brain food, and he has done a pretty good job of convincing Mama of that, too.

I'm standing in the den waiting for Daddy to take his focus off the TV and tell me what was so important for him to interrupt. "OPERATION PROM!" I've been standing here for 3 minutes, so I'm just going to ease into the kitchen with Mama.

"Hey, Mama, do you need some help?"

"Are you feeling well?"

"Ha-ha, you act like I don't ever offer to help you around here."

"Ok, what's going on with you?" "

"Well, Mama, I want to go to the prom this year. And before you say no, remember, Kerry went to the prom as a high school junior!"

I can tell she was not expecting that to come out of my mouth. She is looking at me, kind of happy and shocked at the same time.

Then I hear these words, "go ask your Daddy." Those are the very words I dreaded to hear coming from her mouth! I feel like someone has just pushed a knife into my stomach and was slowly twisting it.

"Sure, I will, but I'm no dummy. I will wait until he eats, and then he will be in a good mood."

"He sure will be in a good mood because I put my foot in this fish!" Mama and I both started laughing while we grabbed plates and silverware to set the table.

Mama made her daily announcement, "Y'all come eat! The food is on the table!"

We are all sitting at the table, complimenting Mama on this delicious meal.

I really don't think I should mention the prom right now. I need to get a better plan together first. Somehow, I'm getting a feeling that everything is going to work out for me, and that brings a smile to my face.

Chapter 2

Tan

"Get up, girl, and get ready for school!"

"Ok, Mama, I'm up."

"Don't let me have to come back in here!"

I'm not ready to start my day. I could use just a few more minutes of sleep. So, I'm turning over and pulling the covers up around my neck, trying not to fall into a deep sleep by keeping my ears exposed so I can hear Mama when she's on her way back down the hallway. I'm not trying to get knocked out before I even get up!

Finally, when I have enough strength to get out of bed, I drag myself to the closet and stand there staring at all my clothes, trying to decide what *on earth I should wear today.*

I'm extremely particular about my closet, so all of my clothes are arranged by color. Starting from the left side of the closet, it's all of my light-colored clothes. The middle section holds all my jeans, and everyone knows that you can never have enough jeans! The dark-colored clothes are hanging on the right side.

My red and white *Coca-Cola* jeans and sweatshirt will be the perfect attire for today. Oh, and this outfit cannot be complete without my red and white oxford style *Reeboks*! Now I'm looking FOXY!

It just hit me. I need to call Janis and tell her to wear her blue and white Coca-Cola outfit. Janis is my best friend at school, and we have been friends since the 9th grade. She would definitely feel some type of way if I stepped up into the school sporting my red and white outfit without her blue and white outfit coordinating with mine.

Mission accomplished! After my speedy call with Janis, she is on board with the matching outfits, and it is understood that we will meet in our usual spot by the band hall. I'm feeling good about today, and for some odd reason, I'm excited to start my school day!

"Tan, get in here and eat your breakfast. It's almost time for you to leave!" I heard Mama yelling, and hearing that quickly distracted me from looking at myself in the mirror.

The wonderful aroma of bacon fills the entire house, especially in the hallway leading to my bedroom. I can never turn down bacon. I think it's my birthmark.

Kerry and JJ have already eaten breakfast and are now walking out the door. Kerry drops JJ off at his school before she makes her way to the university.

I'm sitting and waiting patiently at the table for Mama to place my plate in front of me. She's walking towards me with a plate of food in one hand and a glass of milk in the other hand. I see bacon and scrambled eggs. *Is that what I think it is? I know I'm not seeing things!*

Mama is waiting to see my facial expressions when I discover the cheese toast. My face lit up, grinning from ear to ear, and I'm turning into that adorable little girl right before her eyes.

"Mama, you fixed my favorite, cheese toast!" I practically have to stop myself from jumping around the room to see my favorite food.

She's looking at me, laughing, "I shouldn't have fixed you anything because you stayed in the mirror too long to be able to enjoy it!"

Immediately, I jump up to give Mama the biggest hug I can possibly give. She is peeling me off of her while saying, "your breakfast is getting cold, and you know Mr. Braggs will be blowing his horn soon."

Mr. Braggs is my friend Tracey's father. Tracey and I are also good friends. We ride to school together every morning. Tracey is a grade ahead of me, so that makes her a senior. She's serious about acting and really focused on her studies. Dating is so far from her mind, and whenever I mention it, she always rolls her eyes at me and changes the subject.

As I'm chewing on this good food, my mind is in deep thought about the prom.

Beep! Beep! Well, my thoughts just snapped me back to reality.

"Tan, you hear Mr. Braggs out there!"

"Yes, Mama, I'm grabbing my stuff! See you later!"

There's a long line of cars waiting to enter into the school's parking lot. There are students everywhere. Some getting off the buses, some taking their time getting out of their parent's cars, holding up traffic without a care in the world. Davis High is a really cool school. We are known for our phenomenal basketball team and our jamming marching band.

One thing is for sure: we are the majority here, and there are a precious few of the other races, only because of the magnet/engineering program. My sister Kerry was an engineering student here, and she was part of the first graduating class of the smart students in the program. Those smart students get the best of everything. It's funny how in the front part of the school, where us regular students are housed, it's always either too hot or too cold, but in the new wing where the magnet students are, it's always perfect. Those brainiacs go the extra mile by staying in school an hour later than us regulars, so count me out! I'm not sitting in classes any longer than I have to.

We finally pulled into the school parking lot, and Tracey and I said our goodbyes to Mr. Braggs. We jumped out of the car to get to the specific groups of people that we hung out with. I'm walking really fast, trying to get to my crew, and Tracey is trying to keep up with me like we're racing.

"Tan, Deon told me that you were trying to go to the prom."

"I say, "trying? I'm going!"

"How, Tan? You are a junior, so that means you can't go!"

"Ok, we will see about that!"

Tracey just shook her head and walked off.

Now, I really have to work hard to prove Tracey wrong! I'm walking swiftly through the crowds, trying to find Janis. I finally see her standing by the steps leading to the band hall. We see each other and immediately start smiling and yelling, "Hey, girl!"

Somebody shouted out, "look at the Coca-Cola Twins!"

It's like the crowd gets quiet, and all eyes are on us.

Janis and I are looking too good today. She's cute, super short, caramel brown skin, slightly bow-legged, with a thin build and shoulder-length dark brown hair. Can't nobody tell us that we don't have it going on? As we sashay down the hall, I'm hearing my theme song in my head, "The Men All Pause," by: Klymaxx. I'm sure every girl in this hallway is secretly cursing our names.

Out of nowhere, Janis says, "Tan, guess who just asked about you?"

"I'm afraid even to guess. Just tell me!"

Janis is cheesing real hard, saying, "you know who I am talking about? Think really hard."

My eyes are looking up to the left, trying to figure out who in the world it could be.

"Janis, really, I don't have a clue!"

She's so excited, all in my face, jumping up and down, saying, "Tyler, Tyler!"

"Why are you tripping? You know Tyler and I are just friends!"

I can tell this conversation is about to take off in a direction that I'm not willing to go.

"Friends, my foot! That boy walks you home every day!"

Now she's sounding like Deon. I'm looking at her, wondering why she has to be so loud and country. It seems that Janis may know something that I don't know. *Has Tyler confided in her?*

Millions of questions are crowding my head. *Does he like me, and he's scared to say something? Do I like him like that?* At this very moment, my thoughts are running wild.

"Tan! Tan!"

I squinched my eyes real tight and shook my head a little, responding, "What, Janis?"

"You were in deep thought, Tan, staring into space!"

"I. I," Ring! "I am saved by the bell!"

I barely made it to my first-period class on time. While sitting at my desk, new feelings are surfacing. Could it be that I have uncovered real feelings for Tyler? Have these feelings always been here, and I have ignored them? I'm a mess right now! I can't sit here and focus on Ms. Eve's boring lesson when I have more important things to figure out.

"Blah- blah- blah" is all I hear while Ms. Eve is up there talking about a stupid term paper we are supposed to do. While she's up talking, someone opens the door and sticks their arm inside the classroom, flickers the lights on and off, and takes off running down the hall. Oh well, class might as well be over because everyone is out of control, jumping around, and laughing uncontrollably. I'm sitting here wondering if this type of behavior would be tolerated on the other side of town.

Ms. Eve is a small blonde /gray-haired Caucasian woman about 4 foot 10 inches with a raspy voice.

"Settle down, class, settle down right now!" pleads Ms. Eve, and of course, no one is listening. Year after year, the expectation for her class is to show up to class and just act a complete fool! This is really not okay. After all, I just so happen to love English because someday I want to become a journalist, but this is definitely not a great experience and just a big ole waste of my time! I can only hope that tomorrow will be better.

Time is passing pretty fast. It's already the second lunch, and you can tell because most of the juniors and seniors have cars, so they are headed to the parking lot. I'm moving gracefully through the packed halls, trying to maneuver my way to the cafeteria by the soda machines to meet Janis. While I'm waiting, someone comes up behind me and places their hands over my eyes.

"Hey, Tyler!"

"Wooooooow! How did you know it was me?" Tyler says with a big smile on his face.

"Maybe because you do this at least three times a week!" I can't help but to blush because he's so cute and goofy. I'm thinking to my-self, this time, it feels different. I am looking at Tyler in a whole new light.

Right now, I'm kind of in a daze. Tyler is talking to me, and it's not registering. He interrupts my daze by shoving me.

"Tan, did you hear what I said?"

"Um, no, I'm so sorry. I have a lot on my mind."

"What's wrong with you? You are not even making eye contact while I'm talking to you."

I can't believe he picked up on that! I hope he can't tell I'm getting feelings for him. Tyler notices every little thing. Hopefully, he will miss this one.

Janis yells down the hall, "Hey Tan, come here! There is some-one I want you to meet!"

Janis is walking towards Tyler and me with a new girl. Tyler sees his friends, and he takes off in the opposite direction.

"Tan, this is Shayla, Shayla, this is Tan."

We both smile and shake hands.

"Shayla is new here from Oklahoma, and she doesn't know anyone, so I thought she could hang out with us."

Shala is standing there with all smiles. She's sporting some _Calvin Klein_ jeans with a red and white striped sweater.

"Yeah, that's cool!" Shayla just might be a good addition to our group. Her outfit is blending in perfectly with ours.

Finally, it's the end of school. I'm standing on the track next to the bleachers, waiting for Tyler and Anthony. The three of us always walk home together. Anthony stays a couple of blocks from the school, so he only has a short distance to walk. Here they both come, laughing loudly and walking slowly.

"I heard we have a new girl, and I heard you and Janis are friends with her. How does she look?" Anthony wastes no time asking about the new girl.

We're now walking down the street, and just out of habit, Tyler reaches for my book bag and places it on his shoulder. I never really thought about it in the past, but Tyler is such a gentleman.

Anthony is waiting patiently for a description of Shayla.

"Alright, Anthony, since you are inquiring, Shayla is a little shorter than me, medium size, light-skinned, with short dark brown hair with auburn highlights. She is cute. That's why she fits in with us!"

Tyler and Anthony are laughing, and Tyler says, "The Pretty Girls!"

Anthony has reached his destination, and we say our goodbyes. Then, there was an awkward moment of silence, and I decided to break it.

"So, Tyler, what were you trying to tell me at lunch today?"

"You mean when you weren't listening to me?"

"Ha-ha, I was slightly distracted, but now, you have my undivided attention."

"Tan, do you think I should ask Cassie to the homecoming dance?"

Wow! I never would have thought that's what he wanted to ask me.

"Well, I know you like her. Why not ask her?"

"Do you know if she has a boyfriend?"

"Yes, she does. She was about to break up with him, but he bought her a puppy."

"I think you have a chance, go for it, ask her to the dance!"

"I have a better idea, Tan. Why don't you talk to her for me?"

"Let me get this straight, you want me to be all up in your business? I can definitely do that!"

"Ok, let me know what she says, and don't make me seem desperate because I'm not!"

"I know you are not desperate. You are just afraid of rejection."

This conversation was a little awkward for me because I was thinking of Tyler in a whole other way. Thank God he had no idea! We are walking, high siding, and just enjoying each other's company on this perfect October day. Finally, we are turning on my street, "so Tyler, are you going home, or do you want to hang out for a while?"

"Shoot, I'm kinda tired. I will hang at your crib for a few, and then I will head home."

"Ok, sounds like a plan."

As we get closer to the house, I can see Deon sitting on her porch. I can't help it, but at this very moment, I am regretting that I even had "The Tyler Conversation" with her.

"Alright, Tyler, are you coming inside or what?"

"No, I think I will stay out here and talk to Deon."

I'm thinking to myself that heifer better not mention anything that we talked about!

I'm playing with the doorbell, knowing that it pisses Mama off.

"Alright, you better get off that doorbell if you want me to let you in!" Mama takes her sweet time opening the door.

"Hey, Mama!"

"You know better than to play with that doorbell like that. You know that gets on my nerves!"

I laughed all the way to my room to change clothes. I'm just going to slip on some jeans and a t-shirt and head outside.

"OOOOOOOOH Mama! What is that delicious smell?"

"Smothered chicken, with thick gravy, rice, corn, and corn-bread."

"Can I make the Kool-Aid?"

"I don't care; just don't pour the whole canister of sugar in it!"

"You know I love that ghetto Kool-Aid!"

"Girl, get out of here!"

As I'm walking out, I can still hear Mama laughing about my crazy comment.

As I'm walking across The Franklin's soft, plush lawn, I see Deon and Tyler sitting on her porch, engaged in a deep conversation.

"Hey y'all, what did I miss?"

Tyler looks at me like he knows something. Deon has guilt written all over her face. I'm thinking that she must have let the cat out of the bag. She is looking at me like. I promise I haven't said a word. I'm looking at her with relief on my face because I'm not ready to admit anything.

Tyler quickly stands up, and he's walking towards me, places his right hand on my left shoulder, and says, "I know you hate to see me go, but I gotta make this long walk home."

I'm playfully touching his hand, the one that's on my shoulder, and we both are smiling really hard. Our hands are touching, and now we are hand in hand and swinging them back-and-forth like we are little kids. "Ok, girl, let my hand go!"

"Whatever! You are the one holding on to me!" We both are laughing, and finally, we let go of each other. Tyler takes off running down the street.

I'm just standing in the same spot, and now I'm making eye contact with Dee.

"Don't say nothing, Deon!"

"I won't, but just know Tyler has feelings for you too!"

"Why would you tell me that? I didn't need to know that!."

"Alright then, just act like I have never said anything."

"Move over, Mama, I'm back!"

"Wash your hands. The pitcher and Kool-Aid mix are up in the cabinet. The dipper is in the drawer next to the silverware, and of course, you know where the sugar is. Oh, and don't forget the lemon juice!"

"Yes, ma'am, extra sweet Kool-Aid, coming right up!"

Mama is looking at me out of the corner of her eye in a joking way, and I'm pretending to be frightened.

While Mama and I were playing around in the kitchen, we heard a key unlocking the front door. I look at the clock, and it's 4:30 on the dot. Daddy is always home at the exact same time every day. He pushes the door open, wearing a nice light blue dress shirt with a navy tie, navy pants, and shiny black shoes. He enters yelling, "where is the love of my life?"

I look over at Mama, and she says absolutely nothing! We both are laughing when Daddy enters the kitchen.

"Cathy, you heard me calling for you!"

With a big grin on her face, Mama says, "I didn't know you were talking to me!"

Daddy walks up close to Mama, hugs her real tight, gives her a kiss on the lips, and says, "Who else could be the love of my life?"

I'm looking at them both, just hoping to one day have something close to what they have.

Mama is wiggling her way out of Daddy's arms and making her way to the oven to take the food out and place it on the stove. She begins to fix everyone's plate and yells for us to come to the table for dinner. JJ is the first one to take his place at the table.

"Mama, did Tan make some ghetto Kool-Aid?"

Before Mama can answer him, while poking him in the back of his head, I reply, "yes, I did, and you better not drink all of it up either!"

Kerry comes to the table with a book. She is always reading. She reads for fun. I can't even imagine.

"Hey Kerry, what are you reading?"

"I'm reading North and South."

"North and South?"

"Yeah, it's really good, Tan! You would like it, it's about love and war. I have to hurry and finish this book because next week the mini-series is coming on TV."

"Well, maybe I will watch it with you; hopefully, it will hold my attention."

Kerry places her opened book face down on the table beside her plate.

I'm thinking this may be something cool that I can do with Kerry. I'm kinda looking forward to it.

Chapter 3

Tan

It's just a regular old school day, and I'm sitting in 3rd period with my new friend Shayla. I can tell she's a little uncomfortable because everyone is asking her questions about where she's from and why she wanted to move to Texas. Finally, Mr. Wallace tells everyone to shut up and get to work! Mr. Wallace is our Economics teacher, an average-height white guy, very cool, and his class is usually fun. He has a way of making things interesting. Mr. Wallace tells us to get into groups of fours. It's just pitiful to watch all the guys racing to get to Shayla. So, I CRUNCHED them by grabbing Shayla's arm to get her to be the fourth person in our group. There are a lot of disappointed, ugly boys now. My all-girls group looks over at the boys and says in Unisom CRUNCH! Shayla is confused. She leans over and whispers to me, "What is CRUNCH?" Mr. Wallace's old nosey self overhears her, and he says to me. "Please allow me to do the honors! You see, Miss. Tan here is known for being the Crunch Queen. She came up with that word to use when someone is embarrassed or has said something that is incorrect."

I'm laughing, and I turn around to look at Mr. Wallace and say, "You are so hip, and you have made me so proud!" The whole class is laughing.

"Ok, everyone, calm down, and let's get some work done! In your groups, you are to choose an article from the newspaper that relates to the economy, and you all will be responsible for a presentation." All the groups are very engaged, scattering newspapers everywhere. In every group, there is a facilitator assigning roles and handing out materials. Our group is looking good, we totally have our stuff together!

"Class, we have about 5 minutes before lunch, so let's get this room in order and get ready to be dismissed!"

Everyone is kinda disappointed because we ran out of time. I know my group is excited to present, but we will have to wait until the next class time.

"Ring! Ring!" It's lunchtime!

Shayla and I are headed to the cafeteria to meet up with Janis.

"I sure like Mr. Wallace's class."

"I knew you would, Shayla. He is a great teacher, and he's cool too."

"Yeah, being cool is an added bonus. My other teachers are not fun at all, just plain and boring."

"Wow! You should have consulted with Janis and me before you requested your schedule. We could have made sure that most of your teachers would have been fun, but that was impossible because you didn't even know us then." We both laughed, but it made sense.

While Shayla and I are talking, Anthony walks up smiling hard.

I say to Anthony, "You sure are cheesing hard. What's going on with you?"

Anthony turns and gives me a look like, don't do me like that in front of the new girl. And the whole time, he is looking at her from head to toe!

Ant says, "Ah, excuse me, Tan. Do you mind introducing me to your new friend?"

"Why certainly, it will be my pleasure. Since we are being so formal and whatnot."

"Shayla, this here is Anthony, AKA Ant. Ant, this is Shayla."

"I am very pleased to meet you, Shayla."

I notice that Shayla is trying to keep a straight face while Ant is laying it on pretty thick!

Ant is licking his lips like he is some kind of big-time player, and now he's reaching for her hand. *I know this fool ain't going old school and is about to try to kiss her hand!*

Janis is walking up with a puzzled look on her face. I'm sure she is wondering what in the world is going on. I guess it's time to rescue Shayla from Ant's weak rap. All of a sudden, everything goes black!" Guess who?" Tyler says.

"Come on, Tyler, you know I know it's you!"

Everyone is looking at Tyler. Really?

Tyler is extra hyper today. I can see it all over his face, and he is moving around a lot too.

He walks over to Ant, and they give each other five as if they are the coolest cats alive.

"Say, Ant, what's going on?" Tyler said in a joking way.

"You know me, man, I'm just trying to get to know Shayla."

"Ahhhhhhh, my boy is trying to rap, and let me guess. Tan and Janis are BLOCKING!"

Now Tyler gets right in my face saying, "Tan, why is you BLOCKING?"

Janis and I both are grabbing Shayla's arms and pulling her to our VIP table inside the cafeteria.

Every line in here is long. We need to hurry up and decide what we are going to eat before our lunchtime is over.

The lines finally seem to be going down, so we decide that it's a good time to pick a line to stand in. While we were standing in the Cage Line, where they served hard pizza, dry hamburgers, and almost cheese less nachos, I noticed this guy named Joseph staring at me. So, being the overly confident girl that I am, I say to him, "I don't know why you are looking at me because you can't have me!"

A frown immediately appeared on his face. He has MAD written all over his face!

Joseph gave me the meanest look he could and said, "I can't stand you!"

I turned to Janis and Shayla and said, "Have y'all pick y'all's poison yet?

Janis looks at me with disbelief and says, "I know you are not going to act like that just didn't happen!"

"What?"

"The way you just CRUNCHED Joseph!"

"Yeah!" Shayla adds her two cents.

"Y'all, Joseph and I have that type of relationship where I am well aware that he likes me, and I give him a hard time about it. We are really cool. We are in the same Algebra II class, and we sit next to each other. He always helps me when I'm struggling, and Lord knows I'm always struggling in that class!"

Joseph is a very nice guy. He's not tall, but he's an athlete, and he dresses really nicely. I mean, he wears *Polo* from head to toe! His waves are hitting, too! And he drives to school every day. But one thing is for sure: he is very smart and intelligent! Just last week, we traded *Polo* Jackets for the day, and he told me he wanted to keep my jacket a little longer because he likes the way it smells. Joseph is truly a sweet-heart.

Lunch is over now, and we're back to the rat race. We are all in the hallways trying to make it to class on time. Who am I kidding? Some of us could care less about getting to class on time, and we practice that craft daily.

I'm sitting here in the last period of the day, Journalism. This is one of my favorite classes. Mrs. Terry is our teacher, and she encouraged us to write about something that would get us fired up and make us want to take action! So, I chose to write an article on Homeless in America. I plan to reach out to a homeless shelter to get a general idea of how many people they help a day. Also, how many homeless people are out there that they are not able to help? I'm very passionate about this story because it's a sad situation when you see someone in the heat, rain, or cold, snowy weather without a place in the world to call home. And to think, this is America. How is it possible to have so many homeless people, and it's not a major concern?

Mrs. Terry is calling us up to her desk just to check to see where we are with our articles.

"Tan, I am ready to meet with you," says Mrs. Terry with a kind smile on her face. I stand and gather all my papers and place them in a folder, and I walk to her desk at the back of the classroom. I'm feeling a rush right now because I am so eager to share my ideas. As I'm explaining, Mrs. Terry interrupts me and says, "Tan, I really appreciate your enthusiasm. You are going over and beyond the expectations that I have set for you all. You are most definitely on the right track, and if you need my assistance, please don't hesitate to ask." I thank Mrs. Terry, and I slowly stand up while smiling from ear to ear and gathering my papers to move back to my seat. Before I could take my seat, the bell rang.

I'm walking outside past the crowds and band students rushing with their instruments, playing all kinds of random notes while trying to make it to the field on time for practice. As I weave my way through all of that madness, I can see Tyler waiting for me by the bleachers.

"Hey, Tyler! Where's Ant?"

While he is reaching for my bag, he says, "Hey to you too! Ant had to leave early. His parents got him an early dismissal."

"Hmmmm, I wonder what's that about? Did he tell you anything?"

"Wow! You sure are nosey, Tan!"

"That's not being nosey. That is called being concerned!"

"Yeah, right!"

So, we're walking up the street on the same step. So, I feel like being playful, so I'm trying to lighten the mood by saying," left - left - left - right -left!"

Tyler couldn't help but laugh. He's giving me a slight push and calling me stupid.

"How am I stupid? You are the one laughing at that silliness!"

"Tan, you are so goofy! I swear you are!"

"Birds of a feather flock together!"

"Wow! What are you trying to say?"

"I'm not trying to say anything. You already know we are like the same person. That's why we get along so well."

Tyler looks at me like he wants to say something, but for some reason, it won't come out.

I'm still joking around. "what's wrong with your big head self? Cat got your tongue?"

Tyler quickly finds a distraction. A smashed can by the curb, so he begins to kick it as we walk down the street. I'm thinking to myself, why is he acting like this? What is he trying to avoid talking about? Oh well, I guess I will just leave it alone.

Tyler continues to kick the can a further distance each time, but now I'm sick of him, and that can so the next time he prepares to kick it, I'm going to kick it so far that he'll never see it again.

"Earth to Tyler, earth to Tyler!"

"I hear you. I just have a lot on my mind, that's all."

"I get it, but what I really don't understand is, why can't you tell your best friend about it?"

Tyler catches up with the can, and before he can position his foot to kick it, out of nowhere, I give that can a quick, swift kick right in the drainage sewage!

"Yay! Two points for Tan!" I'm teasing Tyler by laughing and pushing him in the back of his head. He's trying not to laugh, and then he grabs me and holds me really tight. The laughter gradually stops, and silence fills the air. We both are playing it off like that awkwardness did not just happen. I'm trying to think of something to talk about. I know.

"Hey Tyler, you know homecoming is right around the corner."

"Duh! Somebody was supposed to be fixing me up with a certain someone."

The look on my face should give my feelings away. "I'm definitely working on that, my friend."

Ok, now I don't know what to do. The question is: Should I reach out to Cassie and let her know that Tyler wants to take her to the dance? I guess I have to because I gave him my word.

Chapter Four

Tyler

Tan, now that's my girl. We go way back to 6th grade. Back when I was shorter, *Jerry Curls* was beginning to be popular. I always kept a fresh curl. I think that's the reason why she agreed to be my girlfriend then. I can remember that day like it was yesterday. When we first saw each other, we both had the biggest smiles on our faces. I just had to get to know her; she was one of the prettiest girls I had ever seen. There was something special about her. Maybe it was the way she sat in class and twirled her hair while listening to the teacher. To tell the truth, I really believe it was love at first sight.

Here we are years later, and we are the best of friends. I can't recall how or when it happened, but I find myself walking Tan home every day. Our walks home is always fun, and we have great conversations, too. Sometimes, Tan goes overboard with her questioning. Today, we're walking home, and something is clearly bothering me, but I'm trying my best to hide it because I really don't want her to make a big deal out of it. So, as we are walking, I spot a can on the ground to kick down the street to distract myself from the million questions she's throwing at me. Now I can tell she is getting frustrated with me because, out of nowhere, Tan cuts me off by giving the can a swift kick into the drain! I'm looking at her, wondering if that was really necessary.

She was hyped about destroying that can, so she began to do a little victory dance around me while poking me in the back of the head. I can always count on her to lighten the mood by doing something crazy and out of the ordinary. Suddenly, I grabbed her and put both arms around her really tight. I can tell she wasn't expecting that. We are both laughing, and she's squirming, trying to get away, but it's nearly impossible because I have a good grip on her.

After the laughter, there is an awkward moment of silence, and something tells me that I have to come clean about what is bothering me.

So, I finally open up and share. I sure hope I don't regret it later.

"I definitely feel pressured about the homecoming dance. Everyone is making a big deal out of who they're taking and what they are wearing."

"Ok. Tyler, at least you know who you want to go with. and I'm going to work on that ASAP! Do you have an idea of what you would like to wear?"

"That's what I have you for! You know I don't put any thought into things like that. I'll leave that to you."

"You are so lucky to have me. I should consider charging you for my services."

I'm looking at Tan like, yeah right! *This girl is really tripping now.*

We are approaching Tan's Street. I began to take her book bag off my shoulder and place it onto hers, and then I told her that I had to go straight home today. For some reason, she seems to be kind of sad about it.

I touch her chin while giving her a playful smile and say, "Hey, cheer up, girl, you will get to see me soon!"

"Bye, Tyler!" Tan said, with an attitude as she slowly started walking down her street, and I'm doing a slow jog on my journey to the house.

WOMEN!

Why didn't I stay and hang out for a while? To be honest, I really didn't want to face Deon because the last time I was over there and we talked on her porch, I said some things that I really shouldn't have said, and now, the damage is done. Although she promised she wouldn't say anything. I don't know if I believe her. I guess time will tell.

Finally, I made it home! Shaw Avenue has never looked so good. Mainly because I'm hungry and tired. As I entered the house, I could hear my sister, Venus, talking on the phone in the kitchen while warming up the dinner Mom had prepared for us before she went to her evening college class. My Mom is a single mother of four kids with a full-time job while attending college in the evenings. I appreciate everything she is doing for us, and that's why I try not to get in any trouble and work to buy the extra things I want.

Every weekend, I work at the local university as a short-order cook. I can make the best hamburgers with a side of fries in a record amount of time. I have people asking for me by my name because of my cooking skills and, of course, my charm. Now, since homecoming is coming up, I need to work some extra hours because I plan on taking a date. *Hmmm, I'm wondering if Tan is going to make that happen. Will Cassie be willing to be my date? Why is there always so much pressure on the guy? Girls have it so easy; all they have to do is wait for someone to ask them out, and then they have the option of saying that awful word. NO. Why would she say no? I'm nice looking, correction. I'm handsome and athletic, have nice teeth with a winning smile, am of average height, and I keep money in my pocket. What more could a girl want? Maybe a car? Well, I am working on that. Soon, I will be driving to school every day and watching how many girls will be interested!*

I'm sitting on this dark blue velvet-like couch watching TV. A clothes hanger is inserted in the broken antenna on the TV to help assist with the reception. Every now and then, I have to get up and bend the hanger a certain way in order to get the perfect picture. Venus comes into the living room and sits beside me. Venus says, "One of these days, that Coyote is going to catch that Roadrunner!"

"You must be crazy. He'll never catch him. He's too slick!" We both are laughing. I can't believe that we are having a full-blown conversation about a cartoon. Venus is now looking at me with concern on her face; I can tell she is about to ask me something. _Oh no, here it comes._

"What's bothering you?"

I slowly turn my head to look at her. "What are you talking about? There is nothing wrong with me."

Venus starts to laugh and says, "I guess you are just starving because your stomach is growling super loud!"

"Dang! Is the food ready yet?"

"Yeah, it's been ready. I was waiting for y'all to come eat."

"You ain't said nothing but a word!" I jump up from the couch and head straight for the kitchen!

"Ah, man! Not spaghetti again!"

Venus starts laughing, "You know we're going to have it until it's all gone, so eat up!"

I reach into the cabinet, grab a large white bowl, and begin to fill it up to the brim. I reach on top of the fridge and grab some crackers. I'm just trying to make sure we won't have spaghetti anymore this week!

The phone is ringing. _It would ring after I settled on the couch in my favorite spot, right in front of the TV._

Venus yells, "I got it! Hello. Yes, he's here. Hold on. Tyler, it's Tan!"

I place my bowl and crackers on the coffee table, walk to the kitchen, and pick up the phone from the counter. "What's up, Tan?"

"I was just making sure you made it home. I knew you would forget to call like you always do!"

"Man, you know I be forgetting. I get home and, get comfortable, and start watching TV, and before I know it, the phone is ringing, and I think to myself, I know that's Tan."

"Yeah, you should be glad you have a friend that really cares about you."

"I am glad."

"Yeah, right! Oh well, someone's on my other line. I'll talk to you later!"

"Ok." I hang up the phone and walk back to the living room to start back on my meal and watch TV. I just happened to look up at Venus, and she is smiling from ear to ear.

"Is something wrong?"

Her smile had gotten even bigger. Then she says, "Hey, why aren't you and Tan dating? I mean, you are always over at her house, and when you're not, y'all are on the phone!"

As you must know, we are good friends, the best of friends, and we don't even look at each other like that! Besides, I asked her to fix me up with one of her friends."

Venus stands up with both hands on her thin hips, clears her throat, and says, "Oh, my foolish little brother, you are making a very big mistake!"

"Why do you think that?"

"It is so obvious that the two of you like each other, but the problem is, neither of you want to admit it."

Why am I wondering if she could be right? Did I really make a mistake by asking Tan to fix me up with Cassie? My imagination is running wild right now.

Now Venus is pacing back and forth. "And another thing. Don't you walk her home every day? Boy, who are you trying to fool? Because it is not working on me! Hey, are you planning on going to the homecoming dance?"

"I want to go, and that's why I asked Tan to fix me up with this girl named Cassie."

"I'm just wondering why you wouldn't ask Tan to go. Y'all make such a good couple. Hopefully, you haven't messed up your chances with her!"

"What do you mean by messed up?"

"What if she does fix you up with that girl, and it doesn't work out?"

"I don't see what the big deal is! Me and Tan are just friends!"

"Guys are so blind! Y'all never can see what's going on right in front of your face."

I don't know why I let Venus get inside my head. I know Tan is just my friend, and yes, I love being around her, and we always have fun together, but why would I destroy our relationship by trying to date her?

I'm lying across my bed listening to the radio, and the song "Pop, Pop, Pop, Pop Goes My Mind" by Levert is playing. I'm thinking, how did I get myself caught up in this homecoming mess? Maybe I should just forget about the dance and just go to the game with my boys, and that way, I won't have that extra pressure of waiting to see if Cassie will go to the dance with me. I wonder who Tan is going with? *Dang, why am I worried about Tan?* UGH! I hit the bed in frustration. I'm running myself crazy!

Boom! Boom! Boom! Boom! *Is that bass I'm hearing?* I jump up and look out the window, and it's my older cousin Sean in his gray Mustang with a new system coming down the street.

By the time I made it outside, it seemed like everyone on the block was surrounding Sean's car.

He turns the music up, "Peter Piper" by Run DMC is playing so loud that it is rattling all the houses' windows on the street. I slip on my shoes to go outside. I could see that Sean was very proud of his new system, and so were we. I'm rushing to take a seat on the passenger's side so I can check it out more closely. He definitely has a top-of-the-line brand. a Pioneer radio and an amp with some 10-inch woofers in the trunk. *Man! I can't wait to get my ride! People will be able to hear my bass from miles away!*

The older neighbors start coming out on their porches, and out of respect, Sean turns the music down. Once that happens, the crowd begins to dwindle, and it's just a few of us standing around talking now. Everybody, including me, is talking about how they are getting ready to improve their rides and how much bass they plan on having. Sean is looking at me like, what car do you have? I'm more than eager to share the previous conversation Mama and I had the other day.

"I will have my ride real soon. My Mama said if I work and save my money and prove I'm responsible, she would give me her black Firebird."

Sean has a shocked look on his face and says, "Man, if you get that car. Do you know what all you can do about it? It's already a cool car. You really don't need to do much, though!"

"I will definitely have to invest in a system!"

"No doubt! I will help you fix up your ride so you can hang with your cousin."

All this car talk made me anxious to start working more hours, so I could spend money on my car.

Sean announces to the few guys that are left, "Y'all back up! I'm about to take my lil cousin for a spin!"

I'm on the passenger side, and the windows are down, and the music is blasting "Word Up" by the group Cameo.

Sean yelled at the top of his lungs, "Say, Tyler, where do you want to go?"

My first thought was Tan. I don't know why. I knew she was probably outside with Deon because it wasn't quite dark yet.

I shout, "Turn here!" Sean turns on two wheels on Danson Street.

He reaches for the radio and turns it down a bit, "Hey, isn't this the street your little girlfriend stays on?"

Oh, here we go again! What is the universe trying to tell me?

"Tan is not my little girlfriend. She is my friend. That's it, just a friend!"

"Dang! Why are you so upset? What's really happening?"

As we were creeping down the street, I noticed Tan and Deon standing on the curb in the middle of both of their houses.

"There is Tan. Stop so I can mess with her. She won't know who I am in this car."

Sean stops right in front of them, and I say, "Hey, baby!"

They both were trying to see who was occupying the fly Mustang!

Tan had all thirty-two teeth showing. "Is that you, Tyler?"

"The one and only!"

"What are you doing over here?"

"We were just riding, and I wanted to see you. I mean. I wanted to see if Y'all were outside."

I can't believe that just came out of my mouth. Why did I say that?

Deon tries to change the subject by asking, "Who's the driver?"

I'm looking at her like. Good save!

"Oh, this is my cousin, Sean."

"Hey, Sean!" Deon said very seductively.

"Sean, you've met Tan."

Sean gives both of them a nod.

I reach for the door handle to get out of the car. I'm facing both Tan and Deon. Tan's dad is now standing on his porch. It's clear that he is trying to figure out who we are.

"Tan, don't turn around and look now, but. Your nosey Daddy is on the porch."

Tan and Deon both are giggling.

"Hello, Mr. Breakfied, it's me, Tyler, how are you doing?"

I don't know what's gotten into me, but I wanted him to know that I wasn't some random thug trying to talk to his daughter.

"I'm doing fine, and you?" he said very sternly.

"I'm doing alright."

I guess he had all the information he needed because he went back into the house.

Tan was looking at me with disbelief. I guess because I took the initiative to speak to her dad and show him that I was raised right.

The conversation was going well until Deon had to bring up the homecoming dance. I can feel my facial expression changing drastically! Tan notices it right away. "Touchy subject, Tyler?"

"Not at all." As soon as I tried to deliver that lie out into the atmosphere, Cassie and her grandmother drove past us. Now, my anxiety has definitely kicked in!

"Perfect timing! I will go get Cassie so we can see what her plans are for the dance," Tan said.

"Don't expect me to be here when you get back!" I gave Sean a look, and he caught on quickly and said, "Good meeting you, Deon, and good seeing you again, Tan. Are you ready, Tyler?"

"Sure. Alright, later, y'all!" I get in the car, and my heart is beating faster than usual. Sean is looking at me, wondering why you are tripping. As we drive off, I begin to bring him up to speed on the Cassie situation.

"Say, man, why are you asking Tan to fix you up? Why aren't you fixing yourself up?"

"Man, I don't know. I guess I really don't know what to say."

"All you have to do is be yourself. You don't seem to have a problem talking to Tan. Why is that?"

"It just comes naturally. Besides, she's my friend. I'm not trying to ask her out."

"I'm wondering, why not? I thought that was your girl."

"She is, but not in that way."

"Tyler, I think you are confused."

Chapter 5
Tan
Saturday A week Before Homecoming

My alarm clock is really annoying, especially at 6:45 on a Saturday morning. Whose bright idea was it to have cheerleading practice at 8:00 in the morning on a Saturday? Oh well, I guess I played a part in that. At the time, it made sense because the majority of us didn't want to stay late after school, and Saturday morning sounded more appealing. Ms. James, our cheerleader sponsor, does not play. Whenever we have practice on a Saturday, she always reminds us how valuable her time is and if she makes it to practice before, we do, it will be a helluva consequence!

I'm sitting on the side of the bed, trying to get my mind right. I look across the room and see Kerry sleeping so peacefully. Too bad it's about to end because she has to drop me off at practice. Before I can stand up, Mama is standing in the doorway, "Get up, gal, so that you won't be late."

"OK, I'm about to get dressed."

"Hurry up, your breakfast is already on the table."

"Alright."

I walk over to the dresser and try to find some shorts and a T-shirt. It's funny how these drawers can be so organized with everything in its proper place until the day you are in a hurry. I have things scattered everywhere! Oh well, I will have to fix this mess later. As I'm getting dressed in my white cheer t-shirt and my royal blue shorts with the white trim, the phone rings. Mama answers the phone. "Tan, tele-phone!"

I get the phone off the bar in the kitchen. "Hello!"

"Hey Tan, are you up?" Tyler said.

"Yes, I just got dressed, and I'm about to leave in a few."

"Oh ok, well, I have to work today, and I plan on doing some extra hours so I can add more money to my stash."

"Sounds like a plan."

"OK, well, I will call you when I get home."

I said OK and placed the phone back on the bar. I happen to look up, and Mama is smiling at me.

"What?. Did I miss something?"

"That Tyler boy sure is sweet on you."

"What on earth does that mean?"

"Oh, Honey, you will understand it better by and by!"

I'm still lost, so I will just ease on away from this situation and finish getting ready.

"Hey, Kerry, get up so you can drop me off for practice."

Kerry growls and turns over on her side, turns her head back in my direction, and gives me a daring look. I'm standing here watching her to see if she's getting up.

"You don't have to wait for me to get out of bed. I'm getting up!"

I learned a long time ago to leave Kerry alone after you wake her up. She is definitely not a morning person, and it's not worth losing my life over.

A hot bowl of oatmeal and two pieces of crispy bacon is just what I needed this morning. As soon as I took the last bite, I saw Kerry walking towards the front door to leave. She didn't mumble a single word. It was understood to get my butt up from the table and hurry to the car.

My bag and shoes are waiting by the door. "Bye, Mama!"

"Bye, don't forget your stuff by the door."

"I got 'em!"

I'm rushing to get in the car. I'm moving so fast that I forgot to get the cassette tape out of my player to bring to practice. Kerry is putting the car in reverse. We're moving slowly out of the driveway. I take a deep breath and say, "Kerry, wait! I left something in the house that I need for practice!" She exhales, and while slowly pulling back into the driveway, she doesn't make eye contact with me at all; she is staring straight ahead with a stone face. I jump out of the car and run into the house, into my room, to get the tape. I'm back in the car in record time, so Kerry really can't say anything. We start on our way again while riding in silence. I guess I'm being punished for forgetting the tape.

We pulled up at the school, and there were no cars and no one in sight. I don't want to ask Kerry to wait with me, so I grab my bag to get out of the car.

Kerry said, "Is anyone here besides you?"

"I don't think so."

"So why are you getting out?"

"Because I know you want to get home and go back to sleep."

"I'm not going to leave you here by yourself, Tan. Close the door. I'll wait with you."

Right now, I am speechless! *Why is Kerry being nice to me? I can't believe she's choosing me to oversleep!* I'm almost afraid to say anything because I don't want to mess up this Moment.

"Tan, don't forget the series, North and South; come on tonight at 7:00."

"Ok, cool!" I'm really looking forward to spending time with my big sister, and it seems like she is feeling the same way. This is great. I am sitting here having a nice conversation with her. She can be cool sometimes. You just have to catch her at the right moment.

It's 5 till 8:00. Ms. James just pulled into the parking lot. "I sure hate to leave good company, but I must go now." I reach down to get my bag and open the door. "See you at noon, Kerry!"

"Oh, is that your way of telling me to come back and pick you up?"

"Yes, ma'am!"

Kerry gives me a wave and, to my surprise, a beautiful smile.

Ms. James is growing frustrated with us over this dance routine. We have changed the dance several times, and it's difficult for us to agree on the ending. Ms. James stands up and, walks closer to the stage, and says, "When I point to you, just come down and take a seat!"

One thing about Ms. James is that she knows how to get some act right! She has a "no nonsense" look on her perfectly round face as she places her hand on her curvy hips and takes her seat right in the center of the auditorium, where she wouldn't miss anything.

I quickly walk over to the cassette player to push play. Phil Collins' song, "Sussudio," filled the room, and we started moving on cue. As we approached the end, I held up my right hand and made a fist to inform the team that we were sticking to the original routine. There are no complaints nor pushback, mainly because we all know Ms. James isn't playing with us.

"Great call, Captain," Ms. James says as she winks her eye at me, which confirms that she's pleased.

Thank goddess, that went well. Now it's time for us to decide which uniform we're going to wear for homecoming. I grab the megaphone to say, "ok, everyone, let's meet quickly to decide what to wear for the game." Everyone takes their sweet time to gather around for the discussion. "I want to make a suggestion since we have brand new sweaters and the weather is cool now. I think that would be a perfect choice." A few of the girls agreed, and of course, there are some who will never be satisfied just because they didn't come up with the idea. Out of the corner of my eye, I can see when Ms. James begins to stand up while placing her purse on her shoulder. *Oh dear, what is she about to say or do?* She motions for us to come down from the stage. I'm leading the now quiet squad down the steps right in front of our leader to hear her verdict.

Ms. James is standing looking directly into our faces with disappointment written all over hers. " You all make my job so difficult! You can't ever come together and agree on anything! So, since you all have bird brains and are unable to communicate, I will decide what you will wear. You all will wear the new sweater, blue pleated skirt, and long DHS socks. Are there any questions?"

We all are looking around at one another without saying a mumbling word because we know better. Ms. James pauses, gives me a wink, and says, "That's what I thought!"

Now, the practice is over. I need to walk to the front hallway to use the payphone to call home so Kerry can come to get me. I'm digging into the bottom of my bag to locate a quarter to make the call. I'm not having any luck, so I guess I have to make a collect call. I press zero. "Operator, I would like to make a collect call to 451-4157." As soon as the operator announces the collect call from Tan. Mama didn't say anything and automatically hung up the phone because she knew practice is over and someone needed to come get me. I have to laugh to myself because we are totally beating the system.

The school's parking lot is half full now. Many organizations are here practicing and preparing for homecoming. I take a seat on the steps to wait for my ride. At the same time, I'm waiting for the ROTC soldiers to march right past me and stop. The leader yells," at ease! Fall out!"

They were scattered everywhere, and to my surprise, I spotted Cassie amongst the soldiers. She sees me and immediately comes over to me. "Hey Tan! Do you think I can catch a ride with you?"

"Yeah, no problem."

"OK, I'll be right back. Let me go get my things."

A strange feeling has come over me. I am dreading telling Cassie that Tyler wants to take her to the dance. What will my approach be? Should I just come out and tell her, or should I ease into it? Either way, no approach seems to be the right one.

Cassie returns and takes a seat next to me on the steps. Right when I get the nerves to ask her about the dance, the marching band is now coming off the field, and the drums are so loud that they're literally throwing off my heartbeat. The drummers are now in a circle, having a jam session, and everyone is surrounding them, dancing and having a good time. Of course, Cassie and I couldn't help ourselves either because we made our way over there to join the festivities.

The jam session came to an end after the drum major blew his whistle. I feel like crawling back to the steps because I was dancing so hard that I had no energy left.

"Tan, that was so fun! I think we did every dance that was ever created!"

"No kidding! Any dance that popped into my head, I did it!"

"And I was trying to keep up with you the entire time!" Says Cassie.

I can see Kerry's 1982 maroon Monte Carlo turning the corner. Cassie and I both stand, gather our things, and walk to the entrance to get into the car. We both speak to Kerry.

"I hope y'all are not in a hurry to get home because I have to go to Skaggs to pick up a few items for Mama." We both agreed that it wasn't a problem, as if we really had a choice.

Kerry parks and turns the car off. "Are y'all getting out or staying in?"

"We will stay in," I spoke up for both of us because I would use this as an opportunity to see if Cassie would be open to going to the dance with Tyler. Kerry removed the keys from the ignition, got out, and closed the door. I think maybe she thought we would take off and leave her if she took too long in the store, so she took the keys to make sure that wouldn't happen.

I'm just going to come on out and say it! "Ah. Ah, Cassie, what do you think about Tyler? Do you like him?" Cassie has a puzzled look on her face, and she shifts her body towards me and says, "I can't believe you are asking me about him. I always thought he was into you!"

Now, she is not the only one with a puzzled look on her face because I'm wondering how she could fix her mouth to say that!

"No, Tyler and I are just friends, only friends!"

"Well, that's kinda hard to believe because y'all are ways together."

I can't even argue with that. That is a true statement.

"Cassie, Tyler totally likes you. He wants to take you to the homecoming dance!"

"You know I have a boyfriend, and besides, Tyler doesn't have a car!"

At this very moment, I can feel my blood boiling! I will never be able to understand how someone can be so caught up on what someone has or doesn't have, and the sad reality is they themselves don't have it either. Cassie is going on and on about absolutely nothing. I tune her out after the "he doesn't have a car" statement.

Finally, I had enough! I turned my entire body back around, facing the front, looking straight out of the windshield at people pushing and unloading grocery baskets into the trunks of their cars.

"Tan, I do think he's cute, but he's not my type."

"And that is perfectly okay, Cassie because I think you are really missing out on a great guy!"

Kerry enters the car and looks at me and then back at Cassie. "Y'all look like the cat that swallowed the canary. What is going on with y'all?"

My response is, "There's nothing going on. We were talking about the homecoming dance."

"That must have been some discussion because the tension in this car is so thick. You can cut it with a knife!"

The drive to the house is tranquil; no one is saying anything and the radio is so low that I can't even make out what song is playing. As we pulled into the driveway, I really couldn't wait for Kerry to come to a complete stop before I opened the car door to get out.

"Thanks for the ride, Kerry! Hey Tan, what are you doing later?"

Really, you're asking me what I'm doing later? For What? I know you can feel that I'm not too happy with you right now!

"Actually, Kerry and I have plans."

"Oh ok, I was going to ask you and Deon if y'all wanted to hang out or something."

"Maybe another time. See you later!"

Cassie waved bye as she started her way down the street.

I am not looking forward to telling Tyler how my conversation with Cassie went. I know he's going to feel some type of way. *I know Tyler is not going to believe this, but in this case, he has really and truly dodged a bullet!*

Chapter 6

Tan

North and South

"Tan, come on in here. The movie is about to start!"

"Ok," I yell as I'm wrapping up my conversation with Tyler on the phone. He's busy asking me questions about Cassie, and I'm stalling because I don't want to hurt his feelings.

"Tyler, I have to go. It's movie time!" I hang up the phone to make my way to the den to take my place right next to Kerry on the couch.

Mama is in the kitchen making popcorn on the stove. After the last kennel pops, she pours it into a large plastic bowl and passes it to us through the serving window, along with three cans of Coke. Mama is fixing another large bowl of popcorn for Daddy and JJ, who are in the living room watching a football game. She delivered the bowl and returned to the kitchen to get a can of beer for Daddy and a cup of Kool-Aid for JJ. I can hear Daddy teasing with Mama, trying to get her to stay and watch football with him. She assures him she will come to sit with him during a commercial break. Those magic words bring a smile to his face as he watches her walk away to the den.

Kerry is so excited she can't stop talking about how eager she is to see if the movie is going to be as good or better than the book. I am sitting here clueless, waiting patiently, and hoping I can sit through this great adventure. Mama chimes in, saying the book is really good, so that means the movie characters are going to have to work really hard to live up to the characters in the book. Now I feel like someone who hadn't completed their homework assignment when the rest of the class were all well prepared. I am going into this unthinkingly but willing to be open to watching this and spending quality time with my big sister.

"Shhhhh!" Kerry says as the movie starts. And the funny part about that is no one is saying anything. Mama and I excuse her because we understand that this is a huge deal for her. I tune in to see who the actors are in the movie. "OH, MY GOODNESS! Kerry! Why didn't you tell me Patrick Swayze, with his fine self, is in this movie? He alone would be a good reason to watch. I'm definitely watching every minute of this!" Mom and Kerry are both laughing at me and agreeing with me at the same time.

The setting is in the 1800s, and Orry Main, Patrick's character, is from a family of slave owners on a plantation in South Carolina. Love, at first sight is what Orry experienced, and the feeling was mutual for Madeline, his love interest. The two of them met after Madeline's horse and carriage turned over in a ditch, and Orry rescued her. The moment he laid eyes on her, he knew it was love. Unfortunately, he was on his way to the military academy at *West Point* to fight in the Civil War. Orry knew he would be gone for two years and shared that information with Madeline. She appeared to be as hopeful as he and agreed to wait for him. They both promised to write to one another, and Madeline gave Orry a lace handkerchief to keep with him to return to her when he came back safely.

It's a commercial break, and Mama eases her way to the living room, and I follow behind her. She takes her seat in Daddy's lap. JJ is looking like he is so grossed out by the wet kiss Mama planted on Daddy. Mama is teasing JJ by telling him that one day, his wife is going to do him the same way. JJ covers his head with pillows, trying to make himself disappear. I can't resist snatching all the pillows off of him and planting a big, wet kiss on his jaw! "Yuck, Tan!" he says while wiping his face with his t-shirt.

Kerry yells, "It's back on!" Mama and I rush back to the den for more North and South.

Orry makes friends with George, the son of a steel factory owner from Pennsylvania. They are from two different worlds but don't allow it to interfere with their bond. George did voice his views about slavery, making it clear that he did not support it. Orry respected his views and didn't hold it against him.

Love never left Orry's mind. Many nights, he stayed up late writing letters to the women of his dreams. Soon, worry came over him because he hadn't received an answer to the letters that he had written to her. I can't help but think how bro-kenhearted I would be if I didn't get some type of letter, a paragraph, or a sentence from the person I loved.

Orry finally gets a chance to go back home to the south, and his mission is to find Madeline. To his surprise, Madeline is getting married. He's too late to stop it! That was so heartbreaking. I have both hands on my chest in disbelief at this loveless marriage that is taking place. Poor Orry, he's so hurt and disappointed. Madeline sneaks off with Orry to have a private conversation. She reveals to him that she never received any letters from him and thinks that he has decided to move on. Clearly, she sees the hurt in his eyes as he reaches into his pocket and gives her the handkerchief that he cared for, which proves to her that he is a man of his word. My eyes and mouth were both wide open with disbelief when it was discovered that Madeline's father purposely destroyed the letters because he already had planned who he wanted her to marry.

Once the credit starts rolling, I tell Kerry how much I'm enjoying this, and. she interrupts me in mid-sentence, "I know you thought it was going to be boring, but I knew you would enjoy it because it had something to do with love."

While nodding my head up and down in agreement with her, I say, "You are exactly right, and I can't wait to watch more!"

I'm lying in bed reflecting on the movie. It bothers me that Madeline's father withheld her letters from Orry. He had no right to do that! He thought he knew what was best for her, but it was unfair that she wasn't given a chance to be with the man of her dreams. I get it how fathers are protective of their daughters because I'm going through that right now. Daddy has these crazy rules. That started with Kerry. She wasn't allowed to talk on the phone to boys until the eleventh grade, and she was not allowed to go out or have boy company over to the house either. Kerry had to beg and plead with Daddy to let her go to the junior prom with a date. I'm so glad she was the oldest because she has made my experience a little easier. So now I have to get my strategy together and figure out the right approach for Daddy. I'm hoping it won't be a big headache like it was when I wanted to start talking to boys on the phone. Daddy made me keep my room clean for two whole weeks, and guess what? I did it! I'm wondering what ridiculous thing I'm going to have to do before I can go to the prom.

Oh, how I dread telling Tyler that Cassie is still dating someone and that she is not going to the dance with him. I wouldn't dare tell him the other stuff. He doesn't deserve to be hurt. I guess I will go ahead and break the news to him tomorrow, and hopefully, he won't let that get to him. I'm just going to encourage him to go solo or with friends. I definitely won't have a date. Daddy will be dropping me off and picking me up to make sure I won't do anything slick. He always says he has to stay two steps ahead of me, and I joke with him and say you mean two steps behind. For some reason, he doesn't find that funny at all.

It's Monday evening, and Tyler and I are doing our normal routine of walking home together and talking about our day. I know he is going to ask about Cassie soon. I can just feel it.

We are turning on my street now, and I pause, thinking he was going to give me my book bag, but he didn't. He continues to walk to my house, and then Deon comes running up to us from out of nowhere, gets between us, and puts her arms around us. *She really has lousy timing. I know Tyler doesn't want to have a discussion about Cassie in front of her.*

"How are my two favorite people?" Deon says while looking at him and then at me.

"A better question is, why weren't you at school today, Missy?"

Deon removes her arms from around us and starts explaining how she took the day off to go dress shopping for the homecoming dance. Tyler has a confused look on his face. "You mean to tell me you missed school to shop for a dress?" Tyler said as he shook his head.

"I wouldn't expect you to understand. It's a girl's thing!" Deon says with such enthusiasm.

I say to Tyler, "Leave that alone because you are not going to win!"

"Oh, I know that; remember, I have a Mom and a sister!" The three of us are laughing, and for some reason, Deon has a look on her face, and I can tell this is not going to end well.

"So, Tyler, have you asked Cassie to the dance yet?"

I'm looking at Deon. I know you should know better than to ask that question!

Tyler looks directly at me like he wishes he could disappear.

I immediately become defensive and start to speak for him, "No, he's not going to waste his time fooling with her when he knows dang gon well, she's not the girl for him!"

Oh my God! What has gotten into me? What did I just say?

Tyler and Deon are both looking at me in a perplexed manner. So now I have to do some damage control.

Luckily, my girl caught on, and Dee began to say, "Yeah, Tyler, I agree, you deserve someone who will appreciate you."

Tyler still seems to be holding on to my blatant confession, but I'm not going to address that at all. I'm going to move right along and pretend like I never uttered those words.

It's 8:00 at night, and I just did the dishes and cleaned the kitchen. As I walk to my room, the phone starts ringing. Something in my soul is telling me it's Tyler. I grab the phone with the long cord that's sitting in the hallway by my parent's room and pull it into my room to answer the phone. "Hello."

"Hey, Tan!"

"Oh hey, Tyler!"

"What are you doing?"

"Just finished washing dishes and cleaning up the kitchen. What's on your mind, Tyler?"

"You never told me how the conversation went with Cassie."

"Well, it really didn't go well at all. To tell you the truth. She pissed me off!"

I could hear Tyler taking short breaths to prevent from over-heating.

"What do you mean?"

"Basically, she only wants to be with you if it benefits her."

There's nothing but silence on the other end of the phone. I hope he's ok.

"Tyler, you are better off going with friends, and that way, you know you are going to have a good time. You know that's my plan because my dad is not going for the whole date thing!"

That statement kind of lightens the mood because I can hear him laughing.

"Yeah, you're right! Your old man ain't playing that!"

"Oh well, Tan. I guess I will meet your big head there!"

"Sure, and maybe I will save you a dance."

"Or two!" Tyler slid that comment in unexpectedly.

We are both holding the phone. All we can hear now are crickets. We were both mute, so I decided to break the silence. "Good night, Tyler."

"Good night, Tan."

Finally, it's Thursday evening! I am filled with so much excitement because today is the day, I pick up the dress that I ordered for the dance. Kerry is driving Mom and me to Samson South, an outdoor shopping center just a few miles away. We walk into JCPenney and take the escalators down to the catalog department. I hope my dress looks as good as it does in the book. The cashier goes to the back, brings a box, and places it on the counter. I open the box and pull out the most beautiful navy blue, straight, t-strap dress with a hint of silver sparkles on it.

Mom and Kerry both approve of the dress, so Mom pays for it, and off we go.

As soon as we pull into the driveway, Deon comes outside. It's almost like she's psychic or something because she timed that perfectly. She starts walking over to the car as I'm getting out with the box in my hand.

"Hello, Mrs. Breakfeild and Kerry."

They both say hello to Deon.

"Tan, I can't wait to see your dress! After I see yours, you have to come over to see mine."

We walked into the house and went straight into my room, and I placed the box on my bed.

"Open, Open, Open!" Deon says as she is jumping around like a little kid.

"Ok, OK!" I open the box slowly, pull my amazing dress out, and hold it up against my body.

"Oh, Tan! You are going to look so pretty!"

"Do you think so?"

"Shoot! I know so!"

Mom comes in and suggests that I try the dress on so there won't be any surprises tomorrow.

I go into my closet, slip on the dress, and model it for them.

"Wow Tan! That size 1 fits you perfectly!" Mom said.

"Yes, it does. I'm so glad I didn't get the size 3. It would have been too big."

I change back into my regular clothes, and Deon and I walk over to her house so I can see her dress.

I follow Dee into her house to the kitchen where her Mom is. "Hello, Mrs. Franklin!"

"Hi baby, how are you doing today?"

"I'm ok, and you?"

"Oh, baby, I'm doing ok for an old woman."

"Now, Mrs. Franklin, you know you are not old. Stop playing."

She's laughing as she walks into her bedroom and closes her door.

Deon gets two glasses out of the cabinet, opens the refrigerator, and pours us some grape Kool-Aid. We're sitting at the table, and Dee starts to inquire about Tyler.

"So, how did Tyler take the news about Cassie?"

"He's fine. He doesn't need anyone like that in his life. Why would he want to sign up to get used?"

"Yeah, you're right. He needs someone that will appreciate him and someone that really cares about him. He needs someone like YOU!"

I'm going along with everything she is saying. I'm shaking my head up and down, agreeing with everything. Until that last part!

"Wait a minute! What do you mean? Me?"

"Yes, you, Tan! You are right for him! You may not admit it, but I know you've been thinking the same thing lately!"

I just drop my head in hopes that Deon shuts up.

"Let's go see your dress now."

"Ok, but I still meant what I said!"

As soon as we walk into Dee's room, we are greeted by a beautiful black, strapless, chiffon dress trim with pearls across the chest.

"Wow! What a dress! You are definitely going to make a statement!"

Dee places her hand on her chest and says, "Why thank you, ma'am, that is so kind of you!"

"Girl, you are so crazy! We both are going to be gunning in our dresses!"

"For sure!"

In our minds, we were going to be the prettiest and finest chicks at the dance.

"Well, Dee, I need to go home so Mama can start trying to tame my hair for tomorrow."

"Yeah, girl, I know she has to start early trying to tame that mane!"

"Ha! Ha! Very funny!" I say as I'm walking out of her house across the lawn to my house.

As soon as I walked in, Mama said, "Get in here, Tan, so that I can start on your hair. You know this is going to be an all-night thing!"

I exhale and say to myself, "I know!"

It's showtime! I thought this day would never get here! Mama has made the last Shirley Temple curl on my head, and I'm relieved to finally get out of this hard chair and away from the hot fire on the stove. I race to the mirror to admire my hair. I'm smiling at myself because Mama always does a fantastic job! I reach into the closet, take out my dress, and grab my navy blue pumps. My nude pantyhose and slip are lying on my bed. I begin to dress and yell for Mama to come to zip me. As soon as she walked in, she put both hands over her mouth.

"Tan, you look like a doll!"

I can see it in her eyes how emotional this is for her.

"Thanks, Mama," I say with a sweet smile.

"Stay right there. I'm going to get you something. Don't move.

I'm standing here in suspense, wondering what Mama could be getting for me.

Mama returns with the most beautiful diamond earrings, necklace, and bracelet set.

My eyes are lighting up with so much joy right now! I can't believe Mama is letting me wear "THE GOOD JEWELRY!"

"Now, Tan, this is not fake, so you make sure you take good care of my things. And most of all, do not let my bracelet slide off your po wrist!"

I pick up the diamond earrings very delicately and place them in my ears. Mama places the necklace around my neck and the bracelet on my right wrist. All of a sudden, I'm feeling like Cinderella, but all I'm missing is my prince charming.

"John, Kerry, and JJ! Y'all come and see how beautiful Tan looks!"

They all come racing in to lay eyes on me. They seem to all agree with Mama, judging by the big smiles on their faces.

"Tan, get your shoes on and come outside so I can take some pictures before I take you to the dance," says Daddy.

He loves to take pictures with his new professional camera. I have a feeling this photoshoot could last for hours.

"Ok, Daddy, I'll be right out. Remember, Daddy, we only have thirty minutes before I have to leave.

"Ok, if you hurry up, I can get some good shots, and we will be done!"

Now he knows that's not true, but I will play along.

It is not long before Deon and Tracey come to join me in the photo shoot.

Daddy is having a good time, changing lenses and shooting from different angles like he is really a professional.

"Alright, John, that's enough. They will never make it to the dance if you keep that up!" says Mama.

Daddy grins and snaps one more picture, just because. He put his camera away and went to get his keys off the bar.

He says, ok, young ladies, the van is ready to take Y'all to the ball!

Daddy opens the door for Mama, and then he opens the side sliding door for us.

The three of us are looking in our individual compact mirrors, powdering our noses, and applying more lip gloss. I just thought of something, it's the last night for North and South, and I can't miss it, I have to see it!

"Mama, can you and Kerry please record North and South for me?"

"I will if we have a blank VHS tape."

"Just record over something. I have to see it, Mama! I have to know how it ends!"

Deon and Tracey are looking at me, thinking, is it that serious?

I'm taking the time to give them the rundown of the series, and now I believe they can understand why I feel the way I do.

"Tan, before you exit this vehicle, I need to make sure that we have a clear understanding. You need to be out here at 10:00, not on your way out here. you do know the difference, right?" Daddy asked while facing me to make sure there was no way possible for me to be confused.

"Yes, Sir, I understand."

"Deon and Tracey, since I am now responsible for the two of you, I need to know if my expectations are clear?"

"Yes, Sir," they both say while we're exiting the van.

I can't even be embarrassed because my friends are well aware of how strict my Daddy is, and they don't ever say anything to me about it, but they tease me about it from time to time.

As soon as the door opened, the music started blasting from the cafeteria. Everyone starts picking up the pace, trying to hurry to see what's happening. The doors leading into the cafeteria are opened, and the lights are dimmed. This place has really transformed. The tables all have white tablecloths and silver centerpieces with blue and white balloons. Blue and white streamers filled the ceilings, and there was a huge dance floor right in the middle. The DJ is set up in the corner, and he already has a crowd of people around his table trying to request their favorite songs. There's a table in the back full of refreshments, and the teachers are all standing guard behind it. I must say, everyone is looking quite nice tonight, and hopefully, that will prevent them from acting like fools. It's kind of hard to act a fool when you are looking your best.

Deon, Tracey, and I locate a table in a good spot right by the dance floor. Janis and Shayla walk in. Janis is wearing a cute, short, royal blue satin dress with puff short sleeves. Shayla is looking cute, also wearing a long, silver, strapless dress. They are scanning the room, and I stand up and wave my hand. They see me and start walking my way. I meet them halfway, and the three of us hug while jumping with excitement and complementing one another. Everyone spoke, and they had a seat at the table. Tracey is looking very annoyed, probably because she is sitting here with us underclassmen. As soon as her crew walked in, she left us without a word.

The DJ announces that this next song should get everyone up on their feet! As soon as we heard the first tune, we all were hitting the dance floor! "Brass Monkey," now that's my jam!

My crew and I are all in a circle doing the whop. We all have our hands in the air and waving them like we just don't care! This is the first dance, and we are dancing the town down!

Shayla is walking back to the table because she says her makeup is messing up. I'm good; my makeup is light with a touch of blush and lip gloss. Janis is looking at me, wondering if I'm are tired yet. And

I'm shaking my head no while still dancing. Now, she's joining Shayla at the table. And then there were two. Deon and I are serious about this thing. We have made up several dances along the way, and others have joined in on the fun.

Ok, the DJ is really bringing it now. He's killing the rotation! "The Show" by Doug E. Fresh is causing everybody to break out with the prep! *AHHHH,* we are prepping high and prepping low! We are prepping all across the floor! Alright, it's time for me to take a seat now that I feel a bead of sweat on my forehead. Deon is feeling it, too, and follows me to our table. I take my seat and grab a napkin to gently pat the sweat off my forehead. While I'm patting, someone comes behind me and covers my eyes with their hands. *I wonder who it could be.* "Guess who?"

"Oh, I could never guess because it could be anyone!"

"Come on, I know you can get it right with just one guess."

"Ok, but I don't know if this is correct, but I am going to say. Tyler!"

"BINGO!" He says as he uncovers my eyes.

DANG! Tyler looks GOOD! He's wearing navy blue slacks, a crisp white dress shirt with a navy knit tie, a black belt, and black shoes. There is no doubt that he used World of Curls on his hair because every strand was curled to perfection.

"Stand up, girl, let me see your dress!"

I turned to look at my friends, and they were all up in our business.

I don't understand why my heart is beating so fast now. It's just Tyler. What is going on with me?

I hope he doesn't notice. Snap out of it, Tan!

I push my chair back and slowly stand up. Tyler's eyes got big like he saw a ghost. He takes my hand, holds it up, and twirls me around to get the full effect. Something tells me that he definitely likes what he sees.

"Wow, Tan! You look so beautiful!"

I'm blushing, and I can't help it.

"You're just saying that. Go ahead and say SIKE!"

"There's no sike here, I mean it!"

Now, my heart is doing a whole routine in my chest. I can barely catch my breath!"

Get it together, Tan, before he thinks you are crazy!

Tyler leans in real close and says, "Don't forget I want a dance or two with you."

Before I can respond, Deon says, "We were just talking about how cute y'all look, and Y'all are wearing the same color! Y'all need to take a picture. Tan, where's your camera?"

I reach into my purse, get the disposable Fuji camera out, and hand it to Deon. Tyler puts his arm around me, and we both say cheese and the camera snaps. After that, Tyler goes to hang out with his friends. I take my seat and happen to notice all eyes on me.

"Why are y'all staring at me?"

Janis quickly responds by saying, "We think you and Tyler make a perfect couple!"

Janis's statement is interrupted when Deon says, "Look who is walking through the door, and why is she wearing my dress?"

Cassie walks in with her boyfriend, who attends another school, sporting the exact dress Deon has on.

Deon is crushed! No girl wants to have this problem. When shopping for a dress, we really have to go over and beyond to try to make sure that our dress is just that. Our dress! Deon's mood has changed drastically. I'm trying to get her mind off of the dress situation, but that's impossible because here's Miss. Cassie heading our way.

"Hey, ladies!" She says, with a smirk on her face.

Why am I the only one who speaks to her? Deon cuts her eyes at her and proceeds to turn her whole body around to face the dance floor.

"Nice dress, Deon. Let's take a picture together!"

Before words could part her lips, I intervened. "Hey, why don't we all take a group picture!"

Shayla volunteers to take the picture for us. The three of us are standing here with the fakest smiles on our faces. *What a waste of film!*

After the photo op, Cassie walks over to her date, who is in a deep conversation with some guy by the refreshment table.

"Deon, why are you so upset with Cassie? I'm sure it wasn't done on purpose. How would she have known that she was purchasing the same dress as you when she hadn't even seen your dress?"

"Talk what you know, Tan. That heifer saw my dress the same day I showed it to you!"

"Oh, that is so FOUL! How could she do that to you? Yes, it's a beautiful dress, but there are a lot of beautiful dresses out there. I just don't understand that!"

"You wouldn't, Tan, because you are not like that."

The DJ is changing things up by putting a slow jam on, "Computer Love" by Zapp. I'm looking around the room, and the guys are searching for that special girl to dance with. I see Cassie lurking around, looking like she is up to no good.

I know this tramp ain't headed in Tyler's direction! Oh yes, she is! The nerve! She has a boyfriend here and is still after someone else's man! Wait a minute, Tan, Tyler doesn't have a girlfriend. I'm tripping!

While I'm talking to myself, Joseph is trying to get my attention. He wants to dance. I make sure we get close enough that I can keep an eye on Tyler and Cassie. Joseph looks nice tonight. He's wearing some plaid polo pants, a white button-down shirt, and a red polo tie. He's also smelling really nice too. This must be his favorite song because he is singing all off-key in my ear. I guess the look on my face says it all. "What's wrong, Tan? You don't like my singing?" Joseph says in a joking way. I began to smile just to be polite, and the terrible singing stopped. The song is over, and he invites me to the refreshment table. Somehow, I let him distract me because Tyler and Cassie weren't on my mind at all.

Joseph hands me a cup of punch while we are talking, and the DJ thought it was a good idea to play, "Sweet Love" by Anita Baker. I absolutely love her and every song that she sings. Joseph looks like he wants to ask me to dance again, but before he can get the words out. I can see Tyler heading my way. Is he coming to ask me to dance? I don't want to get CRUNCHED, so I look in another direction just in case he's thirsty and he's getting himself something to drink. I walk away from Joseph to throw my cup away, and just like I suspected, Tyler grabs my hand and leads me to the dance floor. It's like magic. I'm on cloud nine. I never thought it would feel this good to dance so closely with my best friend. I laid my head on Tyler's shoulder, and when I raised my head up just to get a little glimpse of him, his eyes were closed.

The music stops playing, and it is time to announce the king and queen. Tyler and I go our separate ways. I'm back at the table, and my friends all have goofy grins on their faces.

"What is it?" I say to them.

Deon suddenly speaks up and says, "If I had a vote, I would totally vote for you and Tyler to be king and queen."

"Wow, Deon, that makes a lot of sense! We are not seniors, so that's impossible!"

"I'm just saying, Y'all look like a fairytale, Cinderella and Prince Charming. Y'all belong together! And while Y'all were slow dancing, I grabbed your camera and took a picture."

"You what?"

I can't believe I didn't notice it. Was I that into the dance that I wasn't conscious of what was going on around me?

"I took a picture. You will thank me later," Deon says, with a devious smile on her face.

I'm so glad my moment of happiness took her mind off the dress drama she had with Cassie. And speaking of Cassie, she's leaving the cafeteria right now with her date. There's no telling where she's going. Out of nowhere, Tracey appears and says, Tan, it is 9:45, and you know what your dad said, so you and Deon better come on to the parking lot now because I'm sure he's already out there. Tracey said what she had to say and walked right out of the door. I look at Deon, and she says, "You don't have to tell me twice!"

Janis is looking at me like I understand, but Shayla has a confused look on her face. What on earth is going on? Janis laughs and says, "I'll see you tomorrow at the game, and don't worry, I'll fill Shayla in."

"Cool!" I say, and begin making my way to the parking lot.

"Wait up!" I hear a male's voice say, and I turn around, and it's Tyler. Deon continues to walk to the parking lot.

"Were you just going to leave without saying anything? Plus, you owe me another dance!"

"I'm sorry, Tyler. I wish I could stay, but my Daddy told us to be outside no later than 10:00."

"So why didn't you tell me? I will wait with you. You're forgetting I know how your Daddy is. I don't mind waiting with you."

Oh, how sweet of Tyler to wait with me rather than be inside dancing or macking on some girl.

"Wow! Don't I feel special!"

"Well, you should!" He says with a big smile.

It's 9:55, and there's the Chevy, burgundy, gray, and black van pulling into the parking lot. Tyler walks us to the van, speaks to my parents, gives me a quick hug, and heads back to the dance.

"I told you that boy is sweet on you!" Says Mama.

"What!" Daddy asks.

Silence fills the van, and Mama strikes up a conversation with Daddy about retiling her bathroom floor. She is brilliant! And quick on her feet! My friends are very amazed at how well Mama redirected Daddy's thoughts.

After getting Tracey and Deon home safely, I'm finally home and getting ready for bed. Today was very interesting and a lot of fun. I will never begin to understand why Cassie felt the need to buy the same dress as Deon. Most of all, I'm so glad Deon didn't deck her! I could tell she really wanted to, but she chose the classy route. And why did I get upset when Cassie was dancing with Tyler? Hell, I can answer that she is not sincere. What I mean is she will hurt him, and I will not allow her the opportunity to do that!

As I climb into my warm bed, I can't help but lie here and reflect on every comment that my friends made about Tyler and me. And most of all, why do I feel like I need to protect Tyler's heart? Could Tyler be falling for Cassie again because of one stupid dance? Well, maybe not because he wanted to wait in the parking lot with me instead of being inside at the dance. Did he choose me because Cassie left with her boyfriend? I'm not trying to be anybody's second choice! What am I thinking? HE'S JUST MY FRIEND!

Chapter 7

Tan

East and West

After a restless night of tossing and turning, it's Saturday afternoon. I can't believe I slept so late. I'm dressed and ready to start my day. As I enter the kitchen, Mama is sitting at the table peeling potatoes.

"Well, hello, Sleeping Beauty!"

I give Mama a warm smile, "Hey, Mama!"

"You must've been tired, sleeping so late."

"I guess I was. I really didn't realize how late it was."

"So, tell me about the dance. Did y'all have a good time?"

"Yes, ma'am, we did. There was some drama with Deon and Cassie."

"Oh my, I hope it wasn't over, some boy!"

"No, worst! Cassie purchased the same dress as Deon and wore it to the dance."

"What possessed that child to do that? That's crazy!"

Should I mention the Cassie / Tyler situation? I better not. Because then I will have to admit that I have feelings for him.

"Now it's going to be awkward whenever Cassie comes around us."

"Oh well, tell me about that Tyler boy. Did you get to hang out with him or dance?"

Immediately, I'm starting to blush. "Yes, we talked, and I danced with him once, right before it was time to leave."

"So, was it a fast dance song or a slow dance song?"

Blushing again. "Oh Mama, it was a slow dance, no big deal!"

"Really? Not judging from the reaction, you are having now," Mama says in a joking way.

"Mama!"

"OK, I'll leave it alone for now. Go ahead and eat something. You have another long day ahead of you."

"Indeed, I do!"

"We want a touchdown, gotta have a touchdown now, hey right now! (clap-clap)"

We are cheering with all our might! It's our mission to win this homecoming game. Davis High-vs-Westview High, the East against the West. Who will come out on top? The crowd is going wild because it's almost halftime, and the score is tied. We both have 12 points, and we have the ball. We have to keep this energy going, so I'm calling for it. Wildcat Beat! I shout out, "Hit it! Clap your hands and stomp your feet and listen to the rhythm of the Wildcat Beat, Go!" Just about everyone in the stands is standing up, clapping, and stomping their feet. Our Wildcats are feeling it now! They scored again! The band was playing our fight song, and we were on the sidelines doing our dance routine.

It's half-time, and I'm walking up to the concession stand to hang out. Joseph approaches me with a white box.

"Hey Tan, I have something for you. I tried to give it to you last night, but you disappeared.

"Ok, what is it?"

We walk over to the side of the stadium and he gives me the box to open.

"Oh, Joseph! It's beautiful! I pull a very decorative blue, white, and silver mum from the box.

"Can I pin it on you?"

"Sure, Joseph, I would love that. I had no clue you were getting me a mum."

"You weren't supposed to."

"Well, at least I can sport it during halftime and then hang it on the fence during the game."

Joseph is so happy right now because he knows he has totally made my day!

"Let me walk you back down to the sideline."

"Ok, that will be nice."

Joseph seems to be so proud at this very moment that someone asks him, is that you, Joseph? He smiles and says, "Man, I'm working on it!"

"Thanks again for making my day."

"Tan, it was all my pleasure!"

I walk the rest of the way to the sideline alone. As soon as I got around the other cheerleaders, they all started to inquire about my mum. I don't comment. I just smile and keep them guessing. I unpin it and hang it up on the fence with the rest of them.

Yay! The East completely whipped the West! Final score: 12 to 25! We are the best! I'm removing my mum off the fence to pin it back on, and I happen to look up and see Tyler.

"What's up, Tan! Nice mum!"

"Why, thank you! So why am I just now seeing you, Tyler?"

"Oh, I've been here. I watched you cheer, and I saw you and Joseph by the concession stand."

"I was wondering if you were here."

"Hey, I will come meet you and walk you to the bus if Joseph doesn't mind."

"Ha-Ha! You have jokes!"

"I don't want him to get the wrong idea about us."

"And what is that supposed to mean?"

The other cheerleaders and I walked together, and then I met up with Tyler.

Thank goodness Joseph is nowhere in sight because I 'm walking with another guy while wearing the other guy's mum! Interesting!

Chapter Eight

Tyler

Homecoming

There's only one week until homecoming. Tan is running out of time to talk to Cassie about going to the dance with me. How hard could that be for her? Because for me, it's considered a difficult task. I really can't explain why I can't talk to her for myself. Just the thought of it brings on a nervous feeling in the pit of my stomach. Besides, I know Tan can do a much better job of convincing her of how great I am.

It's early on a Saturday morning, and I'm sitting on the couch eating a bowl of Captain Crunch cereal and watching the Looney Tunes. Mom and I are the only ones up, so the house is pretty quiet. I get up to get a refill and grab the phone off the wall to call Tan before she leaves for cheerleader practice. She is already up and ready to go. I'm trying to build up the nerve to ask about Cassie, but for some reason, I can't bring myself to do so. Instead, I just let her know that I will be working longer hours today and that I will call her later.

"Tyler, are you ready?" Mom says.

"Yes, I'm waiting for you!"

"Alright, I'm almost ready. Get my keys off the table and go warm up the car."

I push my left foot all the way down on the clutch, then make sure it's in neutral, and start my future car. Ohhhhhh, the sweet sound of this V-6 engine with 107 horsepower is like music to my ears. As I sit here behind the wheel, staring at the large gold bird that stretches across the hood, it brings me great pleasure to know that in the very near future, this very car will be all mine! I reach in the back seat for my cassette tape case and unzip it, looking for the suitable tape because I know Mom can't handle some of my music. Micheal Jackson, yeah, that's a safe choice. Who doesn't like him? I see Mom heading to the car, so there is no time to rewind, so that I will press play. "Billie Jean" came pouring out of the speakers really loud! Mom is using her hands to motion me to move over to the passenger side of the car.

"Tyler, get on the passenger side. I'm in a hurry, so that means I need to drive to ensure that we reach our destination safely and turn that music down!"

I'm moving, but I sure don't want to. I hardly ever get to drive during the week, and now it's the weekend, and she doesn't have time. I'm upset, but it's ok.

Mom is flying up Shaw Ave like she is going to put out a fire! *Slow down, MAD WOMAN! Is this your idea of being safe?* I give her a look, and she realizes that she's driving like a maniac and begins to adjust her speed. *And you wonder where I get it from!*

"Tyler, I'm just showing you what this car can do. But the key is I know what I'm doing because I am a skilled driver! Have you thought about how blessed you are to be getting a car like this?" She reaches over and turns the radio off. *Here we go. a long lecture before work, that's exactly what I needed!*

We are super busy today. I feel like I have made two hundred burgers and fried a ton of fries. If one more person comes in here and thinks they're special by ordering a specialty burger, I'm going to go postal! That only slows me down! I'm programmed to make plain, cheese, or double meat burgers with the usual, such as lettuce, tomatoes, pickles, and onions. In order to cut down on time, you have to put your own condiments on your burger.

Finally, it's my lunch break, and I'm stuck eating one of my famous burgers and fries with a Coke. I'm sitting at a table minding my own business when two of the finest girls on campus walk in. They are regulars here, and they love how I fix their burgers. *They always leave satisfied. That thought makes me laugh.* I have just stuffed about five fries in my mouth, and they seem to be headed my way. I'm trying to hurry and chew fast before they get to me. Too late. They're here!

"Hello, Cutie!" They both say at the exact same time. I'm trying not to look stupid and expose the few fries that are left in my mouth.

"Oh. Ah. Hey, what's up?"

"Did you forget about us? You know we come in here at the same time on the weekend," the taller one says while licking her lips.

I can't help but be distracted by these two beauties giving me the time of day.

"I'm sorry, I've been swamped today and had to take a later lunch. I will fix y'all up right now."

"No, you won't end your lunch for us," the shorter one says, "we will just go order and come back and share a table with you."

Now I must chunk this food down my throat and wash it down with this Coke to try to keep from choking! The things we guys do for beautiful women. When will it ever end?

Here, they come carrying their specialty burgers and sides on their trays. *Funny how their specialty burgers don't ever annoy me.*

By the time they took their seats, I'm done eating my lunch, but I saved enough soda so I could have something to do instead of staring at them.

The taller one is a little bolder than the other one. Out of nowhere, she says, "soooo, do you have a girlfriend? I recall the last time we talked to you, you were planning to ask some girl to the homecoming dance."

I pick up my cup to get a swallow of soda, "actually, I have a friend working on that."

The two of them looked at each other, wondering if he was real.

Now that I think about it. It does sound corny.

"Ladies, I got this. I will give y'all a full report the next time I see Y'all."

"Ok, Cutie," the taller one says, and I head back to the hot grill for the rest of my shift.

It's a trip how I can talk to the two of them all the time, and I also know how they like their burgers, but I don't know their names.

Ant called, and he's on his way over so we can hang out. While I wait for him to show up, I'll call Tan to see if she has some information for me.

"Hello Tan, whatcha doing?"

"Oh, hey Tyler, I'm about to watch a movie with Kerry and my Mama. What's up?"

Now she knows good and well what's up! So, I will play clueless with her!

"Nothing much. Have you had a chance to talk to Cassie?"

Why is this girl stalling? She's trying to tell me about the movie she's about to watch. I couldn't care less about that! STOP WASTING MY TIME! That's really what I want to yell through the phone!

"I have to go now, Tyler. I'll talk to you later!"

Did she just hang up the phone? UGH!

We are cruising in Ant's new car. A white 1985 RS Camera, and it is CLEAN! *Man, I can't wait until Mom releases the Fire Bird to me!*

"That motor is bad man!"

"Oh yeah! If I'm not careful, it will get away from me!"

"Say, man, when you gon invest in a system? You know me; that's my number one priority!"

"Yeah, I know it's a really big deal for you, but for me, I'm fine with just the basics."

"Naw, man! Say it isn't so! You don't really mean that, do you?"

Ant is laughing it off, but I think he is actually serious.

We're at the "Hangout Spot," a parking lot at the corner of Bell and River Street. This is the spot where everyone who's anyone hangs out and just socializes. People are walking around, sitting on cars and trucks, and playing their music. We spot a few of our friends and talk for a while. The sun is about to go down, so it's best not to stick around too long because people start acting ignorant when it starts to get dark. Ant and I walk back to his car and burn out down Bell Street.

As we pulled up in front of my house, Ant turned his car off, and it's evident that something was bothering him.

"Say, Tyler, are you taking Cassie to the dance, or have you given up on taking her?"

"Man. I don't even know. I called Tan to see how their conversation went, but she didn't tell me anything! I'm about ready to say forget it!"

"I know what you mean. I'm just going to go with the fellas and try again next year."

We both are laughing because, at this very moment, we realize that maybe these girls are not worth all the trouble we are going through.

Ant heads home, and I'm walking into the house and going straight to my room. I just don't want to be bothered. I'm not going to call Tan either because I'm in no rush to receive disappointing news. Tomorrow is Monday, and I need to get my clothes together so I won't look like I feel. I locate the iron and the ironing board to iron my Guess jeans. I will wear a light blue Guess sweatshirt, and that way, it'll be less ironing for me. I believe in working smarter, not harder. I can hear Mom in the kitchen cooking something that has a strange smell. I'm not sure what that could be.

"Tyler, come here! I want you to taste something!"

I know it's something that I'm not going to like because I don't even like the smell of it.

"Ok, here I come!"

As soon as I walked into the kitchen, Mom already had my plate fixed. She hands it to me, and I'm walking to the table with an unknown substance on my plate with mashed potatoes, gravy, and corn.

I look over at my siblings, who are also staring at it. I can tell Venus is about to say something crazy.

"Y'all better eat because you know Mom's rule: we keep eating it until it's gone!"

We all had to laugh and come to find out, this unknown substance is LIVER! YUCK!

After I eat everything except for the liver, I take a shower and get into bed. It's challenging to go to sleep because I'm a little unsettled about the dance. Will I have a date or not? That is the question. Maybe I should be more like Ant; just accept the fact that it's not going to happen this year and be okay with it. I can't help but wonder why Tan is stalling. Is she trying not to hurt my feelings, or did she even talk to Cassie? Why am I tripping? Why wouldn't she? I'm definitely going to build up my nerves tomorrow and ask Tan straight up if Cassie is willing to go to the dance with me. I should've just asked Tan to the dance; she is my best friend and it wouldn't be all this extra pressure on me. Why am I thinking about Tan? She always creeps into my thoughts.

It's an ordinary Monday, and we made it through the day. I met Tan at our usual spot, and we walked home. The conversation is going well, and I am trying to figure out when to bring Cassie up. Tan seems to be really trying to talk about everything but that. We are approaching her street, and I'm having a struggle inside my head about whether I'm going to her house or going home. My legs are continuing to walk down her street, so I guess that's what I'm going to do now.

Out of nowhere is Deon, running up, hugging the both of us, and explaining why she missed a day of school to find a dress for the dance. I'm confused. Since when is shopping a legitimate reason to miss school? The expression on my face said it all because Deon was getting defensive and really trying to justify missing school to shop. Tan gave me a look. That meant leaving it alone because I wasn't going to win. So, we move on to the next topic, which is Deon inquiring about me and Cassie. *Why in the Hell does she think it is her business to know whether I asked Cassie to the dance or not? I really do not want to have this discussion with her!*

Tan is ready to spit fire! I have never seen her in defense mode like this before! She quickly snaps and says, "he's not going to waste his time with someone like her. She is not the girl for him!"

I'm shocked to hear those words coming out of her mouth. That only makes me wonder. Who could be the girl for me? The way Tan is talking, she seems to be pretty sure of that statement.

I want to ask her what she means by that, but something is telling me this is not the right time to have this conversation. I can see Tan is speechless and a little uncomfortable now, and Deon puts her two cents in by cosigning everything Tan says.

"Alright, y'all, I have to make this trip. Tan, I'll call you later."

I start a light jog down the street.

I can't get Tan's words out of my head. I have to know what she meant by that! Could it be she feels that she's the right girl for me? Am I just overanalyzing what she said? At this point, I'm not even sure what to think. There is only one solution. And that is to pick up the phone and call her. I glance at the clock, and it's 8:00. That's not too late to call. The phone rings twice, and Tan answers. She told me she just finished the dishes and cleaned up the kitchen. I don't really want to waste time with small talk, so I ask, "How did the conversation go when you asked Cassie if she wanted to go to the dance with me?"

Tan begins to tell me that Cassie only wants a guy if it will benefit her. I really don't know what to say after that. I'm trying to play like this, but it is not affecting me. But Tan can see right through it. She is trying to convince me that I am better off going by myself or with friends like she is because her Daddy is not trying to hear anything about her dating. To make matters a little sweeter, Tan says she will save me a dance. Something takes over my voice and says, "Or maybe two!" I'm glad I expressed myself because being shy clearly will get me nowhere!

It's Friday evening, and I'm waking up from a little nap to find a black garment bag at the foot of my bed. Mom has been here and gone, leaving behind the outfit she purchased for me to wear to the dance. A smile appears on my face as I unzip the bag and see a white dress shirt, navy knit tie, navy dress pants, and a black belt. A pair of black dress shoes and a fresh pair of black dress socks are on the floor by my closet. I can't help but be excited even if I don't have a date. I will make the best of it.

This mirror is telling the truth! I am the most handsome guy on earth! And as soon as I get to the dance, every girl in there will wish they had gone with me. Oh well, I'm so glad Mom thought to get the sales guy at the store to go ahead and tie the tie because I sure can't, and I don't know anyone around here who can either. It's funny that the only person I know who can tie a tie is Tan. Her dad taught her when she was in middle school. She used to wear ties all the time with her button-downs and knit shirts. I liked that look on her. I'm going to be late on purpose. A real player is never on time!

Right before Mom dropped me off at the dance, she took a ton of pictures of me. When I arrived at the school, I could tell that the dance was jumping! I can hear the song "The Show" by Dougie Fresh playing and the sound of people having a good time. By the time I made it to the cafeteria, the song was going off. My eyes wander around the room, trying to locate my girl. Ah, there she is. I'm going to sneak up behind her and surprise her. I'm walking along the perimeter so no one will notice me and ease my way over to Miss Tan. She must've been dancing up a storm because she is sitting at the table with a napkin, patting her face to remove the sweat. I gently place my hands over her eyes because I wouldn't dare want to mess up her make-up.

"Guess who?" I say with a big smile on my face.

She amuses me by trying to fake it like she doesn't have a clue. I love that about her. I uncover her eyes, and when we look into each other's eyes, we both seem to be really pleased. I can't help it. I want to see more!

"Stand up, Tan, I want to see your dress."

She's moving slowly. and when she finally stands, she's breathtaking. And before I knew it, the words, "You look so beautiful," came spilling out of my mouth. It's too late now. I've already said it! So, I grab her hand and spin her around to get the full effect. And I like what I see!

Tan is shocked and blushing because of my word choice. She's trying to laugh it off by telling me that I'm going to say "SIKE!" But I had to reassure her that this was definitely not a "SIKE" moment because I meant every word of that compliment. It's a trip where Tan and I are wearing the same color. We didn't plan it; it just happened. Her friends even think it's cool and suggest that we take a picture. We are standing close together, and I put my arm around her waist. *This just feels right. Let me snap out of it!*

I need to leave this scene ASAP before things get out of hand. Tan takes her seat, and I remind her that I will collect on a dance or two later. I walk away after I spot Ant and a few other friends.

The DJ puts a slow jam on. "Computer Love" by Zapp. I have nobody on my brain but Tan, and I'm trying to make my way to her, but out of nowhere, Cassie grabs my hand! I don't know how to feel or what to think at this moment. She caught me off guard, and I had to try to maintain my cool. I go ahead and lead her to the dance floor, but I'm also looking around for Tan. We stop when we find our spot. We're slow dancing, and here comes Tan. She was walking hand in hand with Joseph. She's close enough that I can keep an eye on her. *Joseph better not try anything! He better be the perfect gentleman, or he will have to answer to me! Cassie doesn't have my attention at all. Maybe that's what she gets for not wanting to go to the dance with me. Where is her man? And why did she go out of her way to dance with me? This must be the extended version of this song because it seems like Tan and Joseph have been hugged up for too long, and I know I'm supposed to be enjoying dancing with Cassie, but my mind is elsewhere.*

Finally, it's over. I'm making my way over to the refreshment table, where I see Tan walking over to the trash can. I'm about to get some punch, but the DJ is channeling my thoughts because he plays an Anita Baker song, "Sweet Love!" My heart is skipping all kinds of beats because I see, as I'm heading in Tan's direction, Joseph is about to sneak another dance. I picked up my pace and beat him to her! *You lost sucker!* A grin appears on my face as I reach for Tan's hand and guide her to the dance floor. That was a smooth move, if I must say so myself. Tan places her arms around my neck, and mine are wrapped around her tiny waist. It's as if Anita is singing live only to us because Tan's head is resting comfortably on my shoulder, and it just feels so good. I closed my eyes, and I found myself slipping off into a fantasy. *Let me stop before this gets weird. I have to remember. I must look cool at all times!*

As the song fades away, the DJ says, "It's time to announce the king and Queen. Tan and I go our separate ways. All of a sudden, I see her and Deon heading out the door. She can't be leaving! She owes me a second dance! I'm rushing after her. "Wait up! I can't believe you were going to leave without saying anything!"

Tan explains how her dad told her to be in the parking lot at a particular time and that she wasn't going to risk being late. I told her not to worry because she knows I know how strict her dad is, and I told her that I have no problem waiting with her. She seemed shocked and happy that I would rather be in the parking lot with her than inside at the dance. When her Mom and Dad pull up, I speak to them both, give her a quick hug, and return to the dance.

When I walk back into the dance, Ant looks like he has something to say.

"What's up, Ant?"

"You tell me, man. If I didn't know any better, I would have thought that you and Tan were a couple out there. Man, I thought I was going to have to pull y'all apart after the music had stopped!"

"Ant, if you don't stop lying! It was just a dance between two friends, that's all."

"I hear what you are saying, Tyler, but you didn't even dance with Cassie like that!"

If Ant noticed that, I wonder how many more people noticed it, too? Maybe he's just messing with me, trying to get a reaction. Or maybe not.

"Well,. Well, Ah. Maybe it looked like that, but that wasn't the case."

"Well, Well. Why are you stuttering?"

I'm just shaking my head. For some reason, I don't even want to be here now. I'm ready to go home.

Ant is giving me a ride to the house. When we pull up, he says, "I think what you and Tan have is special. I wish I had something like that. I opened the car door and ignored that statement, slapped him five, and slowly walked into my house. I hope everyone is asleep because I really don't feel like answering any questions. The TV is on in the living room, and Venus is curled up on the couch, talking on the phone. Her eyes light up when she sees me.

"Look at my little brother! You look so handsome!"

"Thanks, I can't wait to get out of these clothes and these shoes. My feet hurt!"

Venus laughs and says, "Yeah, I feel your pain. New shoes will kill you before you break them in!"

We both are laughing now.

"Did you take pictures?"

"Mom took a lot before she dropped me off, and I took a few at the dance."

"Good! I can't wait to see them."

"Go ahead and finish your conversation on the phone. I'm headed to bed."

Once I'm in bed, I can't help but flash back on the events that happened tonight. Why wasn't I more excited about Cassie wanting to slow dance with me? What was she trying to prove? Why was I even on her radar? She clearly had her boyfriend there. Although he was there, they never danced or interacted with one another, but that didn't stop her from leaving the dance early with him. I will never get the answers to these questions, but somehow, it doesn't matter, mainly because of my best friend / best girl, Tan.

I still can't get over how beautiful Tan looked. She looked like she just stepped out of a fashion magazine. She looked absolutely perfect! Seeing her tonight was like seeing her for the very first time. I let it be known, unconsciously, that I wanted to be in her space. I wasn't shy about letting her know that I wanted to dance with her. I made it a point to wrap my arms around her just right so she wouldn't have to guess how I was feeling. I hope I didn't do too much. The last thing I would want to do is to destroy our friendship.

Ant is out there blowing his horn. He's going to have to wait because I have to check myself out again in the mirror to make sure I am straight. I got my Guess shirt and Guess Jeans on, sporting blue and white, the school colors. *I bet I will get a lot of phone numbers tonight! Hmmm, that reminds me to get a pencil and paper so I can write down all the numbers that I get.*

I snap out of my thoughts when I hear Ant blowing his horn again. Ain't nothing like going to a football game late evening on a Saturday, and it's our homecoming game, too.

Everywhere I look, I see somebody with some mum on. Some of the guys are even wearing something like a mum that fits around the top of their arms. It's not for me. I can do without it. Ant and I are walking around as cool as we can be, and I can see the girls checking us out. Well, mainly me. I suggest to Ant that we walk around and find the perfect spot so the girls will come up to us. He laughs, but he knows it's a great idea. The spot we chose is a win-win because girls have easy access to us, and I have a good view of Tan as she cheers on the side-line. I can hear Tan from a great distance calling her cheers. She takes pride in being a leader. She is really jumping high tonight! That skirt is flying up so much that it doesn't have a chance to come down! And that's a good thing for me.

While I admire Tan from afar, Ant is trying to see what has captured my attention.

"You ain't slick, man!" Ant says.

"What are you talking about?"

"I see you have a good view of Tan and acting like she is giving a private show."

"Man, you are crazy! I didn't even notice Tan until you said something!"

The broad smile on my face is making it very hard for me to convince Ant of my truth.

"Ok, Tyler, if you say so."

We both are having a good laugh about that because we both know I'm guilty!

It's half-time, and we are making our way to the concession stand. As I'm walking, I see Cassie and her boyfriend. She smiles and says hello. I give her a what's up head gesture and walk past her. Two girls from another school have approached me, and I now have two new numbers to add to my collection. I probably won't call them, but it just helps me to feel good about myself when they come up to me flirting.

Wait a minute! I know I have to be seeing things! Joseph is giving Tan a box to open! What in the world could that be? Whatever it is, it sure has her smiling! Why am I watching this?

I'm turning in the opposite direction because I can't watch this anymore.

Well, the game is finally over. We won! The score is 12 to 25. The East has defeated the West! And that's a great homecoming victory! I walk down to the sideline to speak to Tan. She looks excited to see me. She's pinning her mum on while asking me where I've been because she didn't see me at all during the game. Before I answer that, I make sure I compliment her mum. She thanked me and gave me a look that said, don't try to be funny! While we were walking to the bus, I explained to her how I was watching her cheer during the game and how I saw her and Joseph by the concession stand when he was presenting her with a box. She looks confused, wondering how she didn't see me. I'm joking with Tan when I say, "I hope Joseph doesn't mind that I'm walking you to the bus."

She laughs it off, but I can tell that it makes her a little nervous. I know Joseph likes her, and I know he bought her a mum, but I don't know how to feel about that. I have a lot of history with her, and she's very special to me. I don't know if I can stand to see her in a relationship with someone else. What will happen to us? Whoever she gets with will not understand our special relationship. _What am I talking about? I am overthinking this whole thing!_

It's a relief to be in bed finally. I have my radio on during the quiet storm, which is when the radio station only plays slow and relaxing music. "Tender Love," by Force M. Ds, is playing, and I'm not quite sure why Tan's pretty face appears in my mind. It's almost like she's really here. I wish it weren't so late because I wouldn't mind hearing her voice, but I can scratch that thought right out of my head for obvious reasons. I can't help but wonder if she's falling asleep with me on her mind.

Chapter 9
Tan

December My Favorite Time of the Year

"It's the most wonderful time of the year!" I absolutely love Christmastime! It's so much fun to watch Mama go overboard with the tree decor, poinsettias, garland, lights, and mistletoes. I can't forget the lights outside and the plastic decorations in the yard. Oh, and the food! Mama always bakes all kinds of cakes, cookies, pies, and sweets of any sort you desire. You will be able to find it at our house. Apples, oranges, pecans, walnuts, and peppermint sticks will be located in their traditional spot on top of the bar. Mmmmm, Mama introduced us to her favorite treat she enjoyed as a child, which consisted of a bite of pecan or walnut and then taking a bite of peppermint and chewing them together. It's a little piece of heaven inside your mouth.

Let the countdown begin! Although I'm too old to believe in Santa, there is still something magical about Christmas. My siblings and I always count our presents under the tree to see who has the most. Mama and Daddy are usually pretty good about getting us the same number of gifts. I can remember when we were little kids, each of us had our very own section in the den, where we had our very own pile of toys. We would wake up super early on Christmas morning with so much joy and wake our parents up so they could see what Santa had left us. They had to act surprised while trying to hide how tired they were from staying up so late putting our toys together. Santa always ate all the cookies and drank all the milk that we left for him. Those were the good old days.

Now that we are older, we still have lots of presents under the tree, primarily clothes. We also get money, and we can always depend on our grandparents, our Daddy's parents, to bless us every year with a Sears gift certificate. Kerry and I always go to Sears and pick out the cheapest thing to receive the leftover cash from the gift certificate. If I must say so myself, that's pretty smart! JJ isn't so lucky. He always gets a knit hat, scarf, and gloves. Every Christmas, he pretends to be psychic when he opens that particular present, and we all get a good laugh.

There's nothing like having a fireplace! We spend countless hours in the den as a family, so in order for us to stay warm and cozy, Daddy borrows Pops' (his father/our grandfather) truck to load it up with wood, deliver it to our backyard, and stack it up on the side of the storage shed. He makes this a family affair every year, so it's considered a tradition. Each of us has a stocking with our names on it that hangs from the mantle. Santa always fills mine up with jewelry, lip gloss, and fingernail polish. Just thinking about it brings joy to my soul.

Today is the last day before we get out for Christmas Break. These halls are full of anxious teenagers. We all are ready to get these final exams out of the way so we can be out of school for two whole weeks. We are sleeping late and doing the things we want to do. We are on a testing schedule, so I only have two classes today. Lunch will not be served because it is an early release day due to testing. I love days like this. Oh, wait a minute, I probably won't get to see Tyler. All of a sudden, I'm feeling sad.

"Tan!" Janis yells from down the hall.

My spirits are lifted now.

"Hey, girl!"

"Where have you been?"

"I just got here. I figured there's no need to get here early if we are all testing."

"Good point. Oh, by the way, Tyler was looking for you."

I can feel the glow that has appeared on my face. I'm trying to talk while blushing, and I'm pretty sure Janis is going to call me out.

"Dang Tan! You can't hide your feelings for Tyler at all!"

Out of nowhere, Tyler appears. "What's going on with Y'all?"

"Oh, nothing," I hurry and say because I definitely don't want him to know the real deal!

"Y'all just don't want to tell me, but it's ok!" Tyler walks closer to me and whispers in my ear to meet him in this exact spot after my last test.

I can't imagine what he could want or what he has to tell me. How in the world am I supposed to focus on my test? All I can think about is Tyler!

Janis and I are walking to our classes, and she can't help but be nosey.

"What did Tyler whisper to you?"

The look on my face says it all.

"Well, excuse me for getting all up in your business!"

"No, really, I'm confused. He wants me to meet him after our last test."

"For what?"

"Duh! I just told you I don't know why?"

"Girl, he probably is going to tell you that he has feelings for you, or he might have a gift for you. Did you get him something?"

"I don't think that's it, and no, I didn't get him anything."

"Oh, that's going to be messed up when he hands you a gift, and you have nothing to give him in return!"

"Alright, Janis, just stop it. You are making matters worse."

"I'm not trying to upset you, Tan. Don't worry, it's probably nothing."

The first exam was a breeze, but now it's going to get a little complicated.

It's time for Economics. Shayla is already in class waiting patiently to get this test over with.

As I enter the classroom, I say, "Good morning, Mr. Wallace."

"Good morning, Ma'am, he says.

I hurried and took my place at a desk right next to Shayla.

"Hey, girl," I say to her.

"What's up, Tan?"

"I am so ready to get this test out of the way so I can go home and chill for two weeks!"

"I know what you mean. I am overdue for a break!"

"Shayla, don't forget we have basketball tournaments over the break, so that's something else to look forward to."

"Do you have to cheer?"

"Not for all the games. I'll let you know for sure when I find out."

The test has started, and I can't help but have a nervous feeling in the pit of my stomach. What is it that Tyler wants to tell me or give me?

I look up, and Mr. Wallace is standing right in front of me.

"Miss. Breakfield, are you alright?"

"Yes, sir, I am."

"Ok, well, get your head in the game and cut out all that day-dreaming!"

I'm trying to refocus. *I'm so glad no one was paying attention to what Mr. Wallace was saying to me. How embarrassing!*

Shayla is looking my way, wondering what's going on with me. I wish I could talk to her right now, but if I tried, Mr. Wallace would have my head!

Shayla is tearing off a piece of paper; she's writing something on it. She threw the note close to my foot, and out of nowhere, Mr. Wallace placed his big foot on the note, and he bent down to pick it up. Shayla's head drops. This can't be good.

He's slowly unfolding the note while looking directly at Shayla and then in my direction.

"Are you girls trying to cheat on my test?"

Now he has the attention of the whole class. That's just what we needed!

"No, Sir!" Shayla answers while he's opening the note.

"Y'all better hope there is no evidence of cheating on this piece of paper!"

Mr. Wallace is reading the note. He pauses and looks at me with some sort of pity in his eyes. I can't help but wonder what Shayla said on that note. I glance over at Shayla, and she winks her eyes at me with a devilish smile.

"Miss. Breakfield, may I speak to you in the hall, please?"

I immediately stand up and walk into the hall. I slowly turn to face Mr. Wallace. My pulse is racing because I have no idea what he is about to say.

"You poor thing, I can't imagine how hard it must be for you to try and focus on passing your final exam when you have just suffered the loss of your childhood dog."

The look on my face should have said it all. I'm confused as I don't know what! Shayla likes to joke around and write all kinds of crazy notes, so when the teacher intercepts the notes, they often feel really bad about it.

"I'm ok. I will get through it."

"If you need more time to take this test, I will grant it. I know how it feels to lose a pet. It's just like losing a family member.

I assured Mr. Wallace that I was ok enough to complete the test, and I returned to my seat and gave Shayla the side eye. That girl is something else. It is always funnier when her little schemes don't involve me.

The bell rings, and Mr. Wallace dares us to move or talk until all tests are in his hands. As I hand him my test, I can barely look him in his eyes. Shayla is getting a kick out of her prank because she is killing herself laughing out in the hall.

"Girl, why did you do that? You didn't warn me or anything. That completely caught me off guard!"

"Oh, Tan, that's what made it so funny! You should have seen your face!"

After Shayla settles down, I catch her up to speed on my Tyler dilemma.

As we walked and talked down the hall, I spotted Tyler waiting in the exact spot that we were in this morning.

"OK, Shayla, I'll call you later. I can see Tyler waiting."

"Alright, don't forget to call Janis and me on the three-way so you can fill us both in at the same time."

"Ok, I will."

I'm moving at a snail's pace, in no hurry to get crunched or whatever the case may be. Tyler's smile appears to be getting bigger the closer I get to him. Hopefully, whatever he is about to do or say will go quickly since the weather is cold. He's been riding the bus home, and Kerry has been picking me up.

"Say, Tan, can't you walk faster than that? You know I got to get on the bus?" Tyler says, with both hands in the air being all dramatic.

"I'm walking as fast as I can!"

Tyler gives me a look like, be for real!

Now that I'm directly in his face, I can see that he has a serious look.

"So, what is so urgent, Sir?"

"I have something for you."

My eyes are widening. I really don't know how to respond.

Tyler is removing his gold nugget ring off his pinky finger. This is the same ring Tyler has been wearing since the ninth grade. I can remember asking him to let me wear it, and he would, but he would always make sure he got it back.

"SOOO, how long are you going to let me wear it this time?"

"You can keep it!"

"Huh?" I say with a clueless look on my face."

"Yeah, think of it as a token of our friendship."

Before I can say anything else, Tyler takes off, running down the hall to get to his bus.

I'm just standing in the same spot, trying to process what just happened.

Finally, I walk to the parking lot, and Kerry is already there waiting. *I sure hope she's in a good mood.* Ah yeah, she's in a really good mood. She's jamming to "Candy" by Cameo. As I opened the car door, Kerry was doing some dance moves in her seat.

"Hey Kerry, what do you have going on?"

"Hey Tan, I'm getting ready for our Greek Show. We are strutting to this song."

"Wow! I know that's going to be pretty cool!"

Kerry is pledging non-Greek, Gamma Sweet. They are the little sisters of one of the frats. She's always attending all the frat and sorority parties. It makes my day when she allows me to tag along.

"Sooooooo, do you think this will be an event that I can attend?" I'm looking at her with my cute puppy dog look. Kerry is not fazed by anything I'm saying because she's too caught up in trying to remember all the dance moves, she's attempting to do in the driver's seat.

Once the song goes off, she begins to drive off. Kerry turns the radio down and asks, "What were you saying?"

I start speaking slowly while clenching my teeth together, "doooo youuuuuu think I will be able to attend this event with you? And maybe Deon can go also?" I'm closing my eyes tight, not wanting to hear NOOOOOOO!

Kerry looks at me. She blinks a few times and doesn't hesitate to say yes. I am shocked!

"Does this mean Deon can come too?"

"I don't see why not, and ask Cassie if she would want to go."

I didn't see that one coming, but ok, that should be interesting.

Mama is in the kitchen cooking and talking on the telephone with the extra-long cord so she can multitask. I'm being nosey trying to figure out who she is talking to. She reaches into the cabinet, pulls out her cutting board, and begins to cut up an onion. She already has some potatoes cut up in a large silver bowl. Mama pours a little grease in a skillet and allows it to heat up, and then she adds the onions. Now, the whole house smells like a five-star restaurant. She added the potatoes and placed the lid on the skillet. The chicken is already smothered on the stove. The corn and the green beans are boiling, and that means dinner will be served soon. Mama looks at the clock and says, "Oh, look at the time! We have been on this phone for thirty-plus minutes! My long-distance bill is going to eat me alive!" She wraps up her call and says goodbye. She turns and looks at me. She knows I can't wait to see who she is talking to.

"That was your Aunt Mazzy. She'll be here on Sunday."

"Yes!" I am so excited! Aunt Mazzy always comes to visit around this time of the year to do her Christmas shopping. She lets me pick out whatever I want.

"Most beautiful!" Daddy yells out as he walks through the front door.

Mama is doing her usual, pretending not to hear him. Daddy walks into the kitchen, grabs her, and plants a big kiss on her cheek. Mama wipes the kiss off, and Daddy grabs her again, hugs her tight, and kisses her a million times. Finally, he lets go and takes off, running into the den. I'm laughing at them so hard because they remind me of the Looney Tunes characters Pepe' Le Pew and that cat he loves to harass. Mama settles down and begins to prepare for dinner. She yells for us to wash up and come to the table. We are all sitting at the table stuffed! Mom is clearing the table, and Kerry starts to wash the dishes. I guess that means I'm free to escape next door.

I rang Deon's doorbell, and Mr. Franklin answered the door.

"Well, hello, Tan!"

"Hi, Mr. Franklin. Is Deon home?"

He has a look of disappointment while standing about 5'9, muscular, with a pack of cigarettes underneath his white short-sleeved t-shirt. He has smooth, velvet dark skin, with a jet-black Jerry Curl. He eventually told me that Deon was on punishment and he would make an exception for me, so it was ok for me to visit her. Mr. Franklin has always been like a dad to me. He and my Daddy are best friends, and our families do a lot of things together. He steps to the side and allows me to walk past him to get to Deon's room. I knock on her door, and she yells, "I'm not hungry!"

I open her door and say, "That's good because I don't have any food for ya!"

As I enter her room, it's pitch black in here because she has those blackout curtains, so I flip the light switch on. My poor friend is super sad. What in the world could she have done to get herself in this predicament? I'm standing beside the bed, looking at her with her face buried in the pillow. Deon slowly lifts her head, squinches her eyes, and twists her nose while struggling to sit up in the bed.

Quietness fills the room. I finally broke the monotony by saying, "You must have done something really awful to be on punishment!"

This heifer is looking at me like I'm mistaken or something. So, I'm looking at her like, don't play! She's getting herself together to see just how she's going to deliver her drama to me.

"Well, I took the bus to the Northside to see David, the fine boy I met at the track meet last year. I thought since we had an early release and it was the last day before break, that it was the perfect opportunity to do it."

"Wow, Dee, that was bold!"

"Girl, I know, but that's not the worst part. But before I get into that, let me tell you about how much fun we had!"

I take my place in the chair next to her bed, and I'm all ears. *I'm hoping she didn't go all the way with him!*

Excitement is present in her voice and displayed on her face. When Dee says Dav, her whole world brightens up.

"Ahem!" Dee clears her throat to begin telling me about her escapade. "Girrrrrl, we have been talking on the phone since October, and we both agreed that it was time that we meet up and spend some time together. So, I thought it was a good idea to jump my butt on the Citran Bus and go across town to see him."

I'm leaning forward in my chair to make sure I don't miss anything!

"So, he met me at the bus stop, and we walked to his house. His mother was at work, and she was working a double, so we had the place to ourselves. We sat on the couch in the living room and watched a little TV. Then we talked about school and friends. Dav then asked me if I would like to see his room. All kinds of alarms and sirens were going off in my head! I knew better! I told him I would go peek in his room and come back to watch TV. He asked if I was scared to go in there because there was a bed in there. I responded by telling him that I wouldn't feel comfortable in his room and that I thought it would be better to stay in the living room to get to know each other better. He agreed, but he still insisted on me seeing his room. When he opened the door to his room, it was nice and clean. Everything was in its proper place. There was a red, white, and blue plaid bedspread on his bed. A blue lamp and red curtains with white sheers underneath. He had a bookcase that held all of his track trophies, ribbons, and plaques. He was really grinning while he was telling me about each one. I didn't want to sit and risk making bad choices, so after that, we returned to the living room. Oh, and the most important part. He's a really good kisser!" Deon said that last part with a lot of energy, so she meant that!

"So how in the world did you end up on punishment?"

Dee interlocks both hands and places them on the top of her head, with a frustrated look on her face. I can't help but feel bad for her. I'm just hoping that she didn't do anything that she will regret later.

She began to describe how fast time flies when you're having fun. "Dav and I were eating sandwiches and chips, and I happened to look towards the window and wondered where did the sun had disappeared to. That was an indication that it was late and I had missed the last bus to my side of town. Reality hit me pretty quickly when I didn't have any other choice but to call my parents to come pick me up. I dreaded making that call. My dad was pissed! Let's say the ride home was very unpleasant."

I really don't know what to say to my friend right now. She was bold, going all the way across town to meet up with a boy she barely knew and spent time with him alone at his house. I am too paranoid to try anything like that because John and Cathy have zero understanding when it comes to things like that. I can tell Dee is just sick of being on punishment, especially over Christmas Break. I slowly stand and begin pacing the room, trying to think of something I could do or say to make her feel better. Nothing is coming to mind. So, I say to my friend, "I'll be in touch," and make my way back home.

"Auntie Mazzy, you're here!" I'm yelling as I'm running to her, about to knock her down. She held her arm open wide to give me the best hug ever! Uncle Wesley is feeling left out and says, "Why does your auntie get all the hugs?"

I let go of Auntie Mazzy to give my uncle a big hug.

After we all exchanged hugs, we migrated into the den. Mama is showing Auntie all of the brass pieces she has on the fireplace. Daddy puts his two cents in by telling her he is the reason the brass is sparkling. He cleans it twice a month. Auntie Mazzy tells Uncle Wesley to take notes because she can see that in his future. Daddy pats his uncle on his shoulder and tells him, welcome to the club. We all start laughing. I love when they come to visit.

To the mall, we go! We all load up in Daddy's van. Uncle Wesley is in the front with Daddy. Mama, Auntie Mazzy, and her little baby are in the two chairs. Kerry, JJ, Lil Cousin Jr, and I am sitting in the back row. The radio is not playing because they are having a full-blown conversation about the good old days. They make it seem like it was so much fun to have grown up in their error.

My money is burning my pocket. I can't wait to get in these stores and spend! Kerry and I are leaving the group to go about our business. We are going to focus on getting Mama and Daddy's gifts before we buy for each other and JJ. Mama is a collector of many things, so it's not hard to find something that she would like. Daddy is pretty easy to shop for. Whatever we get him, he always pretends that it is the best gift ever.

Kerry and I have purchased gifts for Mama and Daddy, and we found good deals on things that JJ would like. We are heading back through the mall to meet up with Mama and Auntie Mazzy. We finally caught up with them in Dillard's, and they both have bags galore! I can't help but wonder how many are for me. At this point, we are all very tired and ready to end this shopping adventure for the day. As we walked up to the van, Daddy and Uncle Wesley were already there talking and passing the time, waiting for us to finish our shopping. Daddy opens the back of the truck, and it is almost complete to the top with bags. He made the other bags fit, and he quickly shut the door.

Everyone is comfortable just lying around and talking in the den after eating Kentucky Fried Chicken. I use this as an opportunity to sneak into my parent's bedroom to call Tyler. He picks up the phone on the first ring. "Hey Tyler, whatcha doing?"

"Nothing, I just got home. I was out with my cousin Sean doing a little Christmas shopping."

"Oh yeah? I was also out with the family doing the same thing. Did you have a lot of gifts to buy?"

"Nah! I only buy a gift for my Mom."

"Aww, that's so sweet."

"Tan, I'm glad you called. Did you hear that Bobby Brown has a new song? They are supposed to play it for the first time tonight at 11:00, so make sure you are listening to FM 107, The Soul of Texas!"

"I will definitely be tuning in because you know I love me some, Bobby!"

"Whatever!" Tyler said while laughing.

We wrapped up our conversation, and I immediately went to my room to turn on the radio. It was already on the right station. Kerry walks in, inquiring why I am in the room listening to the radio while we have company. Before I can answer her, the DJ says, "Here's a new song by the one and only Bobby Brown, "Girlfriend," and I have a special dedication to Tan from Tyler. Watch out now. I think he is asking you a very important question!"

I cannot contain my excitement. I'm standing in my bed, jumping up and down, and Kerry looks like she is in shock!

"Did that DJ just say your name?"

"Uhhhhh, YES!!! I believe he did!!!!"

I'm jumping like a mad woman! I can't believe Tyler did that! Doesn't he know everyone probably heard that announcement? What does that really mean? I need answers! Finally, I stopped jumping and fell down in bed. Kerry is staring at me like I'm crazy! Then she says, "Is he asking you to go with him?"

I quickly jumped up from my bed to show her the gold nugget ring I had on my right middle finger.

Kerry gasps for air when she sees the ring. "Girl, what did he say when he gave you that ring?"

"He said it was a friendship ring."

"Friendship, my foot! That boy wants to be more than just your friend!"

I'm blushing really hard, and She's looking at me and shaking her head.

We both walk back into the den and blend in with the rest of the family.

I had a good night's sleep after tossing and turning and replaying that song dedication over and over in my head. _Do I call him? Maybe I should act like it never happened. I don't want to hurt his feelings and not say anything, but I don't want to get CRUNCHED either!_

"To be or not to be?" That is the question!

By the time I finished dressing and made my way to the kitchen, everyone was done eating breakfast. Mama had a small plate to the side just for me. While I'm eating, my mind can't help but wonder. Wonder about Tyler. I still need to know why he did that! Auntie Mazzy walks in and says, "A penny for your thoughts."

I drop my head and tell her I really don't know where to begin. I caught her up to speed, and she thought it was so funny. JJ and Lil

Wesley came into the kitchen to get something to drink and took a seat at the bar to drink their juice and have their unimportant conversation. Auntie explains to me why she thinks Tyler did what he did. She seems to believe that he's afraid to tell me himself how he feels, and he felt like that was the best way to do it. She also told me that she could tell that I really liked him because I couldn't stop smiling when I talked about him. She's right. I don't know how she knows, but she knows her stuff. She advised me not to bring it up unless he did, and I assured her that I wasn't going to do that because I was not sure how that would turn out. "I'm so glad we had the chance to talk before you left Auntie Mazzy because I was going crazy!"

"Girl, this is just the beginning. You have a long road ahead." We both are laughing while we hug.

Christmas Eve has arrived! We are so anxious for the clock to strike midnight because Mama and Daddy always allow us to open one present before we go to bed. We have already stacked all our gifts in separate piles, so everyone has their own pile. Mama and Daddy did it again. The three of us have the same number of gifts. They make sure we don't think that they have a favorite child. And if they did, I'm sure it would be me.

We have six more hours before we have to make that difficult decision about which present to open. I'm distracted by the ringing tel-ephone. JJ jumps up and runs into the kitchen to answer the phone as if someone is calling for him. I'm busy picking up presents in my stack, shaking them, and trying to figure out which one is worthy enough to be opened at midnight. I notice that JJ is still in the kitchen on the phone, and then I hear him say, "Are you in love with Tan?"

"Oh, my God! Mama! Tell JJ to give me the phone! I'm wrestling with JJ, trying to pry the phone out of his hands! Mama came into the kitchen, and JJ let the phone go. Now that I have the phone in my hand, I'm really not sure if I want it. Like a frightened mouse, I say, "Hello." the voice on the other end said, "What's up, Tan?" Just as I thought, it was Tyler. I can hear laughter in his tone. He must think I'm an idiot. JJ had no right to ask him that! I could just die! It's taking me longer than I anticipated to get my mind right to have this awkward conversation with Tyler.

"Man, your little brother is so funny. He will say anything!" Tyler said while laughing hysterically on the other end of the phone. This is a good thing. I fall right in line, laughing right along with him. It's working. We are our normal selves and talking about what we think we are getting for Christmas and the upcoming basketball tournament. I must say I am relieved. Now I can exhale!

The clock strikes midnight! "Yay!" we all say together. Daddy says, who's going to go first? JJ grabs a box and tears into it! We all are trying very hard to hold in our laugh because the joke is gonna be on him. A few days ago, Mama, Daddy, and I rewrapped Grandmother's gift in a much bigger box and put marbles inside so JJ would really think he had something good. So Daddy says, with a grin on his face, "Well, it looks like JJ will start us off. Go ahead, son. You are opening that gift like you are a wild animal!" Laughter fills the room, and the look on JJ's face once he finally opens the box is priceless! JJ says, "OH NO! Grandmother got me this time!" We all fall out on the floor laughing uncontrollably! That was definitely the highlight of my Christmas. PRICELESS!

It's Friday night, and my big sister ain't playing! She is leading her line sisters down the aisle to the song "Candy," and they are all struttering their stuff! There are so many different Greek organizations represented wearing all kinds of colors. Kerry and her line sisters are sporting royal blue pants and royal blue and white striped tops with a big royal blue leather belt around their waists. They also had a pearl comb on the left side of their heads just to add a little class. Cassie, Deon, and I can't help but get hyped about that college life. There are so many burgers (fine guys) walking around this establishment, and it is a shame that we don't have guys like this in high school. It's like being in a candy store. Three good-looking guys are heading our way. The three of us are just blushing and really acting our age. It was really smooth the way they walked up to us. As they began to introduce themselves. Out of nowhere came Kerry saying,

"So Y'all have met my baby sister and her two little friends." I hate it when Kerry does that! Now, these guys are no longer interested. They just casually walked away without saying a word. Kerry looked at the three of us while laughing and went on about her business. Although Kerry was blocking most of the night, we still had a good time, mainly because Cassie and Deon had put their differences aside.

The Coca-Cola Tournament is going to be so LIVE! There are going to be so many different schools participating from around the metroplex, different cities, and states. I am happy I don't have to cheer, so I can walk around with my friends, enjoy myself, and be cute. Janis, Shayla, and I are going to wear our form-fitting dresses, and Shayla thought it would be a good idea if we wore a fur coat of some type. I'm trying to see how I'm going to butter Mama up to get her to let me wear her beautiful white and gray fox coat.

AWWWW!!! You can't tell me nothing! I'm looking in the mirror and appreciating what it is revealing to me. Mama came to do her final inspection of my outfit. I say, "I think my outfit needs something. Something like a fox coat, maybe?" Mama is looking at me like I have lost my mind. I hurried up and tried to convince her by telling her that Janis and Shayla's moms were going to let them sport their coats. Mama takes a glance in my direction and walks out of my room. I drop my head and begin to look sad. Mama enters the room like a ray of sunshine with the fox coat draped over her arm. I'm jumping for joy! Mama saved the day!

Mama says, "Girl, you better stop all of that before I change my mind!"

I immediately came to my senses. She assists me with putting the coat on. She is smiling, so I know she is pleased.

"Y'all, better have Y'all's fast behinds out here by 10:15. That's enough time for Y'all to prance around in there," Daddy says as we get out of the van.

"Yes, sir, Daddy, we will be out here and on time. The three of us are what someone would refer to as a "Fly Girl," which means we are looking too good! As a matter of fact,, I can clearly hear that song playing in my head as we walk through the crowds to take our place by the concession stands. We will post here and see how many numbers we will collect. This is just a little friendly competition amongst friends.

I'm looking across the way, and somehow, I make eye contact with Lance. He's an ex from last year, even though I wasn't supposed to have a boyfriend, according to my Daddy. Therefore, our relationship didn't last because my parents were too strict. Lance always said I was the happiest girl he knew. He said that every time he sees me, I'm always smiling and laughing. Lance is walking towards me, just as cool as he can be. "What's up, my little laughing hyena?"

"Hey, Lance," we hugged, and he grabbed my right hand while we were talking. Lance is light-skinned, with brown eyes and brown/sandy hair. He's taller than me and a grade ahead. He is hard-working, and he hopes to have his own business someday. Lance is a nice guy, but he's a little bit too fast for me. He's able to stay out all night long if he wants to, so with that said, there is no way I can hang with that. Last year, he bought me a Texas nugget ring for my birthday, and I bought him some Lagerfeld cologne for his birthday. We realized that we couldn't be in a relationship, but we could be good friends, and that's precisely what we are.

Janis and Shayla couldn't wait until Lance walked away so they could ask me a million questions. While I was telling my business, all of a sudden, it went dark! I know these clammy hands that are over my eyes anywhere. "Guess who?" Tyler says.

"Hmmm, is it? Nah, it couldn't be. I think maybe it is. My best friend, Tyler?"

"Best friend?" Shayla repeats and then says, "I thought he was your boyfriend now! That song dedication said it all!"

Tyler and I are speechless! I thought we were in the clear, mainly because no one had said anything about it up until now. I'm looking at Shayla. Why did you have to open up that can of worms? Janis is tickled to death; she can't stop laughing, and Tyler's friend Ant is finding joy in this, too. I can tell Tyler is uncomfortable because I know I am. This is not the time nor the place to have this discussion in the presence of an audience. Tyler takes my hand, walks me away from our friends, and tells me that he knows he owes me an explanation. I'm trying to play it off like it's not a big deal. We hugged, and we both returned to our friends.

I really can't enjoy myself now. Guys are coming up to me trying to rap, but I'm not interested. I want this night to end. Janis and Shayla are not really having a good time either. I guess my mood is affecting theirs. It's 10:00, and the current game is almost over, so we start heading out to the parking lot because we know my dad is probably already out there. Just as I thought, Daddy is parked right up front by the walkway. We definitely can't miss him.

I've made it home, showered, and now I'm lying in bed. It's time to reflect. First of all, why did Shayla have to mention the song dedication? And why did she think that was the perfect time to do so? It just makes me wonder if she and Janis have had a conversation about it without me. The most important question I have is, what was Tyler thinking when he made the request? I feel like things are going to be awkward between us now, and hopefully, it won't affect our friendship. I wish there were some ways to avoid having that conversation. Maybe he will forget. I don't think I could be that lucky. Oh well, time will tell. To be continued.

Chapter 10

Tan

February

March

It's Monday, February the 2nd, and only a few more days before Valentine's Day. I just got home from school, and the doorbell rings. Mama is talking to someone, and I'm trying to figure out who it is. "Tan! Come here. Cassie is here to see you!"

"Ok!" *What in the world could Cassie want?* I'm walking into the den, and I see her sitting on the couch. "Hey, Cassie!"

"Hey, Tan! I wanted to talk to you about something."

"Ok, what is it?"

"Tory and I broke up!"

"What? Why?"

"Girl, it's really messed up! He found out that I went out with someone else."

"Did you?" *I don't know why I'm asking her this question because I know she probably did.*

"Well, to my defense, I wanted to go to the movies, and Tory had to work, and this other guy asked me if I wanted to go out, so I did. Now Tory is saying that he doesn't trust me anymore."

"I can understand that. Can't you?"

"No.not really."

I'm just looking at her. This is unbelievable! "So, what does all of this have to do with me?"

"Tan, I want you to fix me up with Tyler."

What the Hell did she say? I know I must be hearing things! Why Tyler, and why now? I guess she didn't hear about the song dedication, or she doesn't care!

"Um. Um," I'm trying to get my thoughts together and act like I'm cool with whatever this is, but I'm having a little difficulty.

"Well, ok, I'll talk to him and let you know what he says."

"Ok, hurry up because you know Valentine's is right around the corner." Cassie is really laughing at her so-called joke.

"You know I'm just playing, Tan."

"Of course, you are."

When Cassie walks out, I'm trying to think of what to do next. Who can I trust with this information? Deon is the first person to come to mind. I grab my jacket, slip on my shoes, and make my way next door.

As soon as Dee opens the door, she can see that something is wrong.

"What's going on, Tan? It's written all over your face that something is clearly not right with you."

"I don't even know where to begin!"

"Well, just start talking!"

I'm telling her how Cassie came over and just blatantly asked me to fix her up with Tyler.

Dee's eyes broaden, and the expression on her face says it all: she is disgusted about how forward Cassie is.

"Isn't she dating Tory?"

I'm explaining to her how she cheated on him and how that led to them breaking up.

Dee's eyes are really keen now, she's pissed.

"So now she wants to date Tyler, how convenient. Just in time for Valentine's, so she can send him through the ringer too! AW NAH! That ain't happening, Tan!"

"I know it shouldn't happen, but It's up to Tyler."

"So, what are you going to do?"

"I'm going to tell him."

Dee is spinning out of control. She's going on and on about how Cassie knows that Tyler really is into me, and she says Cassie knows about the song dedication because she told her about it that same night.

We are supposed to be friends! I wouldn't do my enemy like this. What is she getting out of this?

Many questions are going through my mind. I have to realize that everyone doesn't value the same things that I do. Friendship is essential to me. If I call you my friend, I mean it!

"Tan, have you and Tyler told each other how Y'all feel?"

"No, we haven't. We haven't even discussed the song dedication."

"Y'all move slow as a snail! What is taking Y'all so long?"

"I wish I could answer that!"

Rise and Shine! It's a beautiful Saturday morning, and I'm going to take advantage of it. Yesterday, we had a basketball game, and I'm so glad I had to cheer. Tyler came down by the courtside to wave and smile at me. I also know Cassie was there, so maybe she just went ahead and talked for herself by letting Tyler know that she wanted to date him. I haven't made time to tell him, mainly because it is not a top priority. So today, I'm going to clean my room and organize my closet by bringing all of my spring clothes to the front of the closet. Mama will be shocked to see me doing this on my own without her having to tell me to.

The phone is ringing. I'm holding a pile of clothes in my arm, but for some reason, I feel the need to throw them to the floor and run to answer the phone. Oh GREAT! It's Tyler! Usually, I would be excited to hear from him, but today, I am not! I will get this mess over with, and he can do whatever he chooses to do with this Cassie dilemma. After our pleasantries, I decided that I was going to blurt it out. 1 2 3. I can't do it!

"You sure are acting kind of strange, Tan. What's going on?"

Ok, here it goes. "I have something that I need to tell you."

"I'm listening. But first, don't you want to hear why I dedicated that song to you?"

"After I tell you what I have to tell you, that won't even matter anymore."

"You sure know how to get my attention. I'm all ears!"

I start by saying, "Your wish is about to come true."

"How so?"

I began to tell him about the unexpected visit I had the other day. I get straight to the point by telling him that Cassie wants to date him. Now the phone is dead silent!

"Hello!"

"I'm still here."

"I thought you would be bouncing off the walls with excitement. Aren't you happy?"

"Doesn't she have a boyfriend?"

I want to tell him so badly about why they broke up, but that's not for me to tell. He needs to see who she is for himself.

"No, they broke up."

Tyler did not react the way I thought he would, but something tells me that he wants to date her, too. So that things don't get any more awkward, I just give him her phone number so he can call her, and the rest is up to him.

It's the second period, my career/work study class. It's the class I have with Tyler, and I am the only girl, so the guys are very protective of me. I usually enjoy coming to this class, but today is different. Ms. Pye is our teacher. She is an older white lady with lots of wrinkles, glasses on the tip of her nose, and reddish/gray hair. I love her personality. She is very kind and genuine.

Today, we are doing a project that involves career research. Ms. Pye is putting each of us with a partner for the assignment. I'm holding my breath and biting the inside of my lip, hoping she doesn't pair me with Tyler. And she did just what I thought she would do, she made my worst nightmare come true! Tyler and I take our seats at the back table. We both are kind of quiet and unsure of what to say. Tyler is leaning in close to me, and he whispers, "I know your nosey self wants to know about Cassie and me."

I'm laughing, but it's fake. "Sure, you know inquiring minds want to know!"

"Well, we've been talking on the phone, and her conversation is okay. She is clear about what it is that she wants."

"Such as?"

"Meaning what she wants from the guy that she is dating. She is very detailed about what he has to have."

"That's interesting, so how did you measure up to her list?"

"I guess pretty good. We're still talking."

We are both laughing because she has such high demands for the guy, and she never addresses what she brings to the table.

"Tan, I need a favor."

I'm looking at him with my left eyebrow raised, "what is it?"

"Can I give you some money to get Cassie something for Valentine's?"

I begin to talk through my teeth, "it would be my pleasure," I say sarcastically.

It's funny that Tyler didn't notice the sarcasm in my voice.

Ms. Pye walked around to make sure we were all on task, so we immediately changed the subject to focus on our project. As soon as she passes our table, we go back to the subject at hand.

Tyler reached into his back pocket and pulled out his wallet. I'm waiting patiently to see how much money he plans on wasting on her. A nice crisp fifty-dollar bill is now in my hands, and he's smiling like he's "THE MAN!"

"I'm sure you will pick out something nice because you have great taste."

"Yes, I do," I say in a joking manner, and we transition back to working on our project.

This day sure is passing fast. It's lunchtime, and I'm sitting at the table with my girls. And I am debating if I should tell them the latest about my situation with Tyler. I guess I will because I want to see what they think.

I'm deciding to go ahead and do it. I'm spilling all my business at this cafeteria table. Janis and Shayla are both mute. Not a word from either one of them. I'm regretting telling them because they are reacting just like I thought they would.

"How in the world does a song dedicated to you end up being Tyler dating Cassie?" Shayla says in a severe manner. Janis quickly jumps on board, saying, "Yeah, please explain to us how that happened?" After I finished breaking it all down to them. They both agreed that Cassie is not sincere. Now they are looking at me like, what's your plan?

I say, "To be honest, I didn't see that coming myself, but to be fair, Tyler did ask me to fix them up so they could go to the homecoming dance together."

"So! Who cares about that? We all are rooting for you and Tyler, and now you let this happen!" Shayla really feels some type of way about my business. I didn't think it would cause this much drama. The bell rings to go to class, and I am so glad!

Kerry is already in the parking lot waiting when Tyler and I walk outside. He's in a hurry because he has to catch the bus home. He's handing me my book bag while reminding me to shop for his Valentine's gift. I reassured him that I would take care of it. We hugged, and he took off running to his bus.

"Hey, Kerry," I say as soon as I get into her car.

"Hey, Tan!" Kerry says suspiciously.

"I need a favor."

"I knew you were up to something! What is it?"

"Can you run me to Skaggs? I need to get something."

"Get what?"

I have to tell Kerry everything about Tyler and Cassie and how they are dating now. She is looking so confused.

"Wait a minute, Tan, didn't that boy just dedicate a song to you? How in the world is he dating someone else that quick?"

I'm sitting here looking like a duck. I wish I had an answer to that million-dollar question. All I can do is shrug my shoulders in silence.

The store is crowded with last-minute people looking for that perfect gift. I'm trying to figure out what to get based on how they have only been dating for a few days. As I walk down the card aisle, I try to figure out the appropriate card for Cassie. Is she a friend, or is she considered to be someone special? I'm settling for a basic card and a big box of chocolates. So, considering that I have fifty dollars to spend, I think I should treat myself to something nice. Shoot, I deserve it! Cruising around in the make-up section, I make my selection of mascara, lip gloss, and compact powder, and I ease back to the candy section and pick out a nice box of chocolates for me. My job is done now.

It's Friday night, and Tyler is supposed to call me when he gets off work. He is going to inquire about how I spent his fifty dollars, and I'm hoping he will be ok with the choices I've made. I pick up the phone on the first ring. Tyler seems to be very excited to hear about the Valentine's gift I picked out for Cassie. I began to explain to him that since they just started dating, it made sense to keep it simple, and he agreed. I need to tell him that I also did a little shopping for myself.

"SOOO Tyler, I kind of bought a few things for myself," I say, talking and smiling at the same time.

"SOOO, I guess you are trying to tell me that I don't have any change left?"

"Exactly."

"Tan, I know you so well. I knew that was going to happen. That's why I gave you more than enough!"

I love the relationship that we have. That could have gone wrong, but since he knows me so well. It didn't.

Tyler tells me that he will come by my house tomorrow, which is Valentine's Day, and pick up the card and candy to deliver to Cassie. I'm hoping she will be appreciative and not expecting more.

Valentine's Day has come and gone, and now it's time to really focus on "Operation Prom!" It's March and almost Spring Break, so I need to figure out how to bring this up to Daddy in a very delicate manner. The objective is for him to allow me to attend the prom this year. I'm sure he will need a gentle reminder of Kerry attending the prom as a junior. Mama is in the den reading the newspaper and watching TV. I walk in smoothly, take my place on the floor right next to her, and place my head on her lap.

"Ok, what is it?" Mama says while lowering the paper from her view.

I'm whining like an infant. I need to get my way.

"Mama, I want to go to the prom!"

"The only thing that's standing in the way of you and the prom is your Daddy."

"I know that, so can you help me talk to him?"

"First of all, who is taking you to the prom?"

I'm trying to explain to Mama how Deon and I are working on a plan. She's looking at me like she can't believe I'm so dingy.

I continued to explain our plan, and Mama had had enough. She cuts me off, saying, "When you get it together, then involve me."

I guess I can see her point.

Although Tyler is dating Cassie, he and I aren't missing a beat. We talk on the phone every day. Now that the weather is cold, he walks me to the car after school, and we are still the best of friends. So, the little so-called relationship that he has with Cassie is not affecting us at all. It's spring break, and Tyler and I have been talking on the phone really late, after midnight. I sneaked the phone out of my parent's room and stretched the cord to my room. I have to remember not to get carried away laughing loudly because Mama will definitely unplug the phone. I have learned from my past mistakes because she is known for disconnecting a call in a heartbeat.

Tyler is starting to drive more, and he's so happy about that. He shared with me that he has his driver's license, and his Mom is going to release the car to him soon. He is also saying that Cassie's wish list is steadily growing, and he doesn't know if he wants to continue dating her. He is supposed to pick her up today and take her to get something to eat. I know he's not going to have a good time because she isn't me. The only reason I'm saying this is. Tyler can laugh, talk, and be as goofy as he wants when he's with me, and that is why we have always been such good friends. We have so much in common. He deserves to be able to be himself and not have to be nervous and fake to be in a so-called relationship.

We ended our conversation so Tyler could head to Cassie's grandmother's house. I immediately called Deon to tell her to come outside so we could see Tyler when he picked her up. This is right up Deon's alley. She agrees before I can get my words out good. It's a little chilly. Sweater weather, so I grab my jacket before I head out the door. We meet in my driveway and make small talk until we hear some bass coming down our street.

Let me try to hold it together. I'm sure he's in a hurry to get to her.

The music is sounding clearer the closer Tyler gets to us. I prepare to just wave as he passes, but to my surprise, his car stops right in front of my yard. He turns the motor off, and he's getting out and walking towards us. I totally wasn't expecting this.

"What's up y'all," he says with a big grin covering his face.

Dee and I both say at the same time, "Hey!"

Tyler seems happy and nervous. That's probably why he stopped to talk to us so that he could get rid of some of that nervous energy.

I can't help it. I just have to ask. "So, Tyler, is this an official date? Where are you taking her?"

"I wouldn't say that. She just wants to go get something to eat. That's it."

Dee and I make eye contact, and it seems like we are on the same page. When we looked down the street where Cassie's grandmother lives, we noticed the car was not there. That means Cassie just needs transportation.

Hopefully, that's not the case. Wait a minute. Maybe that is not a bad thing. Maybe he will see exactly what she's up to.

I'm playing all kinds of different scenarios in my head. And to think he's going over there and her grandmother isn't there! Now, that is reason enough for me to be concerned.

Dee interrupts my thoughts by asking Tyler what he got Cassie for Valentine's. That was my cue to go in the house for a Moment. When I return, Tyler and Dee are still conversing. They are talking about the song dedication. As I'm walking toward them, I notice my steps are becoming more challenging to make. *I came out at the wrong time.*

Dee shouts, "Tan, hurry over here and listen to Tyler's explanation of the song dedication!"

I'd rather not! I know Dee's nosey self-brought it up. Because, at this point, it really doesn't matter.

Tyler takes one look at me and knows that the conversation should cease. That's the thing about us: we know each other so well.

Dee is clueless about what just happened, but she has enough sense to leave it alone.

Tyler had gotten carried away with us, laughing and talking. We notice Cassie is making her way up the street to see what is taking him so long. He looks at his watch and says, "I've been kicking it with y'all for almost an hour!"

Dee says, "Dang, Tyler! What a way to start off a first date!"

The three of us were laughing, and Cassie didn't really look like she was in a laughing mood. She didn't speak to us, but she made it clear to Tyler that she had been waiting almost an hour, and if she hadn't walked up the street, he would still be talking to us. Tyler had a look on his face that really said it all. He is trying to maintain his gentlemanly status, but Cassie is making it hard.

Spring Break couldn't get here fast enough for me. I'm really looking forward to our mini family vacation. We are going to Galveston, Texas, for the weekend, and we are taking the boat! I love being out on the water in a boat fishing. Mama always makes sure that she packs the perfect picnic basket for the trip. It is a guaranteed thing that fried chicken will be on the menu, and to make sure that our sodas stay cold, Mama wraps each can in foil after she removes them from the freezer and places them in her tote bag. The most exciting part is that Daddy always lets us take turns driving the boat. Our boat is white, trimmed in red, with red leather seats. The front part of the boat has a

U-shaped seating, which is perfect for having conversations. Daddy loves being on the water, too. I think it reminds him of his Navy days.

We made it! Yes! Mama and Daddy is checking us in at the hotel, and Kerry, JJ, and I are waiting patiently in the van. They returned with the room key, and it's like a race to get to the room to change so we can hit the beach! The weather couldn't be more perfect. It's seventy-five degrees, and the view of the beautiful shade of blue water and the sand, along with the breeze we get from riding in the boat, is amazing. Daddy stops the boat far out in the water and begins handing us our fishing poles. Neither of us wants to touch the bait, so Daddy has the responsibility of baiting everyone's hook. This is my family's favorite pastime, just enjoying each other's company and getting away from the everyday disruptions of life.

While my pole is waiting in the water, I can't help but think about the prom. *Is now a good time to bring it up to* Daddy? *Or maybe I should wait and have my stuff together like Mama suggested.*

"Oh! I got one!" Daddy says as he interrupts my daydreaming of the prom.

Excitement fills the boat as we are anxiously waiting for Daddy to reel in his catch. It was a Largemouth bass! Daddy jokes about catching four more so we could have dinner later.

I can't believe it! Daddy is the only one who has luck with catching fish. He says it's because he went to the back of the boat to get away from all of our noise. He may be right because we were doing more laughing, talking, and playing than fishing.

Our mini vacation has come to an end, and we are on our way back home. We are passing a sign that reads one hundred and twenty-five miles to go to reach our city limits. I think I'm going to join Kerry and JJ in taking a nap. I'm going to try to sleep until we pull into the driveway. I wake up to the sound of high-water pressure and Mama and Daddy talking. As soon as we arrive in town, Daddy finds the nearest car wash to rinse off the boat before he puts it back into the garage. I think I will pretend to be still asleep so I won't have to help clean the boat. I wish they would hurry up so I can get home and take care of my business.

I've been gone for two whole days, and I know I missed out on a lot. As soon as I unpack, I will call Tyler to get caught up on his drama, and then Deon will be next on my list.

Mama sees me reaching for the kitchen phone and says, "Ah, have you put away all your things before you get wrapped up in conversation?"

"Yes, ma'am, mission accomplished."

Mama smiles and goes about her business.

I take my place at the bar and dial Tyler's number. His Mom catches me off guard when I hear her voice and not his. She says he's outside, but she would go grab him by his ear and drag him to the phone. I'm laughing because his Mom is always joking around.

"What's up nosey! I know you probably already heard," Tyler says.

"Heard what? I just got back in town!"

"Well, as of yesterday, Cassie and I are no longer dating."

That's music to my ears! Now, I have to act like I care.

"Oh my, Tyler, I don't know what to say."

"You don't have to say anything because I'm over it and have moved on."

I sure would like to know the details, but I will leave it alone for now.

We both are just holding the phone, clueless about what should be said next.

I remember he was outside when I called, so I suggested he go back outside with his company.

Tyler agrees, and then he asks if he could come over tomorrow. I let him know that I would like that very much. We say goodbye until tomorrow.

I thought daylight would never come. Last night, I was so restless, anticipating what today was going to bring. I am so tempted to pick up the phone and call Tyler to see if he is still coming. I reach for the phone and immediately pull back. This I did several times before deciding to go outside and see if anyone was out there. It's a beautiful day in the neighborhood. There is no need for a sweater because the sun is shining and the weather is absolutely perfect. There's a party going on out here, and ain't nobody told me nothing! Kids are in the street throwing a football. Even JJ is out with his jam box playing music. Dee and Tracey are sitting on her porch playing cards. To this day, I hate playing cards, and Dee is the very reason why I do! When we were in middle school, I swear every time I went to her house, she would start dealing cards. It had gotten so bad that I would leave if I saw cards anywhere in the room.

"Hey, y'all!"

They both barely look up to acknowledge me because they are so into their little card game.

"You want next?" Tracey asks me.

Dee starts laughing and falling out of her seat, saying, "Girl, Tan hates playing cards!"

"So, tell her why I hate it!"

"Tan blames me. She claims I was obsessed with cards in middle school."

I take a seat next to Tracey, and I have a good view of her hand. She has a ROYAL FLUSH! Dee is going to be CRUNCHED! Once Tracey hit her with that, GAME OVER! Dee is such a sore loser. She will play one hundred games straight to prove a point.

"Boom, Boom, Boom!" I collect myself and stand right to my feet. Dee and Tracey look directly at me, showing all their teeth. We all know that is Tyler!

I can't contain myself. I'm trying to hide it, but it's nearly impossible.

As soon as Tyler pulled up in front of the house, he turned the music off. He and Ant leave the car to meet us in front of Dee's house. I look over at my house and notice Daddy on the porch, just shaking his head. I know he's wondering why Tyler has to play his music so loud. We all are exchanging hugs, and of course, Dee can't pass up the opportunity to tease Tyler about hugging me a little too long and too tight. There was something magical about that hug.

I hurry to change the subject by asking Tyler about his new system. He suggests that I follow him to his car. So, he lifts up the hatchback and shows me his speaker box. I ask if they are ten-inch woofers, and he is super proud of his accomplishments as he nods his head. Yes, and to my surprise, there is a Pioneer Amp connected to the box as well to help push the bass. We walk over to the driver's side, and he points out the Pioneer equalizer sitting there under the Kenwood radio. Tyler loves his music, and it has to sound just right. He has achieved his goal, and I'm so happy for him.

We rejoin the group, and Dee eases her way over to me and asks me what Tyler and I are talking about. I assured her that it was strictly about his stereo system.

"Girl, when y'all walked away, Ant was telling us how much Tyler likes you, and I know for a fact that you like him too!"

"I do, but we are good like we are. He's like my best friend. I don't want to mess that up."

It's crazy that right now, I'm thinking about kissing him. Where in the world did that come from?

I made the mistake and shared that with Dee, and now she is going to use it against me. I just know she is! While we were talking, JJ came and interrupted our conversation, "Tan, Mama wants you."

I'm kind of glad to get this distraction. Maybe when I return, Dee will have moved on to something else.

"Mama! Did you want me?" I say as JJ follows close behind me. Mama walks out of the kitchen with a paper towel drying her hands, and she says, "Child, what are you talking about?"

"JJ told me." As soon as I say his name, he starts laughing and takes off running back outside. The joke was on me, and that's when it hit me. JJ plays too much! I start to chase after him. I quickly came to my senses, realizing that I must look pretty goofy running after my little brother. My friends are pointing and laughing at us. I am so glad I could be their source of entertainment. JJ is on my list!

The sun is setting, and we're still hanging out. Tyler and I are having a flipping contest, trying to see who can do the most backward flips in a row. I'm dizzy as I don't know what! He will have to win today. Dee is up to something. I can just feel it. I see her giving Tyler some kind of signal. Maybe I am being paranoid. Out of nowhere, Tyler gets right in my face and says in a low voice, "Dee said you want to kiss me."

At this very moment, I could just die! I'm speechless.

Tyler grabs my hand and leads me to the side of Dee's house. He pulls me close to him and places his hands around my waist. My eyes automatically closed, and before I knew it, I was kissing my best friend!

Chapter 11

Tan

April

May

It's a beautiful day in April, and I have so much to do. _Ok, take a deep breath. Breathe in. Breathe out. And repeat._ I'm trying to figure out how to approach Daddy about my going to the prom. I know he's in the den, so I'm peeking at him through the serving window in the kitchen. Mama creeps up behind me and scares you-know-what out of me. "You must not be living right if you're that easy to scare," Mama says while laughing at me.

"I'm trying to build up my nerves to ask Daddy about the prom."

"Child, I am sick of you talking about the prom. Come on, let's go to the den and watch me convince your Daddy to let you go."

"Really, Mama?"

"Yes, really. Now watch and learn," Mama says as she reaches inside the fridge and pulls out a beer. She's leading, and I'm following her to the den.

"John dear, I brought you a beer." I watch as she delivers it with a smile."

"You must have read my mind. I was so comfortable reclining in my favorite chair and reading the paper. I didn't want to move."

"It's a good thing you have such a loving and caring wife!"

"Not just loving and caring, but beautiful too!"

I'm standing here wondering why I have to listen to them be all cheesy, but it will be so worth it if I get to go to the prom.

Daddy puts his newspaper down, and Mama sits on the armrest of his chair. Pops opens his beer and hands it to him.

Now he is all smiles; Mama is working her magic on him!

This is getting interesting, so I take my seat on the couch, wondering what her next move is going to be. Mama looks over at me and gives me a wink, and that is confirmation that I can start ordering my prom dress. Well, since the two of them are so into one another, I guess I will just get lost.

"Tan!" Deon yells as she is standing down the street in front of Tracey's house. I guess I'll walk down there to see what they have going on. The closer I get, the louder Dee gets, telling me to hurry up.

"Girl, Tracey and I have worked your little prom issue out for you. You can thank us later," Dee says with a devious smile on her face.

Tracey interjects by telling me that I owe her big time!

"Ok, before I start writing checks, I need to hear about this fantastic plan," I say to them both sarcastically.

I can tell that Tracey is the brains of this operation because she quickly takes the lead by explaining.

I'm listening while nodding my head up and down in agreement with this awesome plan that my dear friends took their precious time to develop. *This just might be the answer I was so desperately searching for. Now, all I need is a date.*

Cloud nine is the appropriate description that describes me at this moment. Everything is falling into place. Mama sure worked her magic; Daddy has agreed to let me attend the prom. I am filled with joy from the bottom of my feet to the tip top of my head. I just have one major hurdle to jump, and that would be choosing the perfect date. *Who will be the guy that will take me to the prom? Who will be the guy that my parents will approve of? Deon and Tracey took care of the easy part and left me with a significant challenge! I literally have fourteen days to make things happen, and there's no turning back now!*

I find myself in a crowded cafeteria during lunch. It's extremely loud in here. I'm leaning in, almost in the center of the table, to hear the latest news that Shayla is about to deliver. She's telling us that she will be attending the prom with a senior she just started talking to. She is going on and on about her dress and shoes. Tyler is giving me a look. I don't know this look. In the meantime, Coach Jackson is strolling around monitoring and makes a random stop at our table. "So, who over here is going to the prom?" he says while glancing at each of us, one by one. "Oh, that's right, there are no seniors at this table!"

Shayla says, "I'm definitely going. I'm dating a senior!"

Janis says, "Yeah, me too!"

Out of nowhere. "Tan and I are going to the prom together!" Tyler let those words spill from his lips.

"HUH? WHAT?" I say while looking totally lost.

Coach Jackson kind of looks at us like we are both delusional and walks away.

Now we have everyone's attention at the table. Tyler stands and gets closer to me and says, "I have already talked to Deon and Tracey, and they filled me in on everything, so we are going to this prom together!"

Wait! What? I'm trying to wrap my head around this. Why didn't my so-called friends let me in on this part of the plan? How did they get Tyler to agree? I don't know how to feel, but for some reason, I am wanting to start jumping for joy right now! I can't let him know that he has just made my day!

Mama and Daddy is pleased to know that Tyler is taking me to the prom. For some reason, they liked him from day one, and that is so rare for Daddy. This will be my very first date, so I need to make sure that everything is absolutely perfect. I have almost no time to shop for a dress, not to mention my hair. What am I going to do with my hair? Mama and Kerry are being very supportive. They are taking me shopping to find "The Dress!" This is exciting and exhausting at the same time. Finally, I spotted the perfect dress on a bald, faceless, and shiny white mannequin. It's an all-white lace dress with white satin material underneath. It's tea length and strapless with a white satin large bow in the back.

Mama made an obvious observation that I didn't have enough to put into the dress to keep it up. Kerry is laughing uncontrollably in the middle of the dressing room. Mama assures me that she can sew a seam on each side of the dress so I wouldn't have to worry about it slipping down.

My luck is going pretty well because I have located the perfect white heels, white lace stockings, and, to top it off, a diamond tiara to complete the look.

Heavy rollers are weighing my head down as I'm sitting at the kitchen table, painting my nails a pale pink. I can't believe I am going to the prom today! I can tell Tyler is excited, too, because he has called me at least four times this morning. It's not even noon yet. On his last call, he shared with me that his Mom's friend was going to let us use his Cadillac. I could hear how much that meant to him while he was describing the ride to me. We will be riding in style. What a way to arrive at the prom.

The phone is ringing. It better not be Tyler again. I walk to the bar and answer, "Hello!"

"Well, hello, Tandra Ann, how are you?" It's my grandmother, my Daddy's mother. She is the only one in the family who calls me by my first and middle names.

"I'm fine, and you?"

There is a long pause. "I'm well."

She wasted no time in delivering her message. "So today is your big day, huh? Well, that doesn't mean that you are grown! You know it only takes one time. Do you understand what I'm saying to you?"

Wow! I can't believe that we are having this conversation. Why does she think this is necessary? I just want to end this conversation and pretend like it never happened.

"Yes, Grandmother, I do understand." *There's no need to go into details.*

"Ok, I just need to remind you that you are a "Breakfield" and we have class and morals."

"Yes, ma'am, I know."

Before she lets me go, she tells me that she and Sister Carter, her good friend from church, will be over to see me off for the prom.

That's just GREAT!

"OK, we'll see you later. Grandmother loves you."

"Love you too."

It seems like everybody is here to see me off for the prom. I can remember they did the same thing for Kerry. You would think I'm a princess or something, the way they are going on and on about how beautiful I look. I must say, at this moment, I am feeling like royalty.

Daddy is busy snapping pictures of every movement that I make. Everyone is taking turns posing with me. I'm sitting in this straw, tan, Al Green chair in front of the fireplace, wearing white lace gloves on my folded hands that are placed in my lap, with the perfect posture, while balancing a tiara on the top of my head. I glance at the clock and notice that Tyler is running late. *Where could he be? I hope nothing has happened. Should I call him? Hopefully, no one else will notice the time.*

Mama gives me a look of concern. Now my nerves are really bad. I excused myself to the kitchen and grabbed the phone from the bar to call Tyler. He immediately starts to apologize for being late. His Mom's friend was getting the car detailed and lost track of time. Mama enters the kitchen, waiting to hear what is going on. I tell her, and she says, "Let Tyler know that your Daddy and I will bring you over there." We clear the house of our guests and head to Tyler's house.

Daddy made a left on Shaw Ave. My heart is about to beat out of my chest. I'm just realizing that our parents are about to meet for the very first time. Tyler, his Mom, and her friend were already outside walking around the car, inspecting it. My Parents and I are getting out of the van and walking up to them. We all exchange pleasantries, and Tyler looks at me like he sees a ghost.

Tyler's Mom jokes with him by saying, "Son, close your mouth. You're drooling. Go in the house and get Tan's corsage."

Embarrassment appears all over his face. While we all laugh, he makes a getaway inside the house. Tyler returned with a clear plastic container that had a white carnation wrist corsage with black and red ribbons. I absolutely love it! It coordinates with what we are wearing.

Tyler looks so handsome in his black tails tuxedo, white shirt, red bow tie, and red cummerbund. I hand him the red boutonniere and help him pin it on his lapel, and it is the perfect addition to his attire. We are both pleased with what we picked out for each other.

Of course, Daddy has his camera ready to snap pictures.

"Cheeeeese," we both say each time we do a different pose.

Finally, we are off to the prom.

Tyler appears to be comfortable behind the wheels of this 1984 gray Cadillac with a full tank of gas. The ride was really smooth, and I noticed that there was no wind noise. I guess that's why it's a luxury car. Downtown is well-lit. The lights are so bright and beautiful; it's adding to my level of excitement. We are arriving at the hotel and entering the parking garage. It's pretty full, and now we are on the fourth floor. Oh, I guess Tyler thinks he's a professional because he is backing into a spot between a truck and a car. After he completes the mission, he looks over at me and smiles really big. I'm impressed, but I'm not going to stroke his ego. I will just keep that to myself.

Tyler walks around to my side and opens the door. Wow, he is such a gentleman. This is feeling like an actual date.

I'm in awe as we walk through the sliding doors of the hotel. Tyler and I are both looking around, taking in every detail and amazed by its elegance. Suddenly, a tap on my shoulder distracted me from admiring this lovely hotel. It's Tracey, wearing a t-strap, long black formal with a side split, accompanied by a black shawl. Her best friend accompanied her, and they both held an extra ticket in their hands for Tyler and me. The four of us made our way to the sign-in table. Ok, my nerves have kicked into overdrive. I'm hoping there isn't an issue with Tyler and me being their guest. I can tell Tyler's nerves are getting the best of him, too. Three teachers are working the sign-in table, and Tracey's last name just had to begin with the letter B, so therefore we have to sign in with Ms. James. *Just my luck!*

We are all standing before her, waiting for her to acknowledge us. After she flips the pages of her list back to the first page, Ms. James raises her head while looking over her glasses at us.

"Well, hello, Miss Tracey, and party, how may I help you all?"

Tracey and her best friend say their hellos and, in return, hand her the two tickets and tell her that Tyler and I were their guests.

"Tan, please explain to me this little scheme that you all are trying to run."

"Ma'am?"

"You don't think I know that you and this young man are dating?"

"Ms. James, we are not dating."

"Explain to me why the two of you are wearing coordinating outfits?"

Dang, my worst nightmare has come true. Ms. James has figured out our plan! I'm praying that she will show some mercy on us.

She snatched the two tickets and added our names to her list.

"I'm impressed that y'all's little bird brains have come up with a brilliant plan such as this."

We accept the insult and head into the ballroom. Tyler and I pause. I notice that he has beads of sweat popping out on his forehead. We both burst out laughing because that was indeed a close call.

Wow! The prom committee totally outdid themselves in decorating this room. The colors are black and white with crystal accents. The theme must have something to do with stars because silver stars are everywhere. I'm reaching into my purse to get my disposable camera to capture this Moment. Everyone is dressed to kill, and there are many sporting fresh Jerry Curls.

Soft music is playing while we are having dinner. My plate consists of baked chicken, roasted garlic potatoes, and Italian green beans. They taste as good as they look on my plate. We have a choice of tea or lemonade. I am most definitely not having tea.

Now that dinner has been served, it is time for the DJ to get fired up! The first jam of the night is "I'm Bad" by LL Cool J. There is a rush of moving from the tables to the dance floor, and the WHOP is the dance that everybody is doing, and we are all going in the same direction. After we had danced to a few songs, we have decided to leave the dance floor and return to our table.

I spot Janis and Shayla with their dates, and they are headed our way. The three of us are all wearing different types of white dresses. I motioned for Tyler to take our picture. He is quick to inform me that I only have two pictures left to take with this camera. He should know me better than that. I have a backup in my purse. While we were posing, the DJ decided that he was going to slow it down a bit. The moment I heard the first tune, I knew it was my favorite song by Anita Baker, "No One In the World." Tyler somehow read my mind and led me to the center of the dance floor. I don't have a care in the world as I am in Tyler's arms, living out my fantasy, dancing to my favorite song with my best friend. It can't get any better than this. This will always be our song. I am declaring it today!

After the Prom King and Queen were announced, many made plans to leave. They are talking about going to Bennigan's. Tyler and I are following the crowd, walking out to the parking garage. He didn't forget to be a gentleman because he automatically opened my door and closed it, too. As we drove to the other side of town, we reflected on the funny moments of the night and laughed about them. This night is so magical. I wish I could live in it forever.

Out of nowhere, the car starts to jerk and slows down. Panic is on Tyler's face as other cars are passing us up. He carefully steers the car off the freeway by an old abandoned house. It's very dark, and I'm not sure if I should be scared or not. I will wait to see how Tyler reacts. He's looking at the dashboard, and everything is normal. It's not running hot, and there isn't anything that raises concern. Tyler quickly points out that we still have a full tank of gas.

"So, what should we do now?" I asked to see if somehow, he had a plan.

"I'm really not sure. We need to get a phone. We are too far away from the hotel to walk, and we are in the middle of no man's land."

Now I am scared! Just a few minutes ago, I was living in a fantasy, and now it has taken a turn for the worse!

A little time has passed, and we are still sitting in the car, unsure of what our next move should be. Tyler gets out and looks under the hood. I'm not sure if he knows what he's looking for, so I get out also to help him look for whatever it is we are looking for. There is a truck coming towards us. It's a white older guy driving it. He rolls his window down, sticks his head out, and asks, "What seems to be the problem?"

"I'm not sure," Tyler answers, and he goes on to tell him about what took place with the car and how we have a full tank of gas.

The guy gets out of his truck, and he asks Tyler to try to start the car again.

There's no luck with that attempt. The guy says he believes the car is out of gas and that the gas hand may be broken. We both were at a loss for words until the guy had the audacity to say that he could take me to use the nearest phone and then bring me back. Tyler was not going for that. Without any hesitation, he said to the guy, whatever we decide to do, we will do it together. I am so proud of Tyler for speaking up and handling this situation like a grown-up. The guy respects what Tyler says and agrees to take us both. But before we do anything, we both get back and sit inside the Cadillac. There is complete silence, and then Tyler asks me how I feel about getting into a stranger's truck. Without a doubt, I suggest that we pray and ask God to please be with us and protect us.

"Amen!" we look at each other and trust that everything is going to be alright.

As we approached the truck, Tyler opened the passenger side door for me to get in and sit next to the stranger, and he sat next to the door. My dress is puffy, and it's up a bit and, making it awkward for me. I'm using both hands to mash it down so it doesn't get in the way.

"Where to?" The stranger asks, and Tyler responds by telling him the name of the hotel where the prom is being held. Then the stranger starts making small talk by asking questions about our school and the prom. I remain quiet and let Tyler do all of the talking. It seems like time is at a standstill.it is taking forever to get downtown.

The bright lights displayed on the hotel building were so welcoming. We are so thankful to God that this stranger had a good heart and no ill intentions. Tyler and I thank him and walk hand in hand into the hotel lobby. We stop for a moment just to embrace because, silently, we both realize how this could have ended. We now have to make that dreadful phone call to our parents to inform them of our terrible mishap. Tyler picks up a payphone, and I do the same right next to him. We both deposit a quarter. The time is 12:20 a.m., and my Daddy picks up the phone on the very first ring. *I am not surprised at all because I have missed my midnight curfew.* I am trying my best to explain to Daddy to the best of my ability how we could run out of gas, although the gas hand told a different story. Tyler glances over in my direction with a sympathetic look on his face. After both conversations ended, we found a spot in the lobby by the glass windows to sit and wait for Tyler's mom to come pick us up.

I can tell that Tyler feels terrible about the way our night turned out. I reassured him that I had a good time overall and will never forget this for the rest of my life. He cracks a smile and admits that he, too, will do the same. After a half hour of chatting, Tyler's mom and her friend pulled in front of the hotel. Once we got into the car, Tyler's Mom's friend began to apologize for the car trouble, and he told us he would find a way to make it up to us. We still thank him for loaning us his car because it was the right thing to do. I'm sitting in the back seat, thinking about the possible consequences once I make it home. Out of nowhere, I asked Tyler's mom if she could explain what had happened to my dad. She agrees, and I am starting to feel a little better about my situation.

It is 1:15 a.m., and Tyler, his Mom, and I are walking to my door. Before we could step on the porch, the front door opened. Mama and Daddy appears from behind the door. Suddenly, a big lump is in my throat, and my words are trapped somewhere in there. Tyler's mom made her way in front of us and began to explain what had happened to my parents. Mama interrupts her to invite her in. While still running her mouth, she doesn't leave out not one detail as she enters the entrance hall. Finally, Tyler nudges her to stop talking so much, and she says, "I guess I must be running my mouth too much because Tyler just gave me a cue to wrap it up."

I swear she's too funny, and I believe that there is never a dull moment whenever she is around. We all say our goodbyes, and Daddy holds the door open for them. Mama and Daddy must be satisfied with Tyler's Mom's explanation because I made it to my room to get ready for bed without any interference. What an eventful night! This will go down in history, and I'm sure Tyler and I will never forget it. Who knows what the future holds for us? I just hope we will always be friends.

Chapter Twelve

Tyler

Man! This is the day I have been waiting for; it's the last day before Christmas break. I have no problem with getting up and getting dressed this morning. I'm actually ready to walk out the door before my alarm to leave has a chance to go off. As I'm walking to the bus stop, I have a huge smile on my face. Why? Because I have a special gift that I'm giving my special friend today. I know she's going to be shocked. I just can't wait to see her face when I give it to her.

Everyone on the bus is in rare form, excited to get this last day over with! The bus consists of guys with gifts for their girlfriends and girls with much neater-wrapped gifts for their boyfriends. As soon as the bus came to a complete stop in front of the school, we all rushed to get off like it was on fire. I take a second to look back at our bus driver, and she looks relieved that we are out of her life, but the funny part is that she has to do this all over again in a few hours.

Dang, these halls are packed! I see Janis, and that is an indication that Tan shouldn't be far away. "What's up, Janis? Have you seen my best friend?"

"You mean my best friend?" Janis says while hugging me.

"Well, if you see her, tell her that I'm looking for her."

Janis says with a grin, "I most certainly will.

I'm running to my locker to get my notebook, and then I began my search for Tan again.

BINGO! I spot her talking to Janis, so I walk up to Tan, steal her away from her friend, and whisper in her ear for her to meet me at this very spot where we are standing after our last final exam. I could tell she was very curious and confused at the same time. That's the way I intended for her to be. As I walked off, I could hear Janis asking Tan questions, and Tan was getting frustrated with her because she didn't have any answers.

I can't lie. It's tough to focus on my finals. I keep thinking about how Tan is going to react when I give her my gift. Finally, I've completed my last test, and now I am free to leave for Christmas break, but first, I must hurry to meet Tan in the designated spot and then make it to my bus to go home. I'm rushing through the crowds, weaving in and out while trying to make it to **"The SPOT."** OK, I'm here, but there's no Tan. I hope she didn't forget. She's probably running her mouth somewhere. *Should I go and look for her? Would she forget to meet me? Oh, she's coming. Ok, ok, let me get it together!*

"Come on, Tan! I know you can move faster than that!"

"I'm moving as fast as I can," she says as she walks at a snail's pace towards me.

For some reason, I'm feeling kinda nervous, but I don't know why. She's just my best friend.

"I have something for you, Tan." I began to twist off the gold nugget ring that was on my pinky finger. I handed it to her. She assumes that I am letting her keep the ring over the holidays, but I let her know that I'm giving it to her. She seems shocked and at a loss for words. That usually never happens. Tan slips the ring on her ring finger on her right hand, and she gives me the biggest smile. *I knew this was a good idea.* I'm not going to give her a chance to ask me any questions, so I'm taking off to make it to my bus.

This time of year, is not a big deal for me, mainly because growing up, we always got what we needed and not what we wanted. Mom does her best throughout the year to take care of me and my siblings, so I make her a priority every Christmas and buy her a nice gift. Sean is coming over, and we are rolling to the mall to do a little shopping. I decided to wait for him in the living room. As I walk into the living room, I see the half-decorated tree that Venus put up on yesterday. It has different colored lights that are blinking on and off and primarily red bulbs with a few green ones scattered hanging on the branches. Silver garland is wrapped around the entire tree. I guess it adds a special touch. Well, I have a little time on my hands, so I will try to help this little tree out by moving the tree to a corner and removing the decorations from the back to the sides and the front to make it look like it's fully decorated. I step back to look at my accomplishments, and I am pleased.

Sean pulled up, bassing as usual, and came inside the house. He looks at me and then at the tree. I immediately defended myself, "Nah man, I ain't decorating no tree. I just moved it over in the corner for Venus." I couldn't dare lose cool points over a tree! Sean is looking at me like he doesn't believe me. I grab my jacket and say, "Let's bounce!"

Off to the mall, we go! Sean pumps up the bass for the song "Fresh is Word" by Mantronix. I can't lie. His bass is HITTING! We both are bobbing our heads and enjoying the music and the ride. Sean reaches for the volume button and turns it all the way down. *Oh, here we go!*

"Say, who am I taking you to the mall to shop for? Is it ya, girl Tan?"

"Man, nah, I am shopping for my Mom. Besides, I gave Tan my nugget pinky ring."

"What! You gave her that ring? You love that ring!"

"Yeah, I do, but I always used to let her wear it, so I just decided to give it to her."

"What did she say when you gave it to her?"

"Of course, she was shocked, but I told her it was a friendship ring."

"Oh. I got to give it to you. You are smooth! That was a real player's move!"

We give each other five and laugh. *I guess that was pretty smooth!*

The mall is crowded, full of people in the Christmas spirit. The smell of perfume and cologne fills the air and leads me to the counter. *Hmmmm, now what would my Mom like?*

I'm sniffing many samples, trying to decide which one she would like. I think we have a winner: Christian Dior *Poison*. She will love it. Sean is walking my way, holding a bag in his hand.

"What's in the bag?"

"I just picked up a gold rope necklace for Angel."

Sean has been dating Angel for two years, and I'm sure they will marry someday.

I made my purchase, and I'm ready to get out of here before I see something for myself. I need to save my money to fix up my car and to have some money in my pocket. I hate being broke!

The Christmas tree is beaming in the window. It is beginning to look a lot like Christmas around here. I'm trying to hurry and locate the wrapping paper and the tape before Mom comes out of her room and starts asking questions about her gift. As soon as I place the gift under the tree, here she comes, looking suspicious.

"I hope you didn't go spending a lot of money on me, boy!"

I'm about to address her question, but the phone is ringing. I jump up and run to the kitchen to answer it. It's Tan on the other end. She had also been out shopping and just made it in. I'm telling her how I, too, was out shopping for my Mom. As soon as I say that, Mom is walking back to her room with today's newspaper. Now I can talk freely. It was something I wanted to tell Tan, and it almost slipped my mind. "Hey Tan, did you hear the radio station 107.5 is supposed to play Bobby Brown's new song, *I Need a Girlfriend,* at 11:00 tonight? Make sure that you tune in, don't forget!"

I know she will never forget because she loves her some, Bobby B!

"You know I wouldn't miss that for nothing!"

She just doesn't know that I have something up my sleeve that is going to leave her clueless! I can't help but laugh to myself as we are hanging up the phone.

I immediately tried calling the radio station over and over again, and time after time, I received the same busy signal. I'm not giving up. I have to make this happen! I swear I'm not going to give up! It's probably been my one-hundredth attempt, but I finally got through! This song's dedication is going to make her night! I can't wait to hear what her reaction will be. I've been waiting around for 11:00, and finally, it's here! Just knowing that I have made her night brings a smile to my face as I lie in bed, preparing to drift off.

Christmas Eve is today, and it really just feels like an ordinary day. The whole family would meet at my grandparents' house to eat and just hang out. All of my cousins and family friends will be there. We always have a good time. I still can't help but wonder about what Tan thought of the song dedication. I hope it doesn't make things weird with us. I hope she knows why I did it. Dang, I'm not even sure why I did it. Now I'm wondering if I should have done it. Oh well, I can't take it back. It's done now.

It's about 6:00 in the evening, and I want to reach out and call her. I'm listening to the phone ring, and I'm thinking to myself, if there isn't an answer on the next ring, I'm going to hang up. To my surprise, her little brother, JJ, answered the phone. This little dude is so funny.

He's asking me all kinds of things like. Am I in love with Tan? Now this has really caught me off guard, and I can hear Tan freaking out in the background, trying to pry the phone out of his hands. She has to call for her Mama to get JJ to release the phone to her. It's hard for me to control my laughter, so I'm struggling to cut it off. Our conversation carried on as usual, as if nothing had ever happened. I'm glad about that, and I can tell she is too.

Man, I am so glad that Christmas has come and gone. I got a few things I wanted, and most of all, Mom was very pleased with her new perfume. I'm happy I made an excellent choice. Now, my focus is on the Coca-Cola Tournament. This is the last big event before the new year, and schools from all over the city and from different states will be there. So that means girls, girls, girls! I better make sure I don't forget my pencil and paper because I plan on getting a lot of digits! Ant and I will have another competition to see who will collect the most by the end of the night, and I know I will come out on top like I always do!

The parking lot is packed! We should have gotten here earlier. I'm out of the car, ready to take this long walk to the gymnasium, and Ant is still inside the car, brushing on his hair.

"Man, come on! You still don't look any better!"

Ant has a stupid grin on his face as he is exiting the vehicle.

"You're just jealous, Tyler, because my waves look better than yours!"

"You must be crazy! My waves are on yours, fool!"

I'm glad we already have our tickets because that line is ridiculous!

As we moved through the crowds, someone tapped me on my shoulder, and as soon as I turned around, the group of girls behind me turned their heads like they were innocent. I can't lie; they are all fine, and they look good, but they are full of it, so I'm moving on.

"Say, Ant, let's head over to the concession stand."

We are trying to get there, but everyone seems to have the same idea because we are barely moving. I see an opening and quickly rush through, and Ant is right behind me. That was a lot of work, maneuvering our way out of the crowds.

The concession stand area is congested also, but I somehow spot my best friend, and she looks really fly! That dress she is wearing is hugging her in all the right places! Who is that all in her face? Now that's Lance. It looks like he is rapping really hard over there. I hope she's not falling for whatever it is he is telling her. As soon as he walks off, I'm making my way over to her. She doesn't see me approaching her, so I have to make her day by putting my hands over her eyes and asking her, "Guess who?" She always amuses me by trying to act like she's really trying to figure it out. She replies, "Is it my best friend, Tyler?"

To my surprise, Shayla threw a monkey wrench by giving us a friendly reminder of the song dedication I had made to Tan. She went on to say that she thought we were dating now. I may be exaggerating a little, but it seems like the entire gymnasium went silent, and all eyes were on us. Tan looks like she wants to disappear, but she can't do that without taking me with her. I don't know what possessed Shayla to shine the spotlight on that event at this particular moment. It's really kinda messed up right now because our moods have just gone south. There is nothing left to do but just hug and part ways.

February

It's a Friday night basketball game going on, and I am solo to-night. Mom let me drive the car to the game. I'm walking, trying to locate a good seat, and Cassie is heading my way. She comes up to me, says hi, and gives me the tightest hug. This hug feels different from the other hugs before. Maybe I'm reading too much into it. She tells me she's here with friends and will catch up with me later. I locate a seat up high so I can see everything and everybody. My view of the cheer-leaders is excellent. It's a few minutes before half-time, and we are winning. I'm leaving my seat to walk down by the court to wave at Tan so that she knows I'm here. Since we are so far ahead and we just made another basket, I guess I will head home. Cassie is probably preoccupied and has forgotten all about me.

I'm sitting here bored this Saturday afternoon. I don't have one single plan, and no one has called to inquire about hanging out or anything. This is my third bowl of Fruit Loops cereal, and I'm drinking the leftover discolored milk from the bowl. I see the yellow phone on the wall, just waiting for me to call Tan and explain the song's dedication. The receiver is in my hand, and I don't know why my nerves are getting the best of me, so I hang it back up on the wall.

Come on, man! You are making a big deal out of nothing. Just be cool.

I pick it up again, and my fingers automatically start dialing her number. Before I could change my mind, Tan answered the phone. Maybe I'm reading too much into it, but she sounds kinda strange. She will probably be fine after I explain the song to her. As soon as I bring it up, Tan cuts me off by saying, "After I tell you what I have to tell you, that won't even matter anymore."

What is she about to tell me? Does she want to end our friendship? I have messed up big time!

The phone is silent, but I can sense that she is having a hard time conveying her message, so I am waiting patiently for her to get it together.

Finally, the words' part from her lips, "Cassie came over today, and she wants to date you!"

I'm shocked! Never in a million years did I think she was going to tell me this!

Why now? She wasn't interested when I wanted to take her to the homecoming dance. What has changed?

"Doesn't she have a boyfriend?"

Tan began to tell me that they had broken up, but she didn't go into any details.

I'm really speechless, and I don't know how to react. I can tell that Tan is bothered by this conversation, so she's trying to rush off the phone and telling me to get a pencil and paper so I can write Cassie's number down. Now that I have her number, I am unsure if or when I want to call her.

On the third ring, Cassie picks up the phone. She seemed to be waiting on my call. I was worried about trying to keep our conversation alive, but it's going better than expected. She feels the need to keep bringing up Valentine's Day. I think she's trying to make sure that I get her something, although it's just right around the corner, and we are not even dating yet. I don't know what to think about that. I will definitely have to discuss this with my best friend, and hopefully, she will give me some good advice.

Mondays sure roll around quickly. The weekend flew by! It's already second period, and I'm taking my time getting to my career/work study class that I have with Tan. As I'm walking to the classroom, just about everybody wants to stop me and talk to me. I just remembered I only have one more tardy left, so I need to make it to class on time! I cut my conversation short and dashed through the hallway like the building was on fire! "Ring! Ring!" I made it to class by the skin of my teeth! Ms. Pye was just about to close the door, but my foot was already in the class, so she let the rest of me in. I take my seat with my heart beating out of my chest and a big grin on my face.

Ms. Pye is pairing us up for a project. I can't help but notice that Tan is not her usual self today. I wonder what is wrong? Maybe I'm mistaken. I guess it's meant for me to find out because we are partners for this project. We find a table in the back of the class and take our seats. There is no exchange of words between the two of us, so I blurt out, "I know your nosey self wants to know about Cassie and me!" She gives me a fake laugh and pretends like she wants to hear all about it. I'm going on and on about Cassie and me, and finally, I get to the part where I ask Tan to do a huge favor for me and pick out a Valentine's gift for my new girlfriend. I pull fifty dollars out of my wallet and hand it to her. *This is more than enough, and if I know Tan, I know she will spend the rest on herself.* I trust she won't let me down.

Valentine's Day is here, and I am on my way to Tan's house to get the card and the big box of chocolate candy. I'm pleased with Tan's selection, and I'm sure Cassie will be too, but she will never know that I didn't pick the large, red, satin, ruffle box of candy and card out for her. I already explained to Cassie that I was just dropping her gift off because I have to work today. She seems to be okay with that, so I don't press the issue. When I rang her doorbell, she answered it immediately. She's wearing a red T-shirt with a white heart on her chest and some tight blue jeans. As she opened the screen door, I handed her the card and then the giant box of candy. She's smiling, so that's a good sign that she likes it. She then leans out the door to give me a half hug. *Hmmm, that's not what I expected at all. It's like she is trying to rush me off or something. Maybe she has made plans with someone else. I guess I'm better off not knowing.*

March

Spring Break

Just because I'm dating Cassie doesn't mean Tan and I can't still be friends. Our relationship is better than ever, and we still talk on the phone for hours and we still laugh at each other's corny jokes. Tomorrow, I am going to pick Cassie up and take her to get something to eat. I am really looking forward to our date. If that's what you want to call it. I can't lie. I'm really kinda nervous.

Today is the day! I'm ironing my shirt and talking to Tan on the phone. I inform her that in a few minutes, I am going to take Cassie to get something to eat. We talk until I'm ready to walk out the door. I'm checking myself out to give myself one last look to make sure I look GQ. _Damn, I look good!_ I grab my keys off the kitchen table, and off I go to pick up my date.

The bass in my car is hitting! As I turn on Danson Street, I decide to show out and turn my bass up a little. "I Ain't No Joke," by Eric B. & Rakim, is my rap of choice. As I'm driving down the street, I notice Tan and Deon standing on the curb. I'm going to stop and talk to them and see what they are up to. Oh no! I have lost track of time! Before I knew it, I spotted Cassie walking down the street towards us. It looks like she has an attitude. I cut the conversation off and began to speak to Cassie. Oh yeah, she's steaming mad. She's giving me a look like I'm her worst enemy. She didn't even bother to acknowledge Tan and Deon. I'm really trying to figure out if I really want to entertain this.

Once Cassie is in my car and we are driving, she has absolutely nothing to say. I asked her where she would like to go, and she barely opened her mouth to say, Long John Silvers.

Really? I thought this was supposed to be a date. I guess we are not on the same page.

The crazy part about this whole little adventure was that she didn't want to dine in, so we went through the drive-through. I'm not even in the mood to get anything. She ordered her meal, and we pulled up to the window. *I should make her pay for her own food mainly because she is not good company at all!*

This date will probably go down in history as being the fastest date ever! If that's what you want to call it. I sure hope Tan and Deon are not still outside because I don't want to have to explain this to anyone.

It's Spring Break, and I have spent most of my time tending to my car. I washed and cleaned it out and shined up the dash and my tires. It almost looks like it just came off the showroom floor. My stereo system is hitting just right now because I have four new speakers. I can't wait to show it to Tan. She went to Galveston on a family vacation. My grandparents always gather up all the grandkids every summer to take a road trip in their motorhome. We have so much fun just laughing, talking, and playing games with our cousins. I may not get to go this summer because I plan on working more and stacking my money.

I've been talking to Cassie, and as always, it's all about what she wants from me. I don't know if I want to continue whatever this is that we are doing, so I will just fade away gracefully. If I know her, she will be calling soon so I can chauffeur her all around the metroplex. She's going to be in for a surprise today when I discontinue her ride service and go hang out with Ant. As a matter of fact, let me go ahead and disappoint her right now so I can go on about my day.

Cassie answered the phone, and before I could get my greeting out well, she said, "Are you on your way?"

Being so sure of herself, she doesn't give me time to answer, and she quickly tells me before hanging up the phone that she will be outside waiting.

This girl sure has her nerves. I should just let her wait for me to show up, but no, I wouldn't do that. I will give her a call back to let her know I have other plans.

That didn't go over too well at all. She went as far as telling me that she would just find someone else to do it and that I shouldn't get upset if it happened to be a guy or even her ex-boyfriend. It took all I had not to really tell her how I felt. I have enough sense to know this is my "out," so I'm going to take it. Good riddance!

I'm outside with the homies, and Mom yells out the door, "Tyler, telephone!"

Hmmm, I wonder who could be calling me? I went inside to get the phone, and as soon as I said hello, I heard Tan say, "Hey, big head! I'm back!"

I'm smiling from ear to ear. I can't lie, I missed my friend.

"I know you are calling me to be nosey!"

"What do you mean?" Tan says while sounding confused.

I'm just going to spit it out, "Cassie and I broke up!"

There is a long pause, and finally, Tan begins to tell me how sorry she is that we broke up. I'm letting her know that it's really not a big deal and that I have already moved on. I can tell Tan wants details, but I'm not going to give her any, so she's following my lead and moving on. Before I get off the phone to go back out with the homie, I'm asking Tan if it's ok for me to come over to her house tomorrow. That seemed to have made her day because her voice was more high-pitched than usual, so that's how I knew when she was excited about something.

Ant and I are cruising in "The Night Rider," and my speakers are bumping "Looking for The Perfect Beat" by Afrika Bambaataa &

Soul Sonic Force. I stopped right in front of Deon's house, and I immediately turned my music off when I spotted Tan's nosey-ass Daddy standing on his porch shaking his head. We are walking up to the girl's little card game that's just ending, and we all start to exchange hugs. Of course, Deon, with her messy self, has to tease that I hugged Tan longer and tighter. I'm blushing while still trying to remain a G, so to escape that situation, I ask Tan to walk over to my car and check out my new speakers. She seems to be impressed. Our friendship is probably based on cars and systems, and that's why she's so cool for a girl.

When we rejoin the group, I could tell they all wanted to know what we were talking about. I know I'm not going to give them the satisfaction of knowing. Besides, I like to leave them in the dark and just wonder about my business. Deon slides closer to Tan and starts to ask her questions. She is really trying to whisper, but it's not working.

I'm looking over in Ant's direction, and he's looking kinda suspicious. Now I'm wondering what they were talking about when Tan and I left the group. My thoughts are interrupted by JJ when he yells for Tan that her Mama wants her. As soon as Tan walks away, Deon eases her way over to me. She is smiling really hard, acting like she is about to tell me the best secret in the world!

I can't believe the words that are coming out of her mouth! I'm trying to process it. Tan wants to do what? I'm processing it again. Tan wants to kiss me. Is that really what I heard? Deon is looking at me like, what are you going to do about it? I was not expecting her to tell me anything like that. I'm not sure what to do. Deep down, I want to. I really don't have to dig that deep. Sign me up! I want to kiss her, too!

All of a sudden, I see JJ running out of the house, and Tan is right on his heels. She stopped suddenly when she realized we were laughing at them. She's trying to catch her breath and walk back over to us. All she said was JJ plays too much!

After things settle down, we change the mood completely. I challenge Tan in a backflip competition. This is right up her alley; she didn't hesitate to accept the challenge.

We decided to do it at the same time. She was on the left, and I was on the far-right side of the yard. Deon's yard was perfect for this because it doesn't have a tree. Ant walks to the finish line and counts us down to start. Deon and Tracey are counting each flip we do. I'm trying to focus on my number, and now I realize that Deon stopped counting when she got to six. Tracey is still counting for me after I hear her say eight. I came to a complete stop and noticed Tan sitting on her butt in the grass. I'm still trying to continue to stand because I don't want to lose any cool points. I stagger over to her and offer her my hand to help her get to her feet, and I start to brag about being the winner! She's too tired to say anything, so I finally stopped because it's no fun celebrating when the both of us are dizzy as Hell!

It's getting dark while we are standing around talking and high-siding. It's probably time for Tan to go into the house. Deon looks over in my direction and signals for me to make my move. I'm counting in my head, trying not to be so anxious, but it doesn't seem to be working.

My feet just took control, and I began to walk over to Tan. I'm moving close to her, and I say, 'I heard you wanted to kiss me." Before she could try to respond, I grabbed her hand to lead her to the side of Deon's house. I'm not crazy. I know not to let Tan's Daddy catch me!

We're facing each other, and I pull her close to me. Then I place both of my hands around her waist, and she has her arms around my neck. She automatically closes her eyes, and I can't help but see her amazing beauty. This kiss is like no other. Man! I'm actually kissing my best friend!

The other day, I had an exciting conversation with Deon and Tracey. The two of them are very creative. They came up with the perfect plan for Tan and me to attend the prom. I bought into the idea without any hesitation. If I was going to go to the prom, I couldn't think of a better person to go with than my girl, Tan. The funny thing about this is she has no idea that I know about "The Plan."

The school day is going by kinda fast. It's lunchtime, but it seems like I just got here. As I'm walking down the hallway, I can hear the noise from the cafeteria. When I enter, I spot my crew already sitting at our table, talking over one another. I take my seat and join in the conversation.

Coach Jackson is making his rounds monitoring the cafeteria. He is stopping by random tables, harassing and high-siding students, but it's all done in fun. And just as I thought, he's heading in this direction. The look he's giving us lets us know that he is about to say something crazy. He pauses and says, "Who over here thinks they're going to the prom?" Then he gave us all a quick look over and informed us that none of us were going because we were all juniors.

Shayla doesn't waste any time correcting him by telling him that she is going with her boyfriend, who's a senior. Janis chimes right in after her and makes it extremely clear that she is dating a senior also and will be in attendance.

I'm watching Tan and see the look of disappointment on her face, so I speak up and let everybody around us know that Tan and Tyler will be at the prom together! The look she has on her face is priceless. She's speechless right now, so I lean in close to her and share with her that I have already talked to Deon and Tracey about their plan. I can tell she's happy, and I know I have just saved the day!

Coach Jackson shakes his head in disbelief and walks away to the next table.

Let me get ready to be interviewed by millions to explain what just happened. Thank goodness the bell saves me.

Prom

Today, I have so much to do to get ready for the prom. The barber shop will be the first stop so I can get an edge up. The Jerry Curl is still alive and well. I will get the usual. My sides were cut close, and the back was hanging medium-length. It always looks fly. I'm just not ready to get rid of it. "I have curls for the girls!" Who knows, I will probably sport it for at least another year or so.

The barber shop is really crowded. I thought I was ahead of the game by getting here at 8:00 a.m., but I guess everyone had the same idea. As I walk in, I see a lot of familiar faces, and we slap five and I take a seat next to the door. My barber tells me that there are five guys in front of me. That's not something I wanted to hear. I take a deep breath and just prepare myself to be patient. One good thing about this experience is you get to hear and contribute to "Shop Talk."

We have a few old heads up in here that love to give young cats like me advice about life, but mostly about women.

"Say, young man, what movie star or singer do you think is fine?" One of the OGs says while looking directly at me. Without hesitation, I say, "Janet Jackson and Vanity!" Everyone in the place was shaking their heads in agreement and testifying about how fine they both were. The old cat assures me that I have excellent taste, but he had to flashback for a moment to reminisce about who was fine back in his day. The names Tina Turner, Pam Grier, and Diana Ross flow from his mouth proudly as he stands up and gives an old guy across room five. I guess I can relate because at their age now, I can still tell that they were really fine back in their day.

I finally take my place in the chair, and my cut doesn't take long at all. I paid, and now I'm on my way to pick up Tan's corsage. Hopefully, she likes it. I'm pleased with it, but what do I know about a flower?

As soon as I walk in the house Mom and Venus are grinning from ear to ear.

"What's up with Y'all?"

"Go look in your room," Mom says as she stands to usher me in that direction. Venus runs and jumps in front of me and pushes my room door open.

I'm trying to remain calm, but I'm wearing the biggest smile right now!

My tuxedo is lying on my bed, along with a shoe box containing shiny black patent shoes and black dress socks. I check with Mom to make sure that the Cadillac is still our source of transportation, and she confirms that it is.

I need to see what Tan is doing, so I'm calling her number. She answers on the third ring. I have to sound normal and not let her know that I'm very hyped about going to the prom. She's not trying to hide it at all because I can hear it in her voice. I'm pretending that it's an ordinary day and asking her about her plans for today.

"Shut up, Tyler, you play too much!"

I'm laughing at her, and she's not entertaining my silliness at all.

I let her go and grab a quick bite to eat, shower, and get dressed.

My nerves are getting the best of me right now because my Mom's friend hasn't brought the car over yet. _Where in the world could he be? I definitely don't want Tan to panic, so I will hold off on calling her._ My thoughts are interrupted by the ringing phone. As I'm answering the phone, Mom's friend is coming through the door, informing us that he just had the car detailed and wanted us to come outside to check it out. I let Tan know why I'm running late, and she surprised me by being really calm and stating she would have her parents bring her over here.

Tan and her parents arrive and meet my Mom and her friend. I can't take my eyes off of her. She looks GOOD! *Yeah, I'm checking her out from head to toe. I better settle down before her dad notices.*

Mom said something to embarrass me, so that was the end of me lusting after Tan. I excuse myself and go inside the house to get her wrist corsage. When I return and hand her the corsage Tan couldn't be more pleased while showing all thirty-two teeth. The boutonniere she gave me looks great on my lapel. After we give the car one last inspection, I open the passenger's side door for Tan and then I get behind the wheel looking like I belong here. Like it was my car. We are well on our way with a full tank of gas.

Once parked and now, after jumping through a few hoops, we are sitting at the table having dinner. Now dinner is over, the DJ gets it live, and people are racing to the dance floor. Tan and I take a break from dancing and take pictures with friends. The mood suddenly changes when the DJ slows things down with Tan's favorite song, *No One In the World, by Anita Baker.*

I take one look at Tan and read her mind. I'm leading my best friend to the center of the dance floor, and she is melting in my arms. I can't even lie; I'm enjoying this, and I really don't want to let her go. There's no doubt that this will always be our song.

It's time for the King and Queen to be announced. Most of us are planning on leaving as soon as the announcement is over. We are meeting up at Bennigan's. The cool crew pours out of the hotel into the parking garage on our way to part two of our great adventure. Tan and I are trailing at the very end of the caravan. We're both on cloud nine right now, singing just about every song that comes on the radio.

Something isn't right. I can feel it. Is it my imagination, or is this car slowing down? OH NO, NOW THE CAR IS JERKING A LIT-TLE! Ok. Let me try to appear cool. Tan has a puzzled look on her face. I give her a half smile to try and reassure her that everything is under control.

I wish I could believe that. I'm now replaying a previous conversation that I had with my Mom's friend. I remember him having trouble with the gas hand. It wasn't working correctly, and he was putting the car in the shop. So, I asked him about it when I asked him to drive it to the prom. He acted as if I was insulting him by asking him if he had taken care of that issue, so I just left it alone.

This driving experience has gotten worse, and I'm afraid I can't fake it anymore. We are coasting to the side of the road. _I can't even look at Tan right now because I feel like I have ruined her night._

We sit for a moment in silence. _Alright, let me man up and face her and let her know that she is in good hands. The last thing I want is_ *for her to feel scared on my watch.* I turn towards her and tell her that something is wrong with the car, and I point out that we still have a full tank of gas. I'm going to open the hood and check things out. As I turn to open the door, I notice Tan is also getting out of the car. I open the hood, and There's Tan looking harder than me. *I love that about her. Does she even know what she's looking for or looking at?*

"Do you have a plan?" Tan asks.

That's the million-dollar question. "I don't have a plan, but I do know we need to get to a pay phone, and we both know that it is too far to walk to get to one. As we are talking, a white guy pulls up in a pickup truck, asking if we need help. I tell him what was going on with the car and he gets out of the truck to take a look. He asks me to try to start the car. It didn't start. He thought the same thing, which is that the car was out of gas. So, he offers to take Tan to use the phone. *I know DAMN well he doesn't think I'm going to allow him to ride off in the darkness with my girl!* I informed him that we were indeed a package deal. We travel together.

He agrees to take us both, but before we take him up on his offer, Tan suggests that we go back to the car and say a prayer first. She leads us in prayer, and we both say Amen! I look directly at her to let her know I will do everything in my power to keep her safe.

I didn't exhale until the guy let us out in front of the hotel where the prom was held. We thanked him and went inside. It is well past Tan's curfew, so I'm feeling nervous about explaining everything that happened to her dad. As we are walking in the lobby trying to locate the pay phones, I see that Tan is freezing so I take my jacket off and put it around her shoulders.

I pick up the phone and deposit my quarter to call my Mom. She and her friend came to pick us up, and he couldn't stop apologizing about the car. I am just tired and disappointed and just ready for this to be over. Mom made everything alright with Tan's parents. She has a way of finding humor in things that no one else would. _There's only one thing that's on my mind right now, and that is what Tan thought of our, I guess you can say first date. Will she be willing to go on another date with me? Can I get a do-over?_

Chapter 13

Tan

Summer Time

Thank God it's summer! I have a part-time job at the mall, so I can only sleep late part-time. Tyler and I have started dating a week after the prom. We were officially boyfriend and girlfriend, and it felt a little strange. I did grant him a do-over for a first date, so he took me to Red Lobster, and we both ordered popcorn shrimp, fries, and virgin daiquiris. It was the best date ever! We have our dates every Friday, and I always look forward to hanging out with him. This Friday, we're going to Six Flags with Ant and his new girlfriend. I can't let his girlfriend outshine me.so I have to find the perfect outfit.

"Telephone, Tan!" Kerry yells from the kitchen.

I go into my parent's room to get the phone. "I got it!"

"Hey girl, whatcha doing?"

"Oh, hey Dee, I'm chilling. What's up?"

"Do you want to roll to the mall?"

"Girl, you read my mind. I need an outfit for my date on Friday. How are we getting there?"

"My Daddy has to get his car serviced, and he will drop us off and pick us up."

"Well, ok, I will be over there in a few."

I walk into the den, and I see Mama and Daddy on the couch. Daddy is massaging her feet while they're watching TV. It just seems unbelievable because he's the one who has been at work all day, but he's catering to her.

I stand beside the couch and shake my head while looking at them.

"Tan, you better hope you get a man who treats you like a queen and always puts you first."

"Oh yes, sir! That is definitely on my to-do list," I say in a joking way.

Mama adds her two cents by saying, "Yeah, girl, you better hope!"

"Ok, you two love birds, can I go to the mall with Deon? Mr. Franklin is taking us."

"Gone!" they both say at the exact same time.

The mall is not crowded at all. I expected to see teenagers everywhere now that it's summertime. Dee and I really couldn't say too much in the car because we didn't want her dad in our business. I am anxious to get to my favorite store, Contempo. The last time I was there, I saw some cute biking shorts. "Come on, Dee, let's go to my store!"

"I knew we wouldn't be able to leave this mall without going to your store!"

"Ahhh, come on. You know you always find something cute in there."

"Ok, Tan, I'm convinced; let's go in and see what we can find."

As soon as I walk in, I'm overwhelmed by all of the latest fashions. There's a mannequin in the center of the store sporting a complete biking outfit. It consists of a black cropped vest with fitted biking shorts and a cute little cap that brings the outfit together.

I have to find this in my size. There is no way I'm leaving this store without this outfit!

I'm like a fashion maniac, pulling clothes around the racks while trying to find a size one. Don't let me have to look to see what size the mannequin is wearing because they will surely have to disrobe her if it's the size that I'm needing. BINGO! I found both pieces in black and in my size. Dee is walking in my direction to see what I have found. She takes the outfit out of my hands, holds both pieces up and starts to laugh. *I must have missed something because I don't see anything that's funny.*

"Girl, look at these tiny clothes! What size are these? You have to be a stick to fit into this!"

I snatched my outfit back. Dee makes me sick when she makes skinny jokes about me.

I'm not going to pay her any mind. Besides, I'm used to it. I head to the dressing room, and she's right behind me with a pair of shorts and a tank top to try on. I come out to look in the giant mirror outside of the dressing room. *I am gunning! This outfit is hugging my small curves in all the right places! I'm very satisfied with this look!* Dee gives me a thumbs up without high siding, so I know this is a great choice. We make our purchase, and we're off to the next store.

"I need to find some kind of shoes that will go with this outfit."

Dee suggests I buy a pair of "white girl" tennis shoes (KEDS). I do believe they will go well with it. Now that the shoe shopping is done, we both are a little hungry so we're going to check out the food court.

The smell of pepperoni is leading us to the pizza place. We have one gigantic slice on a plate and a drink. This area is more crowded than we thought. It's challenging to find a vacant and clean table. While we are walking and scanning the area my eyes become fixated on the wrong someone. I grab my chest and gasp for air, huh! Dee turns and looks at me, "What's wrong with you? You can't be choking 'cause you ain't ate nothing!"

I'm trying to hurry up and locate a table so I can distract her. Finally, an empty, clean table!

As soon as we sit down, I make a suggestion for us to hurry up and eat so we can make it to Express, before we run out of time. Dee tells me that we have a lot of time to waste because her dad is getting a new set of tires, an oil change, and an AC service.

I drop my head in disappointment. Dee looks at me and asks, "Why are you rushing?"

Dang girl, I'm trying to save you!

I slowly look over across the way to see if the coast is clear and realize that IT has moved closer to our location. *Oh, please don't let this girl lose her mind up in here!*

"You sure are acting strange, Tan. Why are you acting like that?"

The corny mall music is playing, but it's not loud enough to drown out an obnoxious loud laugh.

Uh-oh! The cat is out of the bag now! Dee lowers her drink from her mouth and turns her head quickly towards the direction the laughter is coming from! Her whole expression changes. I swear I can see tiny sweat beads appearing on her forehead and nose. Suddenly, Dee pushes up from her chair while using the table for support and displays a look on her face that could possibly kill. I jump instantly to my feet and grab Dee's arm. "Calm down, Dee! Please don't make a scene."

"Let go of my arm! I guess you think it's ok for this fool to be playing me!"

"I didn't say that. I just need you to calm down before you go over there."

If David has any kind of sense, he will run!

Dee is about to get David's attention. His back is turned to her while his arm is draped across some chick's shoulders while he is leaning in whispering sweet nothings in her ear. The two of them are also accompanied by two other couples, so that's an indication that this little rendezvous was planned. Dee tips up behind him. "Ahem!" She says while clearing her throat as she pokes him hard on his back. He turns around to see who it is, and he snatches his arm so quickly from around that chick's neck and stands in attention like he is waiting on his orders!

Now that was very entertaining!

"David! Introduce me to your new girlfriend!"

"WWWWhatcha talkin' bout?"

"Who is this chick, David?" Dee says as she points her finger directly to that girl's face. The girl rolls her eyes like Dee isn't referring to her.

David is easing away from the problem and trying his best not to make matters worse. He's begging Dee to walk away with him so they can talk alone in private.

Dang, I wanted to hear how he was going to wiggle his way out of that mess!

I'm back at the table, waiting patiently to see what the outcome will be. David's crew are still standing in the same spot, looking like they are in shock.

I'm done eating, so I'm trying to figure out if I should just sit and wait for Dee or use my time wisely and continue my shopping. Express, here I come!

The music in Express is pretty hyped, and the clothes are to die for! A lime green, off-shoulder top catches my eye, along with a pair of Used Jeans with holes and patches all over them. I have to have them both!

I slip into the dressing room, and my outfit is meant for me. I check out and head to my next store, Margos. There is a large red and white sale sign in the window. I can't wait to see what I can find. Oh my, this sale is too good to be true. It's a buy-one-get-one half-off sale. I can totally work with that. I'm buying two tops and two pairs of ear-rings. The thought of saving brings a smile to my face. As I'm leaving the store, I spot Dee and David sitting on a bench talking, and she looks calmer now. I slow my pace to see if I can make out what they are saying, but I can't because all these background noises are interfering with my hearing. I can't wait to get the 411 when she's done. My money is running low, so I need to figure out what to do now. It's no fun shopping by myself. I take a few slow steps and stop right across from the now love birds, and Dee signals for me to come over. *Ok, don't seem too anxious to get over there.* I pretended to be struggling with my bags so I wouldn't appear to be too eager.

They both look relieved, so I guess everything is ok. Dee motioned for me to sit down next to her. As I got closer to her, I could tell that my friend had been crying, and his eyes were watery, too. *I hope he's not playing my friend because she really likes him.*

Six Flags, here we come! *Who is this fly girl looking back at me in the full-length mirror? Oh yeah, it's me!* I laugh to myself and take one last 360-degree spin to give myself final approval. I can't wait for Tyler to lay eyes on me! While I'm preoccupied with myself, I notice an extra person sharing my spotlight in the mirror.

"Hey Dee, I didn't hear you come in."

"Maybe because you were so caught up with looking at yourself that you were totally distracted."

"So, what brings you here, Miss. Franklin?"

"Nothing, really. I know you are about to go on your weekly date and."

"And what?"

"And I wanted to talk about what happened at the mall the other day."

"Ok, I'm listening."

Dee began to tell me that she knows I think she's stupid for believing David when he said nothing was going on between him and the girl we saw him with. I had to interrupt her and ask if she believed her eyes or his words. She kinda gets defensive by saying everything isn't always what it seems. I had to agree with her, but then I said to her we also have choices, whether we're going to believe the truth or the lie. She stares into spaces for a minute. I guess she is replaying the last statement I made. I have to admit, that was an excellent point I just made.

"That's deep, Tan. You have definitely given me something to think about.

My friend is in love, and she really knows deep down that David is a lying snake, but for some reason, she can't resist.

You can't tell me NOTHING! I am looking too good! And how do I know? Because Tyler said so. As soon as we get to Six Flags and we're walking to the entrance, Tyler can't help but walk behind me placing both hands around my waist. He has expressed several times how much he loves my outfit and how good I look. I guess that's why he can't keep his hands off of me. We are holding hands as we enter through the main gate. Tyler spots a bench for us to sit and wait for Ant and his girlfriend. While we are waiting on them, we engage in a conversation about the mall incident. As I'm talking, I'm trying to read his face. Does he think David is no good, or does he think he's innocent? He finally makes a comment. I don't know how to feel about it. He said, "Well, they do live on opposite sides of town, and they attend different schools." He also adds, "They don't see each other often, right?" His statement just kinda killed my whole mood, and he can tell. Tyler stands up and bends down, eye level with me, and he says with a lot of confidence, "I would never do you like that." Those magic words were all I needed to get me back on track to enjoying our date. Ant and his date are walking through the gate just in time before things get awkward with us.

Tyler and Ant are carrying on with their own conversation, acting as if the girls are invisible.

"Ah, excuse us," I say to them both

"Oh, I'm sorry. Let me introduce y'all to my girl," Ant says while putting his arm around her.

We speak and now it's time to ride, eat, play games, and have fun! I'm excited and ready to ride the roller coasters! "Come on, y'all, let's go to the SHOCK WAVE!" Then I noticed all but one of us were excited about my idea. Each individual smile that was displayed on our faces suddenly dissipated. That girl has the nerve to tell us that she doesn't ride roller coasters and really is not fond of anything but eating funnel cake, people-watching, and walking around.

Why is she here? I know Ant could have found someone who is the total opposite of her! She just put a damper on this event. I be dog if I let her ruin my date!

Tyler and I both look at Ant like, what are you going to do with her? Because we plan to have fun, and her type of fun ain't our type of fun. Ant picked up on the disappointed vibe we were giving and told us that they didn't want to ruin our fun and that we should just go on and meet up later.

He doesn't have to tell us twice. Tyler quickly says that we will meet up at 7:00 to eat at Gold Miners for chili cheese dogs and fries.

The lines are so long! I know we have been waiting over an hour. When it's finally our time to get on the Shock Wave, we head for the last car so we can fly up on every dip.

After we rode our third ride, Tyler noticed that it was almost 7:00, so he suggested we start our way to meet up with Ant and his unpleasant date at the designated spot we chose. On the way we stop to get inside a photo booth to take a few goofy pictures. In the first pose, we do a normal smile. Second pose he surprises me and kisses me on my cheek. In the third pose, he puts two fingers up, making bunny ears above my head. We are laughing uncontrollably and almost fall out of the booth. Ant and his date are already at the spot, looking like they are ready to go. Th*ey will not rain on the parade that we have going. We have to find a way to get rid of them!*

As we are eating, Tyler and I are laughing, talking, and acting goofy. They are looking at us like we are crazy. *This is going to be painful and boring if Tyler and I have to stick around with these two!*

Tyler looks over at me as if he's wondering how we're going to get rid of them. I give him a nod to let him know that we are definitely on the same page. To our surprise, Ant stands up and gathers their trash and tells us that they have decided to leave. *Oh, goody!!!! Now, we don't have to figure out how to dump them!*

Fake disappointment appears on both of our faces, and somehow, I bet Ant can tell because he knows us so well.

Now that they are gone, we will continue to have fun for the rest of the evening. What a great way to end the summer!

First Semester

Senior Year

Where did my summer go? It's all a blur because now I find myself back in school, and it's my senior year. Now that is exciting! I'm loving my new schedule. I'm only in school for four classes, and once I find a job through my work-study class, I'll work the rest of the day.

My first-period class is English. I am blessed to have Ms. James for senior English this year, and I know she is ready to load her grade book with zeros and call us up one by one to average our grades on the board. You were either going to be proud or embarrassed after that. I'm glad I haven't experienced that type of disappointment because I'm usually the one with her gradebook, recording all of the zeros for her. Every day, Ms. James has a motto on the board, and you better copy it down in your notebook because one day, when you least expect it, she will conduct a notebook check. Today's motto is: Set some goals, then demolish them. The class discussion is going well today. Ms. James is really giving us something to think about. She says to wake up with a purpose every morning and plan to be your best. That's something that I personally will strive to be more conscientious of doing.

We are all moving about our way to our second-period classes. "Barbie!" Someone is yelling out obnoxiously several times down the hallway. I have to laugh to myself. That has to be Tyler. He finally catches up with me, puts his hand on my shoulder and walks me to my journalism class. He's in a playful mood this morning. Every few steps we take, he kisses me on the cheek. I'm blushing because several people are looking at us.

"Aren't you going to be late getting to your class?"

Tyler laughs and says, "The party doesn't start till I walk in!"

As soon as we reach my destination, Tyler gives me one last wet kiss on my cheek and takes off running and laughing loudly down the hallway. I slide my hand inside my book bag in search of a napkin to wipe my cheek.

Ms. Terry is standing at her door to greet us as we walk in. She has a great big smile on her face. As I'm walking through the door, Ms. Terry says, "Y'all are just too cute!" I smile and take my seat in the back of the room. I only sit back here so I can concentrate on my next big story. There is a rumor that the group Cameo is supposed to be coming to our school. How cool

would that be if I got the opportunity to interview them? As soon as that thought enters my brain, Ms. Terry calls for me and another student to come to her desk. I'm curious about what it is that she wants with the two of us. She confirms that the rumors about Cameo are true. They will be here in two weeks. My eyes are getting large as I wait to hear the task she has for the two of us. Out of nowhere, Mr. Terry says with excitement, "Did you hear me, Tan? I said I would like for the two of you to interview Cameo together!

How in the world did I miss that? I guess I couldn't hear from listening too hard.

It was hard for me to maintain my composure, so it was contagious because the two of us started to scream, jumping up and down while clapping! This is good news! I can't wait to share it!

Moving right along to the third period, home economics. This semester is for cooking, and the second semester is for sewing. We have to take a ton of notes just to prepare to cook French toast. You have to be kidding me. I can fix this in my sleep! Our teacher, Mrs. Marrs, is very serious about us taking notes. She has the transparency sheet on the overhead projector, writing every detail there is about French toast. I will be glad when we make this little simple mess so we can move on to something more challenging. The bell is ringing, and that's the signal to get out of here and get to fourth-period class.

Ms. Pye is sitting in her office that's located in the back of the classroom. A few minutes after the bell, she's in front of the class. She looks as though she has some good news to share.

"Tan, Tyler, and Anthony, Montgomery Wards Distribution Center would like to hire the three of you!" She went on to tell us that they were impressed with the interviews we had last week. I'm speechless! The three of us are astonished by her news. Ms. Pye shared with us that next week, she is going to meet us there so we can get our IDs and work schedules. Tyler and Ant will be working in the warehouse, and I will be working in the office, dispatching and scheduling deliveries. My school day has ended on a good note. This is going to be a great year, after all!

Friday's Pep rally is going to be LIVE! The band is going to play *Bad*, by Micheal Jackson, and the cheerleaders are going to perform. We are wearing my favorite uniform today, which is The white cheer shirt with the blue rim, white vest, and blue and white striped socks. We all made a ponytail with a blue bow. I had a rough start this morning, rushing to get out of the house. *Something seems to be a little off this morning, and I can't quite figure it out. Oh well, perhaps it's nothing.*

When I open the door to the auditorium, most of the cheerleaders are already in their places, ready to go over our dance routine. I'm rushing to put my things down, and I notice, out of the corner of my eye, that Ms. James is giving me a look. *I'm not going to make eye contact with her. I'm just going to hurry up and take my place on the stage.*

"I'm so glad somebody felt like gracing us with her presence," Ms. James says as she walks over to the cassette player and pushes play.

"Wow! I'm impressed!" Ms. James says with a smile on her face. We must have really done great for her to smile like that.

The bell rings, so that means it's almost show time. The band is coming in now to set up. We don't have time to practice the pyramid, and that is what a few of us are worried about messing up. Ms. James tells us that we will do fine so we rush to the restroom to do our final touches on our make-up and hair. We hear the band tuning up, and that is our cue to form two lines at the entrance of the auditorium, making an arch with our pom pom so the football boys can run through. The crowd is up on their feet and ready to have a good time! The football team is all standing in the front row, and now the band is playing the FIGHT song, and we are all on stage doing the routine, and the crowd is doing it with us. Currently the flag girls are getting on stage to do their routine to the school song. Shayla is in the very front, and I'm yelling out, "Go, Shayla!"

She's cheesing super hard! The flag girls are exiting the stage, and the drill team is getting into formation. The band starts to play an old school song, On Broadway, by George Benson, and they begin their high kicks and their ripple turns, which I think is pretty cool. As they wrap up their routine, we are nervously waiting on the steps on the side of the stage. I hope we get through this smoothly. *One, two, three, four, five, six, seven, eight, nine, ten.* I continue to repeat it over and over again until this very moment because it's time!

The first beat dropped, and we are in motion. So far, we are on it! We are all smiles and rocking this routine! Here's the part we are all dreading. The ending, after the dance, we go straight into the pyramid. *OK, breathe, it's going well.* Now, the final piece. Two handstands on each end. I'm responsible for the one on the right side. As soon as I get airborne, one of the cheerleaders grabs my feet.at this moment, my skirt is over my head. I'm hearing lots of ooooooos, and I'm trying to make out what is happening, but I am having trouble figuring it out mainly because I'm upside down. I can see people are pointing, and I think they are pointing at me and laughing.

"Tandra! Tandra! GET YOURSELF OUT OF THE AIR THIS INSTANT!" Ms. James yells as she is clapping her hands at me. When my feet were released, I came down with confusion all over my face. Ms. James is beckoning for me, and I'm making my way to her. She looks frantic. *What in the world could I have done wrong?* She's not saying anything to me, just escorting me out of there into her classroom without one mumbling word. She takes the key from around her neck and unlocks the door. She reaches for the lights, turns them on, and tells me to sit down. *I'm still in the dark.* I'm replaying every moment while being on the stage, and I can't come up with anything! She takes her seat at her desk and she looks at me and shakes her head at the same time. *What did I do that was so disappointing to her?*

"Tandra, I have one question: Did you get your uniform together last night, or did you wake up late rushing and just throw on your uniform and come to school?"

Why is she asking me this? I can't lie to her. I have to tell her the truth.

"I was rushing this morning."

"Yes, ma'am, you were! You were in such a rush that you forgot to put on your cheer bloomers!"

That's why I was feeling like I was forgetting something. I have exposed my polka-dot underwear! I could just faint right now from the embarrassment. How am I going to be able to face anyone?

I begin to see the softer side of her. She is showing compassion. She walks over to her closet and hands me a pair of bloomers. "Tandra, I can't imagine how you must feel right now. If you don't think you are ready to face anyone, you can call someone to come and get you or you can stay in here for the rest of the day, and I will dare anyone to mention that incident in here. It's up to you."

A million things are running through my brain right now. I can't make a decision right now.

"Whatever you decide, you better decide in the next ten minutes because everyone will be going to class."

"Well, Ms. James, I think I need to go ahead and face them now because if I leave today, whenever I return, they will be waiting to laugh and make fun of me.

"It's definitely your choice, but if you need me to help shut them up, don't hesitate to let me know."

I smile, but I know she's not playing at all. I go quickly to the restroom and slip on the bloomers. I take a few deep breaths and return to the classroom.

As soon as I walk in, I see Deon, Janis, and Shayla.

What am I walking in on? Ms. James walks over to me and puts her arm around me. "You really have some good friends. After they had a good laugh, they wanted to come check on you."

She knew she didn't have to say that. "So, the best thing you can do is laugh with them, and before you know it, they will get tired and move on."

That's the best advice. I give her a hug and say, "Thank you, Ms. James."

The four of us left the room and went to the locker to talk.

"You know, Tyler is the one who told us to go find you," Deon says, with imaginary hearts flowing over the top of her head.

Ahhh man! I don't want to face Tyler! I know he will have a good laugh at my expense. I'm just ready for this whole thing to be over with!

My friends are priceless! Although Tyler, Ant and I get out of school at lunchtime, we decided to stay at school through lunch today and then head to Montgomery Wards Distribution Center for our orientation. School lunch is loud as usual and our crew are all at our VIP table. There are flyers posted everywhere about the upcoming talent show to raise money for the seniors.

"Hey, are Y'all girls going to be on the talent show?" Ant asks

I quickly ask, "What are we supposed to do?"

Ant and Tyler both answer at the same time, "Vanity 6!"

Oh, NO, They Didn't Bring Up That Old MESS!

I can't get a word in for Janis and Shayla wanting to know the details. Tyler makes it his duty to break it all down for them without leaving out anything! He shared that it was our eighth-grade talent show. He's so descriptive about everything from the little outfits we wore with the black fishnet stockings, black high-heeled shoes, and, to top it off, a garter belt. Tyler is getting really excited and admits that he had never seen a garter belt in his life before then, and of course Ant had to chime in with his confession also.

Shayla and Janis are wondering why they are just now hearing about this, and Deon has to seal the deal with her version of the story.

What is this? Why do I have to be everybody's entertainment?

I say, "Can't we just move on, Y'all? That's old news."

All of them reply, "NO!"

I'm lying at the foot of my bed, scanning the room. My side of the room is filled with posters and pictures that I cut out of Right-On Magazine and Jive. Of course, New Edition is at the head of my bed, and Micheal Jackson and Prince are usually the first two I see when I wake up because they are on my side wall. The center wall occupies my newborn pictures and yearly school pictures. I look over at Kerry's side of the room, and it is empty. There once lived a large poster of Prince with some little black drawers on while standing under running water in the shower. That all came to an end when Daddy walked by our room one day and ordered Kerry to take that SHIT off his wall! She didn't even try to put up a fight because she knew that battle was already lost. I have to give her credit. She tried it! Now, Prince lives inside our closet. Daddy will never think to look in there.

JJ comes in and interrupts my peace, "Dee and Tracey said come outside."

"Ok, tell them I'll be out in a few."

I drag myself off my bed to see what they want. By the time I make it outside, they are all inside Dee's house. I can hear them from outside of her bedroom window, laughing and talking loudly.

I'm standing on the pouch ringing the doorbell, and nobody is coming to the door. I just walk straight in, and as soon as I open the bedroom door, the noise ceases.

"All of y'all are looking guilty!"

Every heifer in the room burst out laughing!

From my experience, I know whenever you walk into a room, and people are laughing and all of a sudden, they stop. They are either talking about you or something very WILD!

Since the room is filled with girls of various ages, from sixteen to twenty, the older girls who live on the street are friends with Dee's older sister. They are here to give relationship advice. My big sister is not here. She's at home reading one of the many books that she just purchased.

One of the older girls decides to survey the room. "Hey, raise your hand if you are still a virgin." Something in me made my hand fly up in the air with pride. I slowly turn my head to the left and then to the right to find that I am the only proud member of this club. So now everybody is looking at me like I'm some kind of endangered species. _Why_ *did I have to raise my hand? Now, I have to sit here and listen to all this unwanted advice.*

As time goes on, I'm sitting here listening to everybody reminiscing about their first times. Some of the stories were horrible, and some were pretty comical. After a whole lot of laughs, the older girl who posed the question starts to hand out little wrappers.

Is she giving us some kind of candy? I hope it's chocolate.

"Tan, do you know what this is?"

Silence fell upon the room.

At this moment, I am so glad I didn't embarrass myself seconds earlier by saying it was candy.

All eyes are on me now. "Why are y'all trying to insult my intelligence?"

They all look at me with smirks on their faces. I know they could tell that at first, I didn't have a clue, but I caught on pretty quickly though.

Once I get home, I am so paranoid. I go straight to my room with this little wrapper thing in my front pocket. As soon as I enter my room, I start to scan it, searching for the perfect spot to hide this thing. Got it! I will put it behind my newborn baby picture. *How ironic is that!*

I relocate to the kitchen to pour myself a glass of grape Kool-Aid, and Mom walks in as I sit at the bar, swinging my legs back and forth.

"What are you up to Tan? You look like the cat that swallowed the canary!"

"Huh?" *Is it that obvious that I have something illegal hiding in my room?*

I know it's not really illegal, but in this household and at my age, it is!

"If you can HUH, then you can HEAR!" Mom says.

"I'm just having a glass of Kool-Aid, that's all."

"Well, your mind seems to be somewhere else."

JJ enters the kitchen and opens the refrigerator.

"Boy, if you don't get your butt out of my fridge, and you know good and well that you didn't wash your hand after being outside playing!"

JJ quickly came to his senses and, while closing it, went to the bathroom to wash his hands.

Hopefully, she forgets all about the conversation she was trying to have.

Word up! Cameo is here today, and yours truly is getting the chance to interview them. I picked out the perfect outfit that gives off professional vibes. The only thing I'm missing are glasses so that I can look extra intelligent. I have my list of questions and my tape recorder so I don't miss a word. This is an honor. I not only get to meet them; I also get to ask them all kinds of questions. Of course, I won't ask the personal ones.

My classmate and I walk into the conference room, and we're immediately star struck. The lead singer, Larry Blackmon, stands up to greet us and introduces us to the rest of the group.

We take our seats, and the interviewing begins. They are fascinating. They told us that the reason for their visit was to give us a pep talk to follow our dreams and to stay in school. We found out that the group was formed in 1974, and they originated in New York. After many questions and short story telling, our principal came in to let the group know that all the students were in the auditorium and waiting to see them. The interview session ends with hugs and thank you. Then, my classmate and I sat in the front row so we wouldn't miss anything. I know Ms. Terry is going to be so proud of us.

The three of us love working at the warehouse. Tyler and Ant always say I have it made working in the office while they are doing all the heavy labor loading furniture, refrigerators, and washers and dryers. Every chance Tyler gets, he comes by the office window and sticks his head in, smiling and waving. I can't lie. Just that small gesture makes my day.

It's unbelievable how fast this semester is going by; we have already had homecoming, and if I must say so myself, I had the best and the coolest mum. Tyler made sure it stood out. It consisted of a large heart shape full of white flowers that had a chain hooked to a small heart with white flowers. Both hearts had clear lights and streamers with tons of candy, charms, and both of our names in silver. My parents allowed me to attend the dance after the game with Tyler, and we had the time of our lives, but I couldn't stop watching the clock so that I could make curfew.

This was our first Christmas together, and it was so special. I bought Tyler a nice sweater and a cassette tape case. He loved his gift. He totally surprised me with a pair of light blue Guess overalls. That was a great gift. My parents thought it was too expensive, and I was hoping that they wouldn't make a big deal out of it, but they got over it. The best part of the gift was the Christmas card. He signed it with Tan. I love you so much! No one in the world. Love, Tyler.

That made my heart melt. *I know deep down that our love will last forever.*

Chapter 14

Tan

Relationship

My parents make being in a relationship look effortless. This is my first, and I'm inexperienced and new to the game. I have always heard my parents say that the key to a happy relationship is keeping everyone else out of it. I guess they may be on to something because I view what they have as the ideal marriage. They are not only best friends, but they are both family-oriented and love to entertain. They are basically the glue that holds our family together.

Being brand new to relationships has its challenges. You have seen your parents all of your life, so that's really all you have to go on. That's the standard you use for your own relationship. It's like it's already been proven because you have seen it work.

Tyler and I definitely have the friendship part down. We don't go a day without talking on the phone or seeing each other. I love what we have, and so does everyone else. Our friends have been rooting for us for years to get together, and at the time, we couldn't see anything but the special friendship that we had had for years. As we grew up the love, we have has evolved into something so powerful that it's overwhelming sometimes. The beauty of it is that we match well. We are both inexperienced and pretty much just trying to find our way.

If only people would stay out of our business. Stop trying to fix something that's not broken. Tyler and I are OK with going on our dates every Friday, flipping in the front yard, and spending long hours on the phone that's been working for us. But there is this thing referred to as the next level, which we're both not ready for, but peer pressure is getting the best of both of us.

This subject really hasn't come up. It's like we are enjoying each other's company without the complications of that. Sometimes, I wonder if it's going to be an issue for us soon because I'm sure he's tired of hearing about IT and wants to be about IT! I'm hoping that is not the case. But we will soon see.

The Call

It's after ten o'clock on a Friday night, and Tyler and I are on the phone as usual. Earlier today, we went to an arcade and ate pizza. We are both super competitive and decided to make it interesting by betting something. Tyler suggested that if I lose, I had to yell out that I am in love with him. So, I suggested that he had to do the same.

The old games are our favorite, so we decided to start with Pac-Man. The rule was you had to win two out of three games. Before we got started, Tyler began to pop his knuckles, neck, and then his back. He acted like he was getting ready to run a marathon.

It was just my luck to lose first! So, being a lady of my word, I yelled out, "I am so in love with Tyler!" Being the arrogant person that he is. He quickly brought to my attention that I must really be in love with him because I said, "SOOOOOOOO in love!" By that time, we seemed to be getting the attention of other people in the arcade. The second game was close, but I won! Tyler had to amuse me by saying, "I'm SOOOOOOOO in love with Tan!" By that time, we had a large crowd around us. The girls were cheering for me, and the guys were rooting for him. This was the most excitement I've had in a long time, and finally a winner was declared. It was Tyler with his big head self, just gloating and giving himself the title of "The King!" The guys went wild as they celebrated Tyler's win. The girls were saying to me, "That's ok, girl, you'll get him next time."

After we played more games, shared a pizza, and had drinks, we headed home. On the way home, he continued to tease me about being so in love with him. While blushing, I playfully hit him on his arm as we drove on the freeway. He recalled every moment of our date and said he believed that was the most fun we have had on any of our dates. I had to admit that I really had a great time also.

Tyler took his eyes off the road for a split second to glance at me and ask, "Who is your king?"

I didn't hesitate to answer, "JESUS!" We both killed ourselves laughing.

Wow, it's almost midnight, and we are still going strong on this phone. I have to be careful and not laugh too loud so Mama and Daddy won't hear me and make me get off the phone. Kerry enters our room and gives me a mean look, so I know it's time for me to relocate. I'm grabbing the phone and pulling it as the long cord drags behind me. I take my place in the hallway outside the bedroom. I have the perfect view of the den, so I can see when my parents are on the move. They always stay up late on the weekends, and sometimes, they both end up falling asleep in the den with the TV watching them.

"Tan, are you getting sleepy?"

"No, I'm wide awake over here. Are you?"

"I'm a little tired, but there's something I want to ask you."

"OOOH OOOK, what is it, Tyler?" *Random thoughts are roaming inside my brain. Is it something serious? Why can't it wait until another time? Hmmm, it must be important.*

He's taking his time to say whatever it is, like he's taking precautions to choose his words carefully.

"I'm listening, Tyler. Go ahead and ask me."

"SOOO, I was wondering. If you are bored with us?"

"What do you mean? We are not a boring couple at all. We go out on a date every Friday, we are always talking on the phone and we never run out of things to say, and we are always having fun, flipping in the yard, and laughing at each other's jokes. I don't understand where this is coming from! So, I guess the question should really be for you, Tyler, are you bored with us?"

He's silent, but I can hear lite clicking sounds. "Stop biting your nails, Tyler!"

"Dang girl, how did you know that?"

"I know you too well, so whatever you are about to say, it's got you pretty nervous. So, stop wasting time and answer the question!"

"OK, hold on."

I'm hearing lots of crackling sounds on the other end of the phone. This boy is over there, popping every bone in his body.

"Ok, I'm back."

"Are you done popping every bone in your body?"

Tyler burst out laughing, "I can't do anything without you knowing!"

"That's right! And don't you ever forget it!"

Tyler settles down, clears his throat, and says, "Have you thought about us taking our relationship to the next level?"

A lump appears in my throat, and my first thought is of my Daddy killing me. All of a sudden, I begin to get paranoid, and I stand up and start pacing in the hallway while trying to make sure that my parents are still secure in the den. *Why are we trying to fix something that's not even broken?*

"Tan, are you there?"

It takes me a moment to formulate my thoughts to form a sentence to answer his question.

"Why do we need to take this to the next level? What's wrong with the way things are now?"

"Nothing is wrong. I just thought you wanted more."

"How did I give you any indication of wanting that?"

"I don't know. It's just that everyone acts like we should be at that level."

"So, do you agree with them?"

"Yes and no. It's normal for me to want more. Don't get me wrong, I love what we have, and I wouldn't want to destroy it."

"I'm confused. So why bring it up?"

"Just forget I ever said anything."

"I don't think that's possible."

We both are at a loss for words and the silence on the phone is so loud that I can't hardly process my own thoughts. I'm squinching my eyes to see the clock on the dining room wall. It's 1:45 a.m. A faint sound of snoring is coming through the line. "Tyler!" I whisper, but no answer. He has fallen asleep on me. After a few more tries, I'm having no success trying to wake him, so eventually, the buzzing sound from the phone will. I ease into my bed, pull the covers up, and slowly close my eyes.

Should I be worried about us? Am I getting boring or moving too slowly for him? Guess who is not going to get any sleep now? ME!

Second Semester

1988

February

Valentine's Day is on a Sunday this year, and I find myself in church anticipating the song of invitation and waiting to hear the sweet words of one of the deacons: "Shake hands and be merry!" That's when the church is officially over. I can't wait to see what Tyler has for me. As we are walking out of church it seems everyone has a conversation for my Mama. She's just really smiling and thanking the many sisters for complementing her beautiful red dress and pumps and matching purse. Note to self: I might have to borrow the purse and shoes later.

Daddy is sitting at the bar with Tyler, teasing him about making him look bad because he has lots of things for me for this occasion. I am trying to hurry up, getting dressed in my red sweatshirt with a teddy bear holding a heart on it, red sweatpants, red and white socks, with my red and white Reeboks. I can't believe my eyes. Tyler has five red and five white balloons with a vast red heart-shaped balloon in the middle. He also has a heart-shaped cake and a small black velvet box beside it.

"Hey Tyler, Happy Valentine's!"

He stands and greets me back.

"Is all of this for me?"

"Yes, it is."

"Yeah, Tyler is trying to show me up. Now I have to go back to the store!" Says Daddy while laughing and patting Tyler on the back.

I'm admiring the balloons and cake and I pick up the small box and peek inside.

"Oh, my goodness, Tyler, it's beautiful!" I say as I hold the tennis bracelet in my hand.

"Let me put it on you."

I hand it to him and hold my wrist out, and he connects the clamps.

"Wait, let me get your gift."

I had a large cookie cake made for him with: I Love You So Much, written on it.

A smile came on his face as he read those words.

"Do you like it?"

"Yes, Tan, you did good."

We are staying at the house watching TV and talking to my family.

It's after seven, and Tyler is getting ready to go home. I walk him out to his car. Tyler turns to me with a serious look on his face. Before he can say anything, Cassie and her grandmother are driving down the street. Once they get to us, Cassie barely raises her hand to wave. I guess she is in her feelings because Tyler and I are together. I can understand why. Tyler and I don't bother to address it, and he goes on to say that he is having surgery soon. I immediately go into panic mode.

"Are you ok? Are you sick or something?"

"No, I'm ok."

"Then what is it?"

"I'm having a minor procedure on my neck."

"Your neck?"

He moves closer to me and hugs me tight, trying to comfort me and warm me up at the same time.

"Tan, don't worry, I'm going to be fine." He pulls me closer to him and kisses me on my forehead. We are holding each other tightly and slowly releasing our hold so he can be on his way. He gets into his car, and I'm still standing here feeling numb. His window slowly rolls down, and he says the sweetest words ever, "I love you, bighead!"

I wave to him as he drives off into the sunset.

"Come in and sit down like you have some sense!" Ms. James yells as we enter her classroom. "Today is going to be very interesting because I am going to call you up, one by one,

to average your pitiful grades on the board." Now everybody is looking scared and nervous.

Ms. James sure knows how to mess up a good day. She motions for me to get her grade book and help her out with this chore. The first few people that went up to the board only had zeros to average out. "Ms. James, do you want me to read all the zeros?" I ask *because I feel like it's unnecessary.* "Yes, ma'am, I need you to say each one of them so they can get a clear picture of their progress thus far."

I have better sense than to voice my opinion, so I just carry on with this critical task. I don't know if Ms. James realizes that she is causing me to have enemies because my peers are referring to me as her pet. The plot thickens. It's Shayla and Ant's turn to average their grades. Every time I say ZERO, they both turn around and give me a dirty look. I mouthed to them both, _"I'm so sorry!"_

When the bell rings, we are all relieved, trying to run over each other to get out of the door. It's time for my next class, and it is the loneliest walk to my next class because Tyler is not here today. I take my seat in the back of my journalism class and I see the newspapers are ready for distribution. I'm always excited to see my name in print. We are counting the newspapers to pass out to each class. As we complete a stack, someone comes by, snatches them up, and delivers them to a classroom. Ms. Terry is making her point about why timelines are so important to meet because no one enjoys reading old news.

After homemaking and ICT, my school day is over, and it's time for me to head to work.

This week has been kinda bunk because Tyler has been out because he had surgery on his neck. He explained to me that the surgery was imperative due to him popping his neck all the time. Ant and I are riding to work together, and it's just not the same. One of the musketeers is missing. I miss him covering my eyes and asking guess who?

And yelling at Barbie in the hallway and walking me to class. I can't wait to get to work to call and check on him.

As soon as I get to my desk, there's a note that says everyone is expected to work during spring break. I don't know if I agree with that because my family is planning a trip. I will just have to talk it over with my parents to see what they have to say about this. I take my coat off, hang it on the back of my chair, and place my purse in the bottom drawer of my desk. I sit down and pick up the phone to call Tyler.

"Hello," Tyler's Mom says on the other end of the phone.

"Hello, how are you?"

"I'm doing fine, Miss. Tan and you?"

"Oh, I'm ok. I 'm calling to check on the sick and shut-in. How's he doing? Is his neck better now?"

After laughing about my little humorous statement, she collects herself enough to get clarification. "What about his neck?"

I am just asking, "Did his neck surgery go well?"

"Girrrrrrrrl, is that what he told you?" She asks through all of her laughter.

"Yes, ma'am, he did."

"Well, I guess he didn't want to tell you about the special procedure he had."

"Huh?"

"You see, Tyler was supposed to have this thing done when he was first born, but I really didn't think it was a big deal, so I passed on getting it done. Now that he is a young man, he feels like it's necessary."

I'm speechless. Trying to put two and two together.

"Tan, did you hear me? Do you understand what I'm saying?"

Seconds are passing, and it finally hits me! "OH!!!! OH!!! OK!!! I GOT IT NOW!" Some of my co-workers turned around and looked at me strangely, I guess because I said that so loudly. I hang up the phone, and one of the older ladies comes over to my desk and says, "Baby, what's got you saying OH like that? Because back in my day, we said it for a really good reason!" She winks her eye at me and sashays her way back to her desk. EWWWW! I just got a visual of what she was saying. Occasionally I look up, anticipating to see Tyler stick his head in the window to the office, but that's not possible because he's not here. Dang, I miss him!

March

Spring Break is here! Guess who isn't working anymore? That would be me. I talked with my parents about what my supervisor said about everyone having to work during spring break. My Daddy said you are still a child living under my roof that I provide everything for. You are blessed not to have to work, so with that being said, give them your notice and enjoy being a kid because you have the rest of your life to be an adult. It was at that very moment that I realized how blessed I am. So many people my age work because they have to help out at home. I work because I want extra things like designer clothes. My Daddy doesn't believe in buying designer labels. He's always so quick to point out that my polo shirt cost more than his wardrobe.

It's Friday, and it's date night! Tyler and I have missed hanging out for the last two weeks. We've been hanging out at school and talking a lot on the phone. He mentioned that he wants to spend some time alone to talk. But first, we are going to the movies to see *Police Academy*.

"Tyler's here!" I yell as I put on my shoes to get ready to dash out the door.

"Hold up!" Daddy says as he gets up and stands in front of his recliner. "Where did you say y'all were going?

"We are going to the movies."

Tyler is at the door. I wave for him to come in. He's looking scared, wondering what's going on.

"Hi, how are you doing, Mr. Breakfield?"

"I'm fine, and you?"

"I'm ok. So, where are you planning on taking Tan this evening?"

"To the movies."

"And what time will you have her back?"

"By Ten o'clock."

"Ok, that's fine, but Y'all will have to take JJ with Y'all."

Tyler and I look at each other in shock, as if Daddy knew our plans.

There goes our romantic date.

"Is that going to be a problem?" Daddy says.

"No," we both say at the same time.

Tyler and I are getting into his car, and JJ comes running out of the house smiling because he knows we do not want him around.

The popcorn is extra delicious with the right amount of butter and salt. The Coke is extra chilled, and it is a must to have it with the popcorn. I'm sitting in the middle holding the popcorn bucket, and JJ is reaching in every few seconds. Although the movie is quite funny, and I am on a date with my boyfriend, I can't help but wonder why Daddy thought it was a good idea for JJ to tag along. If I know Daddy, he's using JJ as birth control.

Tyler leans over and asks me how is it that your Daddy knew our plans, or is he just physic?

I respond, saying, "It's truly a mystery. You know he always says that he is two steps ahead."

Sometimes, I really believe he is.

Now that the movie is over, JJ gets a refill of popcorn, and we walk to the car. As soon as we are leaving the parking lot JJ asks Tyler if he would stop at McDonalds. I'm trying to explain to JJ that it's already 9:45, and Tyler told Daddy that we will be back by 10:00. Oh, he's mad now. He's in the back seat mumbling something, and all of a sudden, he dumps the whole bucket of popcorn in the back seat. I look over at Tyler, and I can tell he is pissed off. JJ is being a brat. I want to knock him out! As soon as we pull into my driveway, I open my door and raise the seat so he can get out. I tell him he is going to clean up the mess that he made.

Tyler says, "Let him go on, I'll clean it up."

I apologize to him because I'm feeling bad about what happened.

Tyler remains calm while we both are picking up JJ's mess. He scoops up the last of the popcorn from the floor of his backseat, places it in the bag, turns towards me and pulls me close to him as we lean against his car.

"What are you doing?" I ask while loving every second of this. "You know, my Daddy, maybe watching from the living room window!"

"Hell, he should let this one slide since his badass son trashed my car!"

We both are laughing but it suddenly stops as we kiss like we are the only two people here on this earth. He slowly loosens his embrace, and we stare into each other's eyes, which leaves us no doubt in knowing we are definitely meant to be.

I walk into the house, and everything is as normal as can be. *I guess Daddy wasn't looking out that window after all.*

The Incident

Can somebody tell me what the HELL has happened? It's like I'm waking up from a bad dream, and I can't think clearly. All I can remember is this nightmare started when Janis was telling me what she thought but wasn't really sure if her information was correct.

To be honest, I think things got a little questionable after I returned from my spring break family vacation, which was only three days. We left on a Monday and returned on Wednesday evening. So, Friday's date didn't happen because Tyler wanted to hang out with some friends that I don't know and he's been hanging out in their neighborhood since I went out of town. I'm not the smartest person in the world, but I'm so for sure that something is very fishy about this situation.

I need clarification, and the only person that can help me with it is Janis. I'm picking up the phone several times just to hang it up. I'm not sure if I really want to know the truth.

Something Just Ain't Right, by Keith Sweat, is the song that keeps popping into my head. I'm having trouble eating and sleeping mainly because the connection I have with Tyler is slowly dissipating, and I'm holding on for dear life.

That's it. I'm calling her. I need to know what's going on!

Janis picks up the phone on the third ring.

"Hey girl, what are you doing?

"Girl, I'm just watching my little brother and sister. Why? What's up?"

I'm trying to see if I should just blurt it out or just ease into it.

"What do you know about Tyler hanging out over there in your hood?"

"What do you mean?"

"Come on, Janis, please don't insult my intelligence."

"I can only tell you what I've heard. I haven't seen anything."

"Ok, I'll keep that in mind."

"Well, it all started about two weeks ago when this new family moved down the street. They have two kids, a daughter our age and a younger son. All of the guys have lost their minds going out of their way trying to impress her."

"So, what does any of this have to do with Tyler?"

"Tan, what I'm about to tell you, you have to promise not to tell him that I told you."

I'm just wondering if I hadn't said anything to her, would she have told me on her own?"

"Go ahead, Janis, I'm listening."

She goes on to give me a play-by-play of all the rumors she has heard.

I can hear in her voice how it saddens her to tell me this hurtful news.

She starts by telling me that she actually saw Tyler drive down her street with some guys in his car and they all went over to the new girl's house. Her boyfriend Gerry, who is a close friend of Tyler, shared with her that Tyler's other friends all tried to talk to the girl, but she didn't give them any play. So, they bet Tyler that he couldn't pull her. He's been going over there every day, and I heard he took her out also.

And like a dummy, he entertained it.

I am so DAMN mad at him right now!

How in the HELL DID HE FORGET HE HAD A GIRL-FRIEND? Just wait until I talk to him!

A Taste of his own medicine

I find myself going grocery shopping with my parents, mainly because I'm bored out of my freaking mind! I'm trailing behind Mama, minding my business, and this guy who works here approaches me. He is fine! He's tall, dark, with blue contacts and wearing Saucony sneakers. He has my attention as much as I had his. Floyd is his name, and he doesn't waste any time and immediately asks me out. We are exchanging numbers and plan to talk later when he gets off work.

Guilt is trying to creep inside my head as I get ready for my date. Never would I have thought I would be dating someone other than Tyler. *I'm sure he wasn't thinking about me when his bet was going on. I'm going to enjoy my date and not think of my past.*

The ringing phone distracts my thoughts. I'm sure it's Floyd who probably needs directions to find my house. But to my surprise. It's Tyler. It's bringing me great satisfaction to inform him that I'm getting ready for my date. He is quiet and hurt. I guess I need him to feel that same hurt I felt, but the difference is I'm upfront with it. He doesn't have to hear it from someone else. The conversation went cold, and that's my cue to disconnect.

Floyd comes inside to introduce himself to my parents, and off we go to go to dinner and his cousin's birthday party. I'm having a good time, but my mind won't stop thinking of Tyler.

Dang! I'm mad at myself. I just want this date to end. Floyd can kinda sense that my mood has shifted, and he's asking if I'm ready to leave.

Deon and Tracey couldn't wait for me to return. As soon as I get out of Floyd's truck, we hug, and he's walking me to the door; they both come running towards me, out of breath. I have no clue what's going on with them. Deon blurts out, "Girl, Tyler is upset with you! He was waiting for you to get home from your date. He sat on the curb for hours just waiting!"

"What was he waiting on me for?"

"Somehow, he knew you were on a date with somcone else," Tracey says.

"I told him when he called earlier."

"ARE YOU CRAZY!" They both said at the same time.

"Look, Tyler and I are not together, so I am not concerned with him waiting for me, got it!

They're both looking at me like, ok, we think she means business.

"Good night, ladies," and I went into the house.

I know things shouldn't be this way, but that's the way he made them, so now he has to deal with it!

Graduation Time

Class of 1988

Time sure passes fast when it's your senior year. It's graduation day, and I'm incredibly excited, but I can't help but reflect over the last couple of months. In the past, when I thought about this day, I just knew it was going to be a special day for Tyler and me to share, but I guess it just wasn't in the cards for us.

After I found out about Tyler dating another girl. I was heart-broken then and now. He tried explaining how it was just a silly bet between him and his friends, and he expected me to understand. What I needed him to understand was that he was willing to jeopardize the special bond we had over a bet. I sure hope she was worth it. And to add salt to a wound, he had the audacity to take her to the prom. He mustn't have given her a notice because she didn't bother to get her hair fixed. I am not jealous. Just stating facts. Of course, I was the Belle of the ball, and I had a date too. He is just a friend, but he went out of his way to make sure I enjoyed myself.

I'm in a pretty good mood walking around the house getting on my parent's nerves. Every time I'm around them, I tell them, "I'm about to have my GROWN Papers!" The first few times were funny to them, but now they are totally annoyed with me. As I get dressed, I take a long stare at myself in the mirror. I have mixed emotions, excited, scared, and hopeful. My heart smiles when I think of how proud my parents are of me. I'm going to try my best not to let them down.

"Tyler Norman Black," the announcer reads off his name, and I'm clapping for him as tears fill my eyes. *Let me pull myself together before it's my turn to walk across the stage.* It's showtime! "Tandra

Ann Breakfield!" I have a whole cheering section in the middle, yelling and screaming my name. I glance over at Tyler, and he's cheering for me too. This moment is the beginning of the rest of our lives. We are all in the lobby taking millions of pictures, and it's fantastic to see the many proud parents posing with their graduates. I see Tyler's Mom in the crowd. I walk over to speak and hug her. She's happy to see me and is telling me that she is proud of me. She is joking and teasing me to take her son back by telling me that I'm the only one who likes him. It's always a fun time when I see her. Now it's time to celebrate with my classmates!

Once we are all in the backyard of one of our classmates who's hosting the party, Janis, Shayla, and I walk over to the refreshment table. We all have that same look on our faces, the look of excitement and uncertainty at the same time. It's clear that some of us have a concrete plan, and others are still trying to figure it out. I fell between them both; I knew I wanted to be a journalist/writer, maybe for a newspaper or magazine. Also, I have always wanted to be a nurse, maybe work with children or the emergency room. My thoughts are interrupted when someone yells for all of us to get together to take a group picture. The host, a Mom, is about to snap the picture, and out of nowhere, Tyler runs in and hops right beside me while putting his arm around me and yelling, "Cheese!" Everybody is falling out laughing. He turns to me afterward and says I still love you. Our nosey classmates all have their eyes on us, saying, "AWWWWW, Y'all are so cute!" *Please, y'all, don't make this a Tyler and Tan thing. I just want to enjoy my night!*

After a few dances, I'm feeling tired, and my friends and I are just chilling, waiting for the next jam to make us want to jump up and do it all over again. As I'm resting, I can see Tyler trying to get my attention from the other side of the yard. _What does he want? I don't want to do this here and now!_

He slithers over to me and takes my hand to pull me up from my seat. "Come walk with me," he says. We walk and we stop under the street light. He starts off by saying that I hurt him when I went out with someone else. Also, he misses us, asks for forgiveness, and tells me that he wants me back. I stress to him that I will have issues with trusting him, and he's trying his best to win me over. I also explain to him no matter what I say, he's gonna have to go through my Daddy, and that ain't gone be easy. I remind him that he broke his baby's heart. To my surprise, Tyler agrees to talk to my Daddy. _Good luck!_

Going strong is an understatement. We are planning to take our relationship to the next level. Tyler kept his word and talked to Daddy, and it all worked out. Daddy told him that he appreciated him coming to him as a man, and he respected him for that. After that. and on to a new beginning, Tyler gave me a heart-shaped diamond ring and made a promise that he would always love me no matter what. I feel so close to him, and at this very moment, the love I feel for Tyler is more pro-found than it has ever been.

Here's the plan, *"Operation Next Level,"* this weekend, we are going to the Bobby Brown concert, and afterward, we will go to Tyler's house. His Mom is out of town, so he seems to be pretty confident that it will be ok for us to go there for our life-changing event. *I guess I'm ready for this. It's not like I just met him; he loves me without a doubt, and I know I love him. So why am I second-guessing myself? I guess because I don't want any regrets.* As I sit in the middle of our huge sectional couch, in the den, with my legs crisscrossed and bitten off every fingernail I have, my nerves are getting the best of me. I better pull myself together before my suspicious parents suspect something.

My outfit is lying on my bed, waiting for me to get dressed. I'm moving a little slowly. Don't get me wrong, I'm ready for the concert, but I have something weighing heavily on my mind. *How do I prepare for our private after-party?* Funny thing, when I talked to Tyler earlier, he didn't mention it at all. Hopefully, he has forgotten. Who am I fooling? I know good and well that isn't the case.

Deon comes walking into my room, and I know she's here to inquire about my date and the festivities afterward. She calls herself, giving me unwanted advice on what to do and what not to do as if she is some kinda expert. She doesn't know it, but I have tuned her out. I assure her I will follow her advice, and I hurry her right on her merry way.

I hear loud bassing outside. I know it's Tyler in his brand-new blue Chevy S-10 truck. When he found out that I went out with Floyd and he drove a mini truck, Tyler couldn't allow him to outdo him, so he went and got one, too. He seems to think that I'm into trucks. I strut out of my room wearing a white and black polka dot spandex dress, AKA _"Tramp Dress,"_ with the earrings and heels coordinating. Tyler is standing in the dining room talking to my parents, and of course, Daddy has to ask what time he will have me home. Tyler and I look at each other, trying not to have guilt written all over our faces. I immediately grab my black clutch purse from the table. Tyler remains calm and stated by one. Daddy frowns a bit and says ok, not a minute later.

We are in the truck heading to Janis's house so she and Gerry can follow us to the convention center. We're double-dating. This is the first time I have ever ridden with Tyler, and he doesn't have his music blasting. He looks over at me and says, "Do you think your old man is on to us? He was looking at me like, "You think you're slick!"

"I don't think so. I think it's just your conscience."

He agrees with a worried look on his face.

The concert is so live! That Bobby Brown sure knows how to put on a great show! It's intermission, and we all walk into the lobby to take pictures. They had a large straw chair with a high back, and the background was black with a white limousine. I take my place on Tyler's lap and we take the cutest picture. I swear we are the best-looking couple here. Janis and I walk to the restroom to check our hair to make sure we're still cute. She casually asks if I am going to go through with being intimate with Tyler. *Now, why did she have to bring that up? It had finally left my mind, and she had to mess that up.* I tell her that I'm really nervous, and I ask her to pretend that she has something to give me, so Tyler needs to bring me to her house so I can get it.

She agrees to do it, and I'm feeling a little at ease now. We continue to jam with Booby, and now it's over. We are on our way back to Janis' house.

It's 11:45, and I'm inside Jani's house in her bedroom, pacing back and forth. Janis finally says, "Tan, why don't you tell him that your stomach hurts and you don't feel good."

I'm thinking about it, but it doesn't seem believable. "I don't know what I'm going to do or say, but I better get back out there." Janis walks me back out to his truck. Tyler announces the time: twelve on the dot! I get back in the truck and wave bye to Janis. Shaw Ave, here we come!

"Tan, why are you stalling?"

"I can't lie to you, Tyler. I'm scared and nervous." *Plus, I forgot to get that necessary thing we need from behind my newborn picture.*

As we sit side by side in his dark room with the moon peeking at us from the crack in the curtains, he puts his arms around me and holds me tight. His digital clock on his nightstand is giving us a friendly reminder that we only have forty minutes before my curfew. I can feel his heart about to beat out his chest; he's trying to relax so I could be, too, but he's not doing such an excellent job at it. He reaches over and turns on his clock radio. _Nite and Day,_ by Al B. Sure, is playing. I lay back and closed my eyes to become one with him.

That annoying time seems to be brighter, and it's displaying 12:48. It doesn't take long before we both think of my Daddy, and that is all we need to ruin the mood. We are hurrying to get ourselves back presentable so we can pass inspection at my house. Tyler is not wasting any time getting me to the house. It's 12:57, and we hug, kiss, say our love you, and he walks me to the door. Daddy is right there holding the door. I slide in and go straight to my room.

I'm lying in bed with my arms behind my head, wondering if I feel different. _Did that moment change me? I didn't see the fireworks that many have spoken about, but I did feel a deeper connection with my soulmate._

Chapter 15

Tan

Life Changing Events

I'm all packed to spend a week the second week of July at Journalism camp.

Ms. Terry could have chosen anybody, but she chose me to attend. I'm honored that she believes in me and has given me this fantastic opportunity. This camp is being held at the local university where Kerry attends. Just last week, my parents bought me a brand new 1988 Dodge Charger. It's manual, and I can't drive it. I have to learn quickly. Tyler said he will teach me when I return.

Kerry knows her way around this campus with her eyes closed. She drives us straight to the exact dorm where I will be staying for the week. I sign in and get my name tag, and we take a seat to wait for the room assignments. As we are waiting, this short, beautiful brown skin Janet Jackson-looking girl walks in with her dad, and he's carrying two designer luggage of hers. I get a closer look and realize that she's my longtime friend, Rockie from kindergarten. The last time I saw her was in middle, 8th grade at Davis Junior High. I can't wait to catch up with her. She better remember me.

The director of the program came in to introduce herself and assign rooms to us as soon as she read my name, Tandra Breakfield, then Rockie Homes. What a coincidence! My longtime friend looks over in my direction and we both jump up to run to each other. We hug while jumping up and down. Words cannot express how happy the two of us are to reunite. We have a few minutes to unpack our things and meet everyone in the dining hall for lunch. Meanwhile, we both are so happy to be roomies.

Time did not separate us at all. It's like we were never apart for all of those years. We are mostly catching up instead of eating. We will probably regret it later. It's time to meet in the journalism building for orientation and to receive our writing assignments. I hope I get an assignment that interests me. The speaker is going on and on about the millions of stories she has written, and I'm zoning in and out and mostly thinking about Tyler.

"Tan, it's your turn," Rockie says.

"My turn for what?" Now everybody is laughing because it is evident that my mind is somewhere else.

"She asked you what type of stories you like to write?"

"Oh, I like to write editorials."

"Why?" The speaker asks.

"Because I like to voice my opinions also."

"Good answer, Tan. Girl, you made up for that!" Rockie says while laughing.

The time has come to assign stories, and I am very satisfied with mine,

Teenage Runaways. The first step is to gather sources. So, we are relocating to the call center so each of us has the yellow pages of the phonebook and our own phone line. I am having a lot of success. I called *The Welcome House. It*'s a place that takes in teenage runaways to keep them safe and off the streets. Some of their stories gave me a reality check to help me realize how blessed I am. The next step is to go to the library and find articles that relate to my topic.

The feeling of confidence enters my brain, and it's a great feeling.

After dinner, everyone, including the guys, wants to hang out in our room. They are now referring to it as the spot. We have all the good snacks, cards, and a few board games.

The last person finally found their way out of our room at midnight. Rockie and I are too tired to finish catching up, so we call it a night and fall asleep.

Today, we have a little time to work on our stories because we have guest speakers and questions and answering sessions. So far, the speakers have been very informative because I haven't thought about Tyler once, until now. Over lunch, Rockie and I picked up where we left off yesterday. We remember that our birthdays are just a few days apart next month, and she already has plans. She shares that her family is having a barbeque at her grandmother's house in her honor. She says

I should definitely come. When she says Shaw Ave, my mouth drops open.

"Shut up!" I said.

"What?" She says, looking very confused.

"I have one question. Do you know a guy named Tyler Black?"

She goes on to explain that she grew up with him, and their mothers are good friends. After saying that, she holds her head slightly to the side, looks at me, and asks How do I know him?

Of course, I have to tell her about our long journey of getting together. She's really intrigued and wants to know more. Rockie has a permanent smile on her face, and she is clearly loving this new information that she has learned. She tells me that she can totally see us together, and she's excited for us. That's all I needed to know. I can climb back on my cloud now.

Day 5

Is it Friday already? I can't believe that time has passed so quickly. I have had the time of my life while researching, writing, making new friends, and connecting with an old one. Today is supposed to be filled with a lot of surprises and fun. I can't wait! Breakfast was nice.

We all decided to eat together because we knew after today, we probably wouldn't see each other again. After Lunch, we will meet in the journalism building. Let the fun begin!

Four familiar faces were sitting on the platform in front of the auditorium. They are all news anchors for four different networks. One of them happens to be my absolute favorite,

Clara Tines from channel four. She is the one who inspired me to want to become a journalist, and she's beautiful. Oh, I'm really hyped now! I'm hoping I get a chance to talk to her and ask her a few questions. They each shared their stories about their journeys and life experiences. After hearing them present, I'm ready to begin my own journey. Our own stories are in print, and we have a chance to share them and get their professional opinions. This is very beneficial.

Our day has come to an end. This has been a wonderful experience, and I'm so glad I had the opportunity to participate. As I'm saying my goodbyes and passing out hugs, I thought to myself maybe I will meet up with them again, once we all become journalists. Somehow, I know that Rockie and I will never lose touch again.

1989

Suspicion

All is well, and I'm living my best life. I tried going to the local junior college not far from my house, but it really wasn't for me. So now I'm attending *Drex,* the school for certified nursing assistants, and this is the place where I reunited with another childhood friend, Cheraine whom I took gymnastics. She is married and a mother to a toddler and also one on the way. I'm so happy for my friend, and she seems to be happy too. She loves to show pictures of her baby and all of their family pictures. One day, I'm sure I will do the same thing.

Since Rockie and Janis are attending school in another city, and Shayla is doing her own thing, Cheraine has become my best friend. We are constantly out shopping or hanging out at our parents' house. She's just like me, spoiled and very family-oriented. Everybody thinks we look alike. We both are average height, skinny, with long, natural curly, sometimes straight hair.

It's a Friday, and it's date day! Our date starts at lunchtime because my school is right around the corner from his job. Tyler still works for Montgomery Ward Distribution Center, and he has gotten a promotion to start training to deliver. Today, he is bringing me Taco Bell, a Mexican pizza, a soft taco, and a drink. We are sitting in his truck talking, making plans for our future. He is asking me if I think it's too soon to get engaged. This is taking me by surprise. Why is he thinking about an engagement, and he just made me a promise with a ring?

For the rest of the day, I can't stop thinking about our conversation.

My class is almost over for the day. I'm wondering if I should pick Cheraine's brain about my new dilemma. I really don't know if she's the right person because she's worse than me for being a hopeless romantic. And just as I thought. She was ready to plan the wedding!

Wow! I'm falling for it, too. I'm sitting here daydreaming about my perfect wedding.

Red Lobster has a more serious vibe this time around. Tyler is telling me that his cousin Sean is about to get married. *Oh, now it's making sense. That's why he wants to know how I feel about getting engaged.* I'm just listening, trying to figure things out. He goes on to explain to me how much he loves me and wants to make sure I understand it. I'm shaking my head every time "yes" and verbally saying it, too, but he's still trying to convince me. *This is getting a little annoying! Where in the Hell is this coming from? At this point, I'm picking at my food, and the conversation is dying.* He can tell I'm frustrated and he tries to change the subject.

On the way home, it's still kinda awkward, and he's making small talk. I'm just nodding my head every now and then, so he will think I'm listening. I have checked out because deep down, I just feel that there's something he isn't telling me. He pulls up in the front of the house and turns his truck off. He looks at me and asks, "What's wrong?"

I quietly said, "Nothing."

He's not crazy. He knows that there is something truly bothering me. We both get out of the truck and walk to my porch. We kiss and we hug much longer than usual. This hug feels like it could be the last one.

The "S" Has Hit the Fan!

It's funny how a few months can pass and everything that I've wondered about somehow is getting revealed to me now. There was this feeling that I had deep down in the pit of my stomach that my life was getting ready to make a turn but not in a good direction, and I wasn't even sure why I was feeling that way until now.

When your best friend calls you and tells you to come next door right now! You go!

Whatever it is. It can't be good. Let me brace myself for the worse.

I just walk right in and push her bedroom door open. Dee, Tracey, and Gayla, our other friends who stay on the opposite end of our street, are all sitting on the bed. This looks like an ambush. This cannot be good. *Do you mean to tell me that the news is so bad that it takes three of them to deliver it?* I ease over to the chair that's beside her dresser and take a seat.

It seems as if they are having a hard time deciding who's going to tell me what's going on.

Hell, don't be shy now. Speak up and let me know what's up!

Deon stands up and says, "Well, the three of us have all heard the same rumor, and we know this is something that you need to hear. And before I tell you, I want you to know that if it were me, I would want y'all to do the same thing."

Ok, now I feel like I need to throw up. How bad could this be?

I look at Tracey and Gayla and they are both in agreement.

"Well, ok, let's hear then!"

Deon nods at Gayla. I guess that's her clue to take over. Deon takes her place back on the bed, and Gayla stands and looks directly at me with her eyes extra magnified. She begins by reminding me of where her boyfriend stays. I'm nodding, indicating that I know, so she goes on to ask if I remember a girl we went to school with named Karen Slater. I respond, "vaguely. Why?"

She goes on to say that there is a rumor going around that she is pregnant.

I look at her like, what does that have to do with me?

Deon interjects by saying, "With twins, and they are saying they are Tylers!"

Well, just blow me down!!!!!!! I sure wasn't expected to get sucker punched like this!

The three of them are looking at me like I'm some kind of wounded dog with fleas.

I know one thing: they will not get a reaction from me! I wish I could just get up and walk out, but my legs will not cooperate. I'm stuck!

Tracey finally says, "So what are you going to do about it?"

The three of them are really sitting here waiting for an answer.

I'm furious! It wouldn't be wise for Tyler to call or come over. For his safety, he better steer clear! And that GIRL! There are no words! I definitely wouldn't have put those two together in a million years. While I play different scenarios in my head of how I will choke Tyler, he has the audacity to call. He is in a playful mood. He notices that my energy does not match. I advised him to come over because there is a matter that we need to tend to. Without hesitation, he's on his way.

I can tell he senses the seriousness of the matter because there is no bass when he pulls up. I hurry to meet him outside because I don't want anyone in our business. I greet him without hugs or kisses. I'm just sitting in the truck, trying not to blink so tears won't fall from my eyes.

"Tan, talk to me! What's wrong?"

"I hate you, Tyler! How could you do this to me?"

These tears are flooding my eyes, and I have no other place to go but out.

Confusion is all over his face and he's tearing up too.

"What did I do, baby? Please talk to me!" His voice is full of concern.

"You have me walking around here looking like a fool! You've been lying up with some random heifer! And to top it off, She's pregnant by you with TWINS! I liked you a whole lot better before you had your special little surgery!"

Tyler cuts his eyes at me and drops his head. He suddenly raises his head and suggests that we pay Karen a visit. I wonder how he thinks that's a good idea?

There, she sits on the back of a truck, swinging her legs and feet. She has a look of excitement until she sees that Tyler isn't alone.

She immediately tries to straighten her appearance and fixes her posture. We're both walking towards her, and she looks embarrassed as she looks everywhere except at us. Tyler just assumes that we know each other. I haven't ever said one word to her. Never had a reason to. I take a good look at her, and her stomach is huge and I look at him and just shake my head. This is the worst situation I think I have ever been in.

Tyler doesn't waste any time trying to clear his name. He directly says, "Karen, tell Tan that those are not my babies!" She doesn't even hesitate before she says, "No, they are not!"

Nah, she answers that too quickly. I'm not buying it! "Well, then, why are there rumors that they are his? You had to put that out there! Why would people just make that up?"

Finally, she makes eye contact with me, looks me dead in my eyes and says, "They are Marlon's babies."

"I'm still not satisfied.it is a fact that y'all slept together, and ain't no telling how many times. So, my next question is for you, Tyler: why in the Hell were you sneaking around with her?" He has a dumb ass look on his face like he's shocked that I figured out that he laid up with her.

"I'm being honest, Tan, it was only once."

"Is that supposed to make me feel better because it was just once? You have got to be kidding me!" *My blood is boiling! I could slap both of them!*

He knows better than even to attempt to defend himself.

Now it's her turn. "Didn't you know that he has a girlfriend?"

It's amazing! She is speechless also.

"I have had enough, Tyler. Take me home!"

As soon as he starts the truck, the song, *Saving All My Love for You,* by Whitney Houston is playing. How ironic! "A few stolen moments is all that we share. You've got your family, and they need you there." Those words are coming through the speakers as if it was meant just for me. Tyler reaches over and snaps it off! *Don't be mad at Whitney because you got yourself in this mess!*

The Engagement and Marriage

1990

It's a beautiful spring day in May, and we are having a wonderful date at one of

our favorite places, the Botanical Gardens. The birds seem to be chirping extra loud and the flowers are absolutely perfect.

"Tandra Ann Breakfield, do you want to be my wife?"

"What kind of question is that? And what are you doing down there?"

"Girl, I'm trying to be romantic. I'm trying to propose to you?"

"Stop playing, Tyler. You don't even have a ring!"

"Oh, I don't!" He says as he takes a small black velvet box out of his pocket.

Both of my hands cover my mouth in disbelief.

As he places the ring on my finger, he whispers, "No one in the world."

I wish I could live in the moment forever because I know it can't possibly get any better than this.

What's Done in the Dark

"Congratulations, Honey, you're pregnant!"

"Ahhh, I didn't come for that. I just came to get a complete blood count and pee in a cup!"

This nurse must have me mixed up with somebody else. I'm trying my best to explain to her that I didn't come here for that and how this is all just a big misunderstanding. The white walls are closing in on me. I can barely breathe. And all I can hear are those words, "You're Pregnant! You're pregnant!" Over and over again in my head.

"Honey," the nurse says while holding my arm to ease me into the chair, "do you understand that there is no mistake, and you are going to have a baby?"

I can't respond. Information overload! While she's talking, my mind has taken off full speed ahead. I can already see my belly big as a beach ball and my nose spreaded across my face. My thoughts are interrupted when I hear her say, "Do I need to call someone to be with you?"

I'm snapping out of it so I can collect myself and make my way to my car.

Not sure of what my next move should be, leads me to pull in at the Taco Bell's drive-through window. For some reason, I am extra hungry. I'm ordering my favorite: Mexican pizza, two soft tacos, and a Mountain Dew. I know the perfect place to eat would be the park.

I'm sitting here with me and my thoughts, just trying to figure out a game plan. How is Tyler going to take this news? *Who can I trust with this secret? How are my parents going to react?* I have to handle it the best way I know how. HIDE IT!

While I'm eating, I'm replaying the scene in my head when Tyler asked my Daddy's permission to marry me. Of course, he proposed first and then asked for my Daddy's permission afterward. Daddy gave him a speech about what it means to be a husband and a man. He also asked Tyler if he thought he could give me the lifestyle that I'm accustomed to. Daddy also shared with him that it wasn't going to be an easy journey, but Tyler and I just looked over at each other and smiled. Mama and Daddy both looked at us like we were clueless. *Now that I have a chance to think about it, we really are.*

I can't keep this to myself. I have to lean on somebody. This is not something I can keep. That would totally send me straight to the crazy house.

Guess What?

Sleeping is the only thing that's on my mind right now. As soon as I get home, I just want to fall into my bed in a deep sleep without any interruptions. The only complicated thing about that is I can't get caught sleeping because that's not my norm. If Mama were to catch me, that would raise a red flag. This particular time, I get carried away because it's that kind of sleep that's so good that I can taste it. I'm in bed, covered up around my neck and having the craziest dream ever, and suddenly, I feel a tap on my foot. My eyes open enough to see that it's Mama.

"Tan, why are you sleeping? Are you sick?"

"No, Mama, I'm just tired."

She looks at me in a very concerned manner and says, "Gal, are you pregnant?"

"Mama, why would you ask me that?"

She's looking very suspiciously at me, and she turns around and walks out the door.

Oh no! Now my conscious is really going to eat me alive! I'm up now! Who can sleep after that?

My first thought is to call Tyler. *How do I tell him?* I'm just going to blurt it out. I don't have the time to pretty it up. I need to get this secret out!

Tyler cannot stop smiling after hearing the news. He's asking me questions like: Are you sure? When will it be here?

I responded by saying I'm very sure and it will be here some-time in January.

This guy couldn't be happier. He's the happiest I've ever seen him because January is his birthday month. He's going on and on, telling me how every year he and our son will celebrate together.

"Excuse me, "HIM!" What makes you so sure we're having a boy?

"I'm a "G" I make boys!" he says while hugging me tight.

Now it's time to rain on his parade. He has forgotten that we have to tell our parents.

It's funny how quickly his expression of joy changes to stress.

"So, what's the game plan?" I ask.

"It really shouldn't be that bad because I already had the marriage talk with your dad, and he knows we plan to be together."

I'm seeing his expression change back to joy because he realizes it's really not that bad.

"So, what do you think your Mom will say?"

He looks like I'm asking him a silly question.

"My Mom will be cool about it, you'll see."

Breaking The News

This is one of the hardest things I've had to do. To look at my parents and see the hurt in their eyes is so heartbreaking. I can barely lift my head to look at them. My Daddy is one of the strongest men I know; he's my hero, but to see my Daddy cry. I can't stand to see it.

After Tyler left, I'm here alone to deal with the aftermath. It's dinner time, and Mama and Daddy are not really themselves. They are kinda quiet and trying to just get through the day. Mama has prepared a wonderful meal as usual, and we are all sitting at the table waiting in silence. She's fixing our plates by placing our favorite choices of fried chicken, mashed potatoes, corn, and green beans. OH, my goodness! This meal is extra delicious today. Mama gave Daddy his beer, her and my siblings Kool-Aid, and, for me, a tall glass of milk for obvious reasons.

Out of nowhere, JJ says, "Is Tan pregnant or what?"

I want to take this fork that's in my hand and poke him in his arm! Why would he want to bring this up now? Daddy seems to have lost his appetite because he gets up and goes to his room without finishing his dinner.

Boy, do I feel bad!

Marriage

August 1990

Wedding day jitters plus morning sickness is not my idea of a blushing bride. I'm getting married today, and it's a little difficult to feel excited because my Daddy is so sad. He has begged me not to marry, telling me just to wait and not rush. He has even offered to buy me a brand-new Mazda Miata. Now, that's a little hard to turn down, but the truth is, I love Tyler.

Mama has a different approach. She makes it very clear that I am not the first person to get pregnant without being married and I dang shol won't be the last! She says, "If that's why y'all are rushing to get married, then don't!" I'm grateful that my parents want me to wait and offer their support, but it's a little shocking because all we heard growing up is. How we better not get pregnant, or they would put us out! They had fear in us, and now that I'm grown, that tune has changed.

Daddy couldn't take being at the house because he knew I wasn't going to change my mind, so he went on to work early because it saddened him in his opinion that I was rushing into something. It hurts my heart to know that I'm hurting my Daddy.

I'm scared! I hope I know what I'm doing.

Mama enters my bedroom with a warm smile, carrying a garment bag. "I have something for you."

Her warm smile is what I need to help me through this day.

"Oh, thank you, Mama," I say as I open the bag and see a beautiful off-white satin pleated dress.

She's happy because I'm happy. As I'm dressing, Mama lifts my hair and places her good pearls around my neck. I can remember how special I felt when she let me wear them to the dance.

The phone rings, and Mama answers it. I hear her say, "No, John, she hasn't changed her mind, and yes, he has called to tell us the time to meet him and his Mom at the courthouse."

I guess Daddy had to check one last time to see if his wish had come true.

Mama came back into the room with tears in her eyes. *I guess the sadness in Daddy's voice triggered it.* She grabs me and holds me very tight. I can feel her heart beating. These words came from her mouth, "You will always have a home here! Don't ever think you can't come back home! You will always be my baby girl!"

That's the reassurance I need to start my journey. It just feels good to know that my parents love me unconditionally, and that's price-less!

Reality is setting in now. I'm scared! My whole life is going in a whole new direction. All of this is brand new. I've never been a wife or a mother. Will I be good at both? I guess now it's too late to doubt myself because I'm about to hit the ground running! *Breathe in, breathe out. Ok. It's going to be alright, it's showtime!* One last quick look in the mirror, and Mama and I are on our way to my destiny.

Tyler and his Mom are already here. I see his Mom's Cadillac parked up front. I found a parking space a few cars away from hers. I turn off the ignition and exhale. Mama reaches over and pats my shoul-der to remind me that I'm not alone. *What would I do without her? I hope I never have to find out.*

There's a special sparkle in Tyler's eyes as I enter the room. He's looking at me like I'm the most beautiful woman in the world. *Don't ever stop looking at me like that.* He compliments my hair, which is straight and flowing, and he tells me how pretty my dress is, too. I return the favor by telling him how handsome he looks in his gray suit, but I notice he isn't wearing a tie. We all exchange hugs, and his Mom takes his tie out of her purse and hands it to me. As I'm wrapping the tie around his neck, I'm feeling his energy. It's a feeling of warmth that's filled with hope with a splash of excitement. "Perfect," I say as I give the tie a little twist to strengthen it. Tyler hugs me tight and whispers, "I can't wait for you to become my wife."

That statement didn't escape his Mom's ears because she states, "Son, you sure can't whisper!"

Both of our mothers find that to be hilarious.

The justice of the peace walks in and introduces himself. "So, who's ready to tie the knot?" Tyler grabs my hand, and we follow behind him to the front of the courtroom.

"Can I offer you all a little advice before we start?"

Tyler and I both agree to hear what the judge has to say.

"Always remember that love conquers all. No matter how rough things get, remember why you both fell in love in the first place and that will make your journey together much sweeter.

"Do I have y'all's word?"

"Yes sir," we say in Unisom.

We're really doing this. We are about to make a lifetime commitment to each other.

I read Tyler's lips, "No one in the world," and that made my heart smile.

The "I dos" went smoothly, and now the kiss. We are so into it that we've forgotten we had an audience. The three of them are clearing their throats while laughing so we can get the hint to cut it off. Our eyes slowly open, and we are slightly embarrassed while blushing. The judge signs our marriage license and wishes us a happy ever after.

Honeymoon

New Orleans is our destination, and we are making the eight-plus hour drive. It seems like every hour, I need Tyler to stop so I can pee, but other than that, we are having a good time. Periodically, he looks at me and says, "Hey, Mrs. Black," with a big grin on his face. I don't think I will ever get tired of hearing that.

Static is all we can hear when we turn to local radio stations, so that means I can DJ.

Tyler is wondering which cassette tape I am going to pop in. I chose *"My Fantasy"* by Guy. Oh yeah! He is pleased. We are both jamming as we sing every word of the song. Dang, all this singing got me hungry. Tyler looks at me and says, "Are you hungry yet?"

"You must be reading my mind. Let's stop and get some seafood!"

The sign reads, "Welcome to Vicksburg, Mississippi." Just reading the sign makes me believe that we have come to the right place to find some good food. I spot a billboard that says, "All you can eat is fresh catfish," and instantly, my mouth starts to water.

"Tyler, we have to go!" I say as I bounce up and down in my seat.

"Ok, calm down, old hungry woman!"

The aroma of fried catfish hits us right in the face as we walk through the door. I can't wait to see what this fish is all about. The waitress sits the golden perfectly fried catfish, shrimp, and fries in front of us. We look at each other, and it's on now!

After all that good eating, we have another three and a half hours to go. I'm in the driver's seat now and waiting for Tyler to get me some good music to roll to. He made an excellent choice, *Poison*, by B.B.D.

"AHHHH YEAH! We are in business now! We're both trying to act out the video while on this road. Who can get sleepy while jamming this hard? The answer is NO ONE!" We decide to listen to the whole tape and that is keeping us in party mode.

OOO Wee! I have never been so glad to see New Orleans city limits. Tyler gets the Mapsco out to map out the directions to the Holiday Inn on Royal St. I park near the entrance. I'm so tired! I have to find a way to peel myself out of this truck because I've been sitting too long. Tyler walks around to the driver's side and places his arms underneath mine to help me stand.

I can barely feel my legs and feet. I have to give myself a few minutes to try to walk.

The hotel lobby is very exquisite! We both are pleased. I take a seat while Tyler goes to the desk to get the keys. As we step into the elevator, we notice that the number thirteen is missing. It's because they believe that number to be bad luck. We're getting off on the fifteenth floor, and the view from our room is breathtaking! We both don't have the strength to take another step, so we fall on the bed to get a little rest. The plan is to recharge and then go sightseeing.

The nap turned into a deep sleep. It's after eight at night, and we're out looking for food. "Gumbo sounds great!" and he agrees. While we are waiting for dinner, this older couple comes over to our table and asks if we are on a first date or honeymoon. We are looking confused, wondering why it matters. The women went on to say that they had been watching us, and they could just feel the love that we have for one another, so it had to be a fresh new love or a next-level love. It's funny how we go through life, and we don't know who's observing us.

We're back in our hotel room now, and my mind is set on soaking in the jetted tub. After what seems like hours of soaking, Tyler is giving me the best full-body massage ever! He is working the soreness out of every muscle and joint that I have. *I am going to sleep like a baby tonight in my husband's arms.*

Suddenly, the curtains are opening and the sunlight is across my face. There standing with a tray is my husband. "Rise and shine, Dear; I have breakfast. You were sleeping so good, and I didn't want you to miss breakfast, so I decided we would have it in bed."

"Wow, you are off to a great start. Are you trying for husband of the year already?"

He can't help but grin, and he kisses me on the lips and then starts removing the lids off the plates. Pancakes, scrambled eggs with cheese, sausage, bacon, and orange juice.

"You did good!"

"Anything for my favorite girl!"

Before I can swallow the last of my orange juice, Tyler is rambling about all the things that we are going to do today. So, I'm getting up and getting ready for our great day that he has planned. Every time I attempt to put on a piece of garment, he takes it out of my hands and kisses me softly on my neck and shoulders. "Boy, you better stop before you start something!"

Evidently, that is a challenge that he welcomed because it's an hour later, and we are still in bed.

Wow! There is a Daiquiri shop on every corner. They must be pretty good because the lines are out the doors. "Just because I can't have one doesn't mean you can't enjoy one, Tyler."

"That wouldn't be fair."

"Come on now, I insist!"

I didn't have to do too much convincing because now he's walking around sipping on a strawberry daiquiri, and I'm sipping on water. Yay!

As we walk down Bourbon Street, he sees an arcade, "Hey Tan let go in so I can whoop you like old times!"

"I'm all for it! Let's go!"

We walk in, and every game that we love to play is occupied.

"Why are all these kids in here?" He said.

"You do know that it is an arcade, and kids love to play games."

"True!"

Oh no! There's the motorcycle game.

"Come on, Tan, get on!"

He jumps on the blue one, and I'm on the red one. He drops the tokens in, and we both burn off! We're leaning, crashing, and rolling over. Oh, what fun!

Lunch was delectable. I think we must have sampled every seafood dish they had. I was completely satisfied with my choice of the crawfish etouffee; it was extremely flavorful. Tyler just wanted his usual fried shrimp. We're back in our room resting up for this evening. He has a surprise for me. *I wonder what it could be.*

"What should I wear to this surprise?"

"Just put on a sundress, you know I love you in a sundress!" He says as he hits me on my behind.

"Well, ok then, your wish is my command."

As we are walking down the street, I'm feeling so excited about us. The sun is setting, and we are heading in the direction of water. Tyler's surprise is a romantic dinner and music on the Steamboat Natchez. We are cruising from New Orleans to the Mississippi River and back. Oh my, the view is absolutely beautiful, and the band is playing jazz tunes with couples up slow dancing and having a great time. I can't help myself; I have to order the gumbo again. I can't resist. Tyler orders the same.

This has truly been a night to remember, and I'm looking forward to millions of nights like this with my husband.

Baby Shower

December is going to be a busy month for me. My baby shower is next weekend and two weeks after that is Christmas. My two good friends are back home for the holidays, and I can't wait to see them. The shower will be here at our apartment, so I have to make sure that it's spotless. Cherine has been a big help. We are always out shopping. She has helped me organize all the tiny outfits and accessories I have for the baby.

My parents have really spoiled me. I don't want for nothing! Whatever I want to eat, they make sure I get it. Last month I found out that it's a boy. Tyler is on cloud nine. That's all he talks about is his son, like he's already here. Cheraine is excited that I'm having a boy because she has two. So, my baby already has two friends.

Baby blue, yellow and white are the colors for my baby shower. "It's A Boy" signs are hanging over the front entry, by the gift table, and over the bar area where the food is. I'm wearing a baby blue jumpsuit with a baby blue bow tied around my long ponytail.

Pass the toilet paper roll! I'm looking at my family and friends like, Y'all know my stomach ain't that big. They are supposed to tear the tissue the length that will wrap around my tummy, and I swear

Kerry's tissue looks to be a mile long. I'm standing up with my arms out, waiting for each one of them to try their luck. *Ok, we have a winner!* "Yay, Rockie!"

You would think she has won a million dollars the way she's jumping up and down. She reaches into the prize box and pulls out a small, clear baby bottle filled with candy.

The food is so good. Mama made chicken salad sandwiches and extras to go on Ritz crackers. Cheraine is obsessed with Mama's chicken salad, and she admits she has lost count of how many she has eaten. There are meatballs, pasta salad, fruit, and vegetable trays. Mama has made my special punch with grape juice. I'm sitting here feeling super full with my plate resting on my stomach. Now that my tummy is bigger, I use it as my own personal table.

Janis and Deon make it known that it is time to open gifts. Rockie grabs a pencil and notepad to make note of the gifts and who they were from. Cheraine moves a chair by the gift table so I can sit and open gifts. This is the moment I've been waiting for. I have never seen so many cute blue little outfits in my life! I have more than enough receiving blankets and washcloths. Glass bottles seem to be very popular. I will be washing bottles for days! I have diapers for months, and it seems like I will never run out. I'm so grateful for family and great friends. I am so BLESSED!

Welcome to the World

January 1991

Tyler can't believe that it's happening, and it's happening on his birthday! I'm trying to make sure I have everything I need for the baby and me. I can't depend on him because his head is so far up in the clouds, so he can't be of any service to me right now. Ok, I believe I have everything. I interrupt Tyler's pacing back and forth in the kitchen, "I'm ready now."

He grabs my bags and tells me to sit while he loads the car and warms it up. As I'm sitting on the couch, I look at the clock, and it's 4:30 in the morning. My head is spinning, and my nerves are getting the best of me, but just knowing that Mama is going to be with me as I enter into motherhood brings me peace.

I'm in a divine birthing suite that consists of cherry wood furniture accompanied by lavish drapes, and the most exciting feature of them all is the jetted tub! Just like the one we had in New Orleans. I couldn't have chosen a better place to have my baby because this is also my place of employment. All of my coworkers have been coming in and out of here all morning long. *The next person comes in and says, "Girl, you haven't had that baby yet?" I'm going to strangle them!*

It's afternoon, and I'm really feeling the pain now. The nurse comes in to check me and reports that I've only dilated to three and a half centimeters. *Is that all? Dang! I'm never going to have this baby!*

I need to have him before The Cosby Show comes on. I can feel myself growing more frustrated by the minute. Every few seconds, someone comes through the door. I have a room full of family, friends, and coworkers.

I am hungry as Hell! I'm lying here not saying anything while Tyler is feeding me ice chips and rubbing my head. I wish I could join in on the conversations, but I don't have the strength, and this pain is really kicking my butt! The time is 2:00 in the afternoon and now I'm six centimeters. The nurse says it won't be long now.

"Knock - Knock!" My sister-in-law Venus walks in with a Burger King sack and some flowers, and she says, "Girl, you ain't had that baby yet?"

She definitely is supposed to get strangled for asking me that annoying question and tackled for bringing in food! I guess I will let her make it since she brought such pretty flowers.

The doctor clears the room because I have dilated enough to get the Epidural. I'm so scared, but I am ready to meet the little person who's been kicking me and keeping me up at night for months. As I lean forward, I feel a stinging sensation in my lower back area in a matter of seconds, causing me not to feel anything from my waist down. I'm glad to get some relief now. I just have to focus on pushing, and soon this will be all over.

Tyler is a real trooper. He has been by my side every step of the way. He is very attentive, holding my hand and whispering, "No one in the world," when things start to get rough. I just hope he doesn't pass out like some husbands do during the delivery. I have heard so many horror stories about that.

"PUSH!" That is all I have heard in the last hour or so. I don't ever want to hear that word again! My eyeballs feel like they're about to pop out! I feel like I have been pushing for days! When will this unpleasant part end?

"You are doing good! I can see the head." says one of the nurses.

All this pushing, and that's all you can, see? I will probably be pushing until this time tomorrow before they can see his shoulders! I just want to hear my baby cry out into the world and know that he is healthy.

This is going to be my last push. I'm going to push with all my might. I'm going to push so hard that my teeth are going to all fallout!

The nurse counted, "One, two, three, and PUSH!"

"Thank you, Jesus, for hearing my cry! My baby boy is here, and he has a good set of lungs, too.

Tyler is cutting the cord, looking like he's a pro. We both have tears of joy rolling from our eyes. We will never forget this experience; it will truly be a cherished memory.

All Good Things Must Come to an END!

Six Months Later

It's been a joy for us to watch Baby TJ grow. He has a personality now. I now know exactly what to do when he's sleepy, which is to lay him across my lap and pat his tiny bottom until he drifts off to sleep. He also likes to get his hair brushed. It relaxes him. He's the perfect baby. He's a little bundle of joy that's always smiling. This baby wakes up with a smile on his face. He looks so much like Tyler. It's hard to tell that I had anything to do with carrying him. It seems like Tyler had him all by himself. I guess they look so much alike because they share the same birthday. Tyler is so grateful for that. He always says you won't ever be able to top that gift. He has a good point there.

Things are going so well at the Black's household. We have our little routine down. Tyler gets up too with the baby when he needs feeding and changing during the middle of the night. I'm back working at the hospital, just part-time. We are so grateful to Mama because she keeps Baby TJ every day and doesn't charge us a dime. There is no better feeling than to know that your baby is going to be well taken care of by his grandmother, who loves him dearly. This baby has really brought a whole lot of joy to our family.

On the weekends, we share our time with both sides of our family because we want Baby TJ to know them both. Kerry always teases us by calling us "Happy Family." She really gets a kick out of that.

It's a rainy Friday night, and Tyler is out with friends, and I'm home with the baby, just chilling and getting ready to put him to bed. For some reason, Baby TJ cries every time I try to put him in his crib. I think I have spoiled him because he just wants to be across my lap. That's when he gets his best sleep. So, I'm not going to keep walking back and forth; Baby TJ will be accompanying us tonight.

The news has gone off, and there is no sign of Tyler. *Should I be worried? Why hasn't he called me?* Something just doesn't feel right. I hear him at the door now. I hear him coming in. It sounds like he is carrying a lot of things. I can't get up to see because I don't want to wake the baby. He's going into the baby's room, and I hear him on the baby monitor. He probably thought Baby TJ was in there. *It's taking him a long time to figure it out. What could he be doing there?*

Finally, he comes into our bedroom. I reach over and turn on the lamp. Tyler walks over to me, kisses me on my forehead, and does the same to Baby TJ. I mentioned that I was worried when he wasn't home earlier. He has a strange look on his face as if it's something he's not telling me. I immediately ask him what is going on with him. He has a crazy look on his face. *I have a feeling that whatever it is, it's not going to be good.* Tyler takes a seat next to me on the edge of the bed. *Lord, what is this man about to tell me?*

Tyler began to stall by telling me how much he loves me and how he didn't want anything to come between us. *What the HELL has he done now?*

While He's bracing himself to spill whatever has been weighing him down, he's interrupted. This unexpected interruption took me by surprise. There is crying coming from Baby TJ's room, and he ain't even in there. My eyebrows automatically point straight up.

"Tyler, what the HELL is going on? Why do we hear crying in the baby's room, and our baby is right here asleep? Please explain! And make it good!"

Tyler quickly stands to his feet, very confused about what his next move should be. I can tell he's not sure if he should stay in here with me and try to explain or run into the other room. I'm not giving him much of a choice to come clean because now I am getting out the bed to see what the disturbance is in the nursery. He's following behind me like a little kid who is in trouble, trying to explain before I witness whatever it is for myself.

"I just be DAMN! Are my eyes playing a trick on me, or what? Do I see two toddlers standing, holding the rails of my baby's bed? *He got me F'ed UP!*

"Tan, give me a chance to explain!"

I really don't want to hear shit he has to say because now I am feeling betrayed. How can I trust anything that will come out of his mouth? I just want to get my baby and run to my parents, but I don't want them in my mess. I need a minute. I can't deal with this extra Tyler has forced on me. I'm walking back into our bedroom, and I close the door behind me. My baby must know Mommy needs him to get his rest while she tries to hold on to her sanity.

An hour later, I hear a faint knock at the bedroom door. *He knows better not to wake up this baby.*

I take my pissed-off time getting out the bed to open the door. *I can't even look at him. There is nothing he can say to make me understand, so he can just shut up talking to me.*

Tyler and I are in the dining room, sitting across from each other, unsure what our next move should be. The silence is so thick that you could cut it with a knife, and finally, he begins to present his case. I have made up my mind to just hear him out and not comment until he is completely done. I want him to get everything out before I let loose.

In the midst of his storytelling, I feel myself about to explode. Nothing he is saying makes any sense. How can you try to convince me that it is ok for you to take ownership of not one but two babies because no one else was man enough to do it? I'm explaining to him that the problem I'm having is he did not once take into consideration how his actions could affect me and us as a couple. And also, I say, "What made you think that your approach of bringing them here tonight was wise? You really could have found a better way!"

Tyler drops his head and takes a moment to process my concerns. I think he has a clear picture of the damage that his actions have caused.

"Tan, I am so sorry that I hurt you like this. That was not my intention. I just wanted to take the responsibility as a man and still be your husband and Baby TJ's father, too."

"Well, that's very noble of you wanting to save and rescue Karen and her twins. So, you never said that they were yours or how you and she decided that y'all were going to do this together because the last I heard, both of y'all lying asses said that you weren't the father, and yet here we are today with you stepping up as their pappy! How long have you been going on behind my back, playing happy family with them? And most importantly, how am I supposed to trust you moving forward? You should have never married me if you knew you were going to sign up for this!"

Oh, the tension is real in this room now. Tyler is feeling the heat, and he knows I want every last one of my questions answered.

He stands and clears his throat several times, and when he makes eye contact with me, I notice the stream of tears flowing from his eyes, and the apologies start back.

I can't be weak. I must demand that he give me an explanation. If not, he will lose all respect for me and Lord knows what could be next.

It's two in the morning, and we're both stressed and mentally drained. I head back to the bedroom, and Tyler grabs a blanket from the closet and makes his bed on the couch. It hasn't been thirty minutes since I got in bed, and I hear crying from the nursery. I can hear him in there trying to calm them down, but they are giving him the blues. I'm trying to lie here as if I don't care, but that's not even my spirit, so I get up and walk to the nursery. Tyler has two sippy cups in his hand, and the twins don't want any parts of him or the cups. One look at their innocent, teary eyes, my heart just melted. I decided to pick one of them up. The other one reaches for me, and as I pick her up, the crying stops. I transitioned to the living room on the couch where Tyler had previously made his bed, and the four of us just sat in silence. These sweet, precious babies just don't know how they have worked their magic on me, which has softened my heart to try to make this work. *Maybe I'm delusional or just plain sleep-deprived, but whatever it is, I think Tyler and I can work through this. I pray he doesn't make me regret this later.*

Six Months Later

Happy Birthday, Baby TJ! I went a little overboard with the Sesame Street decorations, and I found the perfect Sesame Street outfit for him. Mama and Kerry are busy decorating and blowing up the balloons, and Rockie is getting her video camera together so she doesn't miss a moment of Baby TJ.

He's taking a nap, resting up for his important event. I can't wait to see his reaction.

Mama says, "Don't be surprised if he is afraid of his cake because you sure were!"

I can't believe I almost sat on my cake on my first birthday! That is too funny! Hopefully, he doesn't take after me.

The food is ready, and the decorations are on point! Let's get this party started! Guests are coming in one after another. My small apartment is full to capacity. It has taken some getting used to being in a smaller place now that Tyler and I separated. I can't believe it had to come to this, but things just got out of hand. It started with the twins. Then he started clubbing and staying out all times of night. I couldn't take any more disrespect, so I made the best decision for me and Baby TJ and that was to leave. The funny part about leaving Tyler was his Mom was very supportive. She told me if I were serious about leaving him, she would help me. So, every month on the first, she has money for my rent in a coat pocket in the back of her closet. She instructed me to get it even if she wasn't home. I love her for being understanding and not taking sides. She is genuine and loyal, and I greatly appreciate her for that.

Someone is awake now. Kerry is walking down the stairs with Baby TJ in her arms. He is confused by the decorations and all the guests who are yelling, "Happy Birthday, Baby TJ!"

This crazy baby is scared out of his mind and starts to cry. Rockie is tickled and capturing every moment. I'm trying my best to distract him by showing him all the gifts and his cake. None of these things phases him. All he wants to do is lay his head on my shoulder and peep at everyone. When the music starts playing and the kids start to move around, Baby TJ starts to warm up and wants Kerry to put him down. He's running around and playing with his cousins and friends.

There's a knock at the door, and Rockie opens it, in walks Tyler and Ant, who is not only Tyler's friend but also Baby TJ's Godfather now. They're both carrying lots of gifts.

"Where's Baby TJ," he asks as he kisses me on the forehead.

"He's running around playing. Happy Birthday to you!"

He smiles, and before he can respond, Baby TJ notices his dad and breaks away from the crowd to give his dad the best greeting. The birthday boys are so happy to be in each other's presents. It is a happy and sad feeling all in one. *If only things could have been different.*

1993

On and off is a way to describe this so-called marriage we have. This is getting so exhausting, trying to be a full-time mother and a part-time wife. Tyler is really trying to talk me into getting a house with him, and we start over, but deep down, I just know he's not going to do right, so I'm not going to entertain that thought.

Before Tyler and I separated, I started noticing changes in him. Besides his obsession with clubbing, he also developed an appetite for other women and fast money. His lifestyle was becoming too much for me, so I knew it was necessary to make my exit. The final cue was when Tyler and I were out one night and returned home, only to find our front door lying on the living room floor. I knew then that me and my baby were out! I felt like the least I knew, the better off I would be.

The two of us agreed to try again. Baby TJ is always happy to see his parents together. He squeezes in the middle of us and has the biggest smile on his face. *I wish my baby could grow up with his parents together but I don't think that's going to be the case.*

Tyler is adamant about proving he wants me and only me. He wants his family. So, to prove it to me, he takes his truck to the paint shop and has it customized. I can't believe what I'm seeing. This man has gone over and beyond to prove to me that he chooses me/us. Never in my wildest dreams would I have thought that he would get a giant portrait of me painted on the hood of his truck. This is very impressive, and it leads me to believe that any other woman would be stupid as Hell to want to ride around with a married man with his wife's face on the hood of his truck.

Today is just like any other day at my job, working as an administrative assistant for a home health agency. One of my close coworkers and I decided to walk across the street to Sound Warehouse to look for a new CD that she wanted. I spot Tyler's truck in the parking lot. I had been telling my coworker about how my husband has gotten my face painted on his hood, and now she can witness it for herself and check out the inside because he had it redone also. So, we're walking into the store on a mission to find my husband. I'm sure he's probably with Ant or one of his other friends.

Oh, but to my surprise. This is the ULTIMATE CRUNCH! Tyler is in this record store with some HEIFER! *I can't show the hurt that is suffocating my heart right now. I have to put on a front. I know one thing. He will never know how much I want to cry and break something over his head right now.* My coworker is looking confused, but I keep my cool and tip up on Tyler with his little girlfriend looking right at me.

"Hey, husband!"

Tyler looks like he sees a ghost.

"Give me your keys so I can show my friend the truck. I'll bring them back when we're done."

Tyler's mouth is open, but no words are coming out, so I grab his keys and we make our way out to the truck.

Oh, he's worried. I can see all over his face. It's bringing me the satisfaction to know that he knows that he is BUSTED!

Before we can return back into the store, Tyler and his little date are headed to the truck.

"Hello, Tyler is so rude not to introduce us. I'm Tan, his wife, and you are?"

Her large eyes are about to pop out of her head. She finally locates her voice and says, "Hi, I'm Sherry."

"Well, Sherry, here are the keys. You and my husband go ahead and enjoy the rest of y'alls date.

It took all I had not to act a fool. I must say I am very proud of myself for not going off and just moving on!

1994

Emotional Rollercoaster

My baby is now three years old, and he is attending private school. I did tons of research to find the perfect school to educate him. This particular school has a great curriculum, which has proven to teach children to read and write in cursive at the tender age of three. When I heard that, I was like, "Sign him up!" Now that he's going to school, he considers himself to be a big boy, so he says he's not a baby anymore, so drop the Baby and just call him TJ.

It's TJ's first day of school, and I am very emotional. My little baby is growing up, and he's growing up too fast for me. His first day-of-school outfit is just too cute! He has on a Barney t-shirt and jeans, purple and white Jordans, a Barney lunch kit, and a Barney mat for nap time. He is so excited. He says he can't wait to get to school to make friends.

I'm driving and looking in my rearview mirror at my big boy as I struggle to look through my tear-filled eyes. It seems like yesterday that we were bringing him home from the hospital. As I'm parking, TJ has already unfastened the straps on his car seat and is trying to get out. I guess I am moving too slowly for him.

We walk into the classroom, and there are two sets of kids. There are the ones who are calm and the criers in the corner sitting on a stack of blue mats. It's going to be interesting to see which group TJ will join. I'm talking with his teacher, and TJ is sticking to me like glue, and I'm sensing that there is going to be some trouble when I try to leave here without him. I'm getting ready to leave, and his teacher is trying to distract him by showing him some toy cars and trucks. It may have worked for a split second because I'm turning to make my way to the door, and out of nowhere TJ grabs my hand tight and tries to leave with me. I'm trying to explain to him that Mommy has to go to work, and I need him to be a big boy and stay here at school. My baby is crying so hard, as if I'm telling him that he will never see me again. Time is not on my side right now. I'm going to be late if I don't figure something out. TJ is looking at me like, Mommy, please don't leave me. I'm bending down to pick my baby up, hug and kiss him and sit him right beside another little crying boy who is crying just as hard as he is. I know that sounds bad, and it's probably going to disqualify me from being the mother of the year. My whole mood is messed up now. *I want to go back and get my baby.*

Being a Mom is the highlight of my life. I have my TJ to take my mind off my troubles. Tyler and I are co-parenting and dating occasionally. He spends quality time with TJ and picks him up from school. I don't want to confuse TJ or get his hopes up by thinking his parents are together. Sometimes, I sit and reflect on what could've been and the sad reality of my fairytale being destroyed. For the life of me, I don't know where it went wrong. One minute, it's all about the two of us. Then we became parents and also, an unexpected bonus, twins. Also, things began to become more important than family, such as club-bing, money, and women. Finally, I had to make the necessary decision to leave our dysfunctional home and make a life for me and my child. I wonder what made Tyler so money-hungry and a skirt chaser? In my mind, we were perfect. But I guess I am delusional for thinking we could live happily ever after together.

So, for now, moving forward, I am going to put my foot down. Lord knows I am weak behind this man, but I have to love me and my child more. This on-and-off mess is going to stop, and I can't leave it up to him to do it. I will have to do it. The longer I buy into it, the more he will try to get away with it. So, I am making a promise to myself to let the past go because if Tyler really wanted me, he would have cleaned up his act by now.

Change Of Plans

My parents insist that I move back home because I am wasting money paying rent at an apartment that I hardly ever stayed in. TJ and

I are settling in nicely and we both are being spoiled on a daily basis. Mama is always cooking our favorites, and she and Daddy are like a little cleaning service because they are always tidying up our room. I never realized how good I had it growing up until life threw me several curve balls. Now, I'm just trying to figure out what life is without who I thought was the love of my life. I know it's not going to be an easy journey, but a necessary one. Tyler wants to come over and talk. I think it would be a bad idea to talk here so I told him I would meet him at the park.

The conversation I'm having in my head is very conflicting. One minute, I'm rehearsing my "Let's stay together" speech, and the next minute, I'm giving a farewell speech. I pull into the park and see Tyler is already here, leaning against his truck.

Ok, Tan, do not show any signs of weakness and don't let him sweet talk you.

As I'm walking up to him, I see that big smile, the one that's hard for me to resist, displayed right on his face. And before I can get a word in. Tyler takes me into his arms and kisses the life out of me. Whatever I had planned to say to him has gone right out the window!

It's my birthday! I'm ready to celebrate! Mama and Kerry made plans to take me out to eat and shopping. Those are my two favorite things. The Dallas Galleria is the best shopping experience. They have all the high-end stores and the nicest restaurants. My mission is to find the perfect outfit for tonight. Tyler is taking me out. I feel like I'm back in high school, getting ready for a first date.

An outfit in the window of Lord & Taylor jumps out at me. Tyler will absolutely love me in this red, form-fitting, spandex mini dress. I'm checking myself out first in the dressing room mirror. Ok, I'm liking what I see! Thanks to my baby TJ for these nice-sized breasts and curvy hips. When I walk out to show Mama and Kerry, they both say, "that's the one!" I'm blushing because I haven't had the desire to look sexy. Now I must find some cute red sandals to go with this dress.

This has been a great birthday so far, and dinner was excellent. We went a little crazy in the mall, but it's ok because it's my birthday! Once we get back home, I start getting ready for my night on the town.

Lady in Red is the theme for the night. The doorbell rings, it's my date! I can hear Daddy letting him in and trying to have a conversation while TJ is jumping all on his back, ready to wrestle. By the time I walk into the room Tyler is out of breath. I can't help but laugh. He did have enough strength to tell me how good I looked. Even TJ says I look beautiful. We finally got the opportunity to leave when Mama fixed TJ a bowl of chocolate ice cream. That was a nice distraction.

There is a red convertible Corvette with the top down in front of the house. We are walking towards it, and he's opening the door for me. When Tyler gets in, he asks, "Do you like it?"

"Like it? I absolutely love it!" I can't stop smiling. We are off to a great start.

We are having dinner and listening to a little jazz at the Caravan of Dreams downtown. Tyler is doing a good job with my birthday festivities. He has always known exactly what I like and I haven't had not one complaint about anything he has planned for me.

Now that dinner is over, we are on a carriage ride throughout downtown. This is nice and romantic. Tyler tells me that he knows he has put me through a lot, and he is sorry for that. He's also trying to explain to me that he has a lot going on, and he really wants to be with me, but I need to let him do what he needs to do. That's an interesting statement. It seems to me that somebody wants to have their cake, ice cream, cookies, and punch! So, I'm just nodding while he's talking because deep down, I know the harsh reality. It's over for us, and I have to be ok with it. The song *End of The Road,* by Boyz II Men is playing on the radio as soon as he cranks up the car. How ironic is that! This song seems to be preaching to us, and it's bringing tears to my eyes. I'm looking over at him, and I can tell he is feeling the same way.

The night ends with the most soul shaking kiss ever and a soft whisper in my ear, "No one in the world!"

Life Goes On!

We're going about our daily business as usual. With me dropping off TJ every weekday morning at school and going to work, it leaves me no time to focus on my crushed dreams. TJ is not missing a beat because he gets to see his Daddy every weekday when he picks him up from school. Sometimes, Tyler has the gull to have his girlfriend, Sherry, in the car when he drops TJ off at his wife's parents' house. I can't lie; I feel some kind of way about that, but I have to learn to be just like him and not have a conscience. It's funny how Tyler wants to do his dirt and doesn't want me to do anything. He dared to tell me if I ever had sex with someone else or got pregnant by someone else, that he would be done with me. The way I'm feeling right now. Guess who's about to test that theory?

Although my marriage is now a joke, Tyler and I are decent to each other, and we support one another. Today, I received a phone call from Karen. I'm wondering what she could want with me. I still don't know to this day what occurred between her and Tyler for him to step up to help raise the twins. The way I look at that situation now is. That is not my problem! So, I'm ok with whatever. She is calling to see if I would allow TJ to attend the twins' birthday party.

Breathe in and breathe out. Why isn't she communicating with Tyler? And a better question is, who gave her my number? Let me stop tripping.

I shouldn't have a problem with her. We never crossed paths until that day Tyler and I went to her house. But don't get me wrong. I wanted to hate her because, to me, she was part of the problem with my marriage, not to mention this other chick, Sherry and all the others that are running around with my husband. My mamma told me that I shouldn't be mad at them because none of those women committed to me. It took me a while to process that, and that's because I wasn't mature enough to comprehend that, but now I am, and it has made my life less stressful.

So, this is why now I can have a conversation with Karen and not want to choke her. I agree to either bring TJ myself or let Tyler do the honors. I will look at the positive side of it, which is a reason to buy two cute little dresses.

The lack of social life is getting the best of me. I am ready to start living, meeting people and doing some things that interest me. Don't get me wrong, I love being a Mom, but there is more to life than taking your child on play dates and watching PG movies. I miss being in a relationship. I miss being held and wined and dined. It's time for me to be set free.

Am I wrong or selfish for wanting to matter to someone other than my child? That's it! I'm making my next move!

Mrs. Tandra Black, "the lawyer will see you now."

I stand and follow the receptionist to the conference room where the lawyer is already sitting in there with a stack of papers in front of him. He immediately stands when I walk in, shake my hand and pull a chair out for me. I exhale while waiting for the questioning to begin. He starts off by asking me why I want a divorce and if there's any way that my marriage could be saved. I'm sitting here with him, sharing my heart's disappointments. It is painful to admit that there's no saving this marriage. It's over. I am making the decision to have him served because I know he will not cooperate and sign peacefully. My lawyer assures me that it will get done.

I'm hopeful and just ready to disconnect from this nightmare.

My weekend started earlier this morning when I dropped TJ off at school and came back home just to rest and clear my head. *I'm making a life-changing move, and it feels great!*

The only thing that kind of gets to me is that there is really no one who can relate to what I'm going through. Cheraine is my only married friend who's married, and I don't think getting a divorce has ever crossed her mind. So, I will have to keep this to myself.

The server contacted me because he is having trouble locating Tyler to serve him the divorce papers. He is saying every time he goes over there, Tyler's truck and other cars are there, but whoever comes to the door always says he's not there.

Hmmm, let me think like a man right now.

I instructed him to change up his strategy by sending a nice-looking sister to serve him. I assured him that it would work, so he was willing to give it a try.

B-I-N-G-O! It worked! Tyler fell for it! The woman that they sent with the divorce papers was able to serve him. The server was laughing when he contacted me and said you know him so well. I'm glad that's over with, and I can finally get a court date and be on my way to freedom.

I have gotten used to my new norm of not being with Tyler in any shape, form, or fashion and out of the blue, he calls to see if I would accompany him to Jamaica. He's practically begging me to go as if I'm divorcing him. Deep down, I want to say yes. We have never taken a trip like that together, but I know I cannot get involved again. I have come too far; besides, Tyler's lifestyle scares me. He's throwing money around like it's nothing and driving all kinds of nice cars. Nah, I'm going to have to pass on the trip. I can tell he's hurt, but not for long. I'm sure someone else is on standby.

February 1995

I'm FREE! This is a new beginning, and it sure feels good! TJ comes first, and then it's all about me. My parents have been so supportive, as also Tyler's Mom. I am feeling blessed! Although Tyler and I are not a couple anymore, we don't allow anything to interfere with us being there for our child. He always picks him up from school, attends programs and takes him places.

Something doesn't seem quite right this morning. I can feel it in my spirit. Even TJ seems to be a little off. He's irritable and says he doesn't want to go to school today. I'm having the hardest time trying to convince him of how much fun he's going to have at school and how all of his friends are waiting to see him. Finally, he agrees to go, and he enters his classroom, walking slowly with his head down. His teacher notices it right away. I explain to her that he is just having a hard time this morning for some reason.

It's after 4:00 in the evening, and I have been in meetings all day. I'm walking out of the conference room, and the receptionist is telling me that TJ's school has called twice. All of a sudden, I panic, wondering why the school is calling? Is TJ hurt, or did something bad happen?

My hand is shaking really badly while I'm dialing the number. The secretary answers the phone and informs me that TJ hasn't been picked up yet. She went on to say that he is always picked up every day by 3:00, and she has also tried calling his dad, but there was no answer. I'm trying to process everything she is saying while grabbing my purse, briefcase and keys. I'm leaving my job right now to pick TJ up.

When I get inside the school, I find TJ sitting at the front desk smiling and eating gummy worms. They told me that they still weren't able to get in touch with his dad. This is so not like him. I hope nothing terrible has happened to him. Once I get home and get TJ settled, I will try to locate him.

I called him several times and got no answer. I paged 911 a few times and still no response. I'm getting a bad feeling. Deep down, I can feel it; something bad has happened. This explains the feeling I had this morning. It's just not like Tyler to disappear and not pick up his son. He would have called me. He would have reached out.

What has happened to Tyler? I'm scared!

Chapter Sixteen

Tyler

When Life Catches Up With You

DAMN!

www.ingramcontent.com/pod-product-compliance
Lightning Source LLC
Chambersburg PA
CBHW070409310726

48977CB00003B/615